W9-COG-782

Dear Mystery Reader,

A major new talent on the mystery scene, Martha Lawrence is one of our most exciting and original DEAD LETTER authors.

For her debut mystery, MURDER IN SCORPIO, Lawrence was nominated for Edgar, Anthony, and Agatha awards. Critics and mystery readers alike fell in love with her parapsychologist P.I. Elizabeth Chase and clamored for more. Now comes Lawrence's sophomore effort, THE COLD HEART OF CAPRICORN, a spellbinding continuation of her psychic detective series.

Chase's talents are extraordinary. Elizabeth can actually "see" details from crime scenes...before they occur. She uses her gift and sharp wit to solve some of the toughest criminal cases in Southern California. This time out, a violent rapist is terrorizing San Diego. Baffled by the lack of physical evidence, a desperate police force turns to Elizabeth for help. Utilizing astrology, precognitive dreams, and hypnosis, Elizabeth must muster all her paranormal expertise to track down the elusive rapist. But when Chase looks to the stars, all signs point to murder...and the next victim may be Elizabeth herself. It's "X-Files" meets Sue Grafton in this mesmerizing mystery.

Enjoy!

Yours in crime,

Joe Veltre
Assistant Editor
St. Martin's DEAD LETTER Paperback Mysteries

Other titles from St. Martin's **Dead Letter Mysteries**

Dead Letter is also proud to present these mystery
classics by Ngaio Marsh

Critical acclaim for Martha Lawrence and...

THE COLD HEART OF CAPRICORN

"Run, do not walk, to your nearest bookstore, for THE COLD HEART OF CAPRICORN, Martha C. Lawrence's second book...I loved every word."

—*Washington Times*

"Lawrence proves her initial success was no fluke, with her second—and even better—thriller."

—*The San Diego Union-Tribune*

"Elizabeth proves to be a worthy protagonist: smart, mature, funny and sensible, as well as 'sensitive.' Looking into the future, I predict that we'll see this series continue for a long time as Lawrence fans continue to grow steadily."

—Minneapolis *Star Tribune*

MURDER IN SCORPIO

"One of the most engaging mysteries I've ever read. There's no tougher critic than a Virgo and this Virgo says MURDER IN SCORPIO is flawless."

—Nancy Pickard, author of *Confession*

"Lawrence demonstrates the storytelling skill of a veteran, and with this taut and suspenseful tale gets the Elizabeth Chase series off to a rousing start."

—*The San Diego Union-Tribune*

"Fine prose, a matter-of-fact approach to some rather extraordinary perceptions, and a wry sense of humor characterize a remarkable first novel."

—*Library Journal*

"An innovative and exciting new mystery featuring a private eye with a difference...Peopled with fascinating characters and a well-crafted plot, this is a terrific read."

—Janet Dawson, author of *A Credible Threat*

ALSO BY MARTHA C. LAWRENCE
Murder in Scorpio

The COLD HEART of CAPRICORN

MARTHA C. LAWRENCE

St. Martin's Paperbacks

The characters and events in this book are fictitious. Any similarity to real persons, living or dead, is coincidental and not intended by the author.

Grateful acknowledgment is given for permission to reprint the poem by Emily Dickinson, "After Great Pain, a Formal Feeling Comes." Excerpted from *The Oxford Dictionary of Quotations* by Oxford. Copyright © 1980. Reprinted by permission of Oxford University Press, Inc.

THE COLD HEART OF CAPRICORN

Copyright © 1997 by Martha C. Lawrence.

Library of Congress Catalog Card Number: 96-30718

ISBN: 0-312-96294-0

Printed in the United States of America

St. Martin's Press hardcover edition/January 1997
St. Martin's Paperbacks edition/January 1998

St. Martin's Paperbacks are published by St. Martin's Press, 175 Fifth Avenue, New York, NY 10010.

10 9 8 7 6 5 4 3 2 1

To those who've been there—
from one who has also

ACKNOWLEDGMENTS

I thank Hope Dellon and Kelley Ragland for their guidance, Gina Maccoby for her diligence, Howard LaBore, George Brennan Hayes, and Candace Ward-Davis for their expertise, and Maggie Griffin and Harlan Coben for the much needed laughs.

I especially thank SDPD Officer E. R. Martinez and Deputy District Attorney Pete Deddeh. It's been more than ten years now, but the memory of your caring remains.

After great pain, a formal feeling comes—
The Nerves sit ceremonious, like Tombs—
The stiff Heart questions was it He, that bore,
And Yesterday, or Centuries before?

Emily Dickinson

I'm a little wounded, but I am not slain;
I will lay me down for to bleed awhile,
Then I'll rise and fight . . . again.

From *Dryden's Miscellanies*, 1702

The COLD HEART of
CAPRICORN

PROLOGUE

I wish only my good premonitions came true.

My name is Elizabeth Chase, and I am a psychic. It's not an easy calling. For starters, I don't even like the word. It conjures up images of glowy-eyed soothsayers mumbling vague predictions for undeserved fees. Yet from an early age I've known outcomes before they've happened, seen people whom others can't see, heard voices that others can't hear.

Longing for normalcy and social approval, I kept most of this information to myself, did my best *not* to know, see, or hear. It didn't work. My experiences intensified, culminating in the sighting of a ghost in broad daylight on the Stanford University campus during my sophomore year. I figured I was crazy, but just to be sure I abandoned my premed program and threw myself headlong into the study of psychology and parapsychology. Two Ph.D.'s later I concluded that I might not be crazy after all and that while I might never understand them to the satisfaction of my rational mind, my strange perceptions could have practical applications. Finding lost children. Recovering stolen property. Fingering scumballs.

At some point I realized that a private investigator's license would come in handy toward these goals, so I got one. People started calling me a psychic detective. I loathed that hokey label, so much so that one of my twisted friends printed up business cards stating same, just to razz me. I decided to stop taking myself so seriously and started using them. It felt like destiny.

This last investigation, the case of the serial rapist, almost killed me. Literally. Had I seen it coming? Yes, I'd seen glimpses of the dark days ahead. So why didn't I use my precognition to avoid the nightmare?

Because sometimes the only way to escape evil is to turn and face it head-on.

1

I take a lot of ribbing about being a witch, so it's no wonder that Halloween is not my favorite holiday.

And what a Halloween it was. An unseasonably wet and cold one, especially for Southern California. The rain had stopped shortly after nightfall, but the damp gusts rattling through the palm fronds outside threatened more showers to come. I'd had just two waves of weather-hardy trick-or-treaters: a passel of five tiny dinosaurs with one grown-up human hovering behind their plush fabric tails and, much later, a seductively made-up group of post-pubescent Draculas looking like they were trolling more for action than candy. Other than that all had been quiet. I figured I'd give it until midnight and turned on the eleven o'clock news to pass the time.

The local news station was covering the Ken Theater's annual Hallow's Eve screening of *The Rocky Horror Picture Show*, an event that each year draws a lively gathering of leather enthusiasts and cross-dressers. A reporter stood before the bizarre crowd giving a tongue-in-cheek minidocumentary about the cult classic. In mid-sentence her mouth gaped open. A half beat later she announced that the station would be cutting to the scene of a rape and attempted murder that had just occurred only blocks away. The video cut bumpily to the exterior of a private residence, where cops and paramedics had converged. The camera then panned around the broad back of a uniformed officer and focused on the doorway.

Seconds later medics emerged carrying a stretcher and hurrying toward the ambulance.

I couldn't see her face. The victim's head had been covered with a nonstick surgical bandage, to put pressure on the wound and stanch the bleeding. Her long dark hair hung limply over the side of the stretcher. One of the medics had wrapped a blanket around her shoulders, but it fell open as she was loaded into the ambulance. The camera took full advantage, zooming in on a white nightgown dramatically drenched in blood.

I stood before my television with my arms crossed over my chest. This wasn't the first incident. For the past eight months I'd been reading about a series of rapes—nearly a dozen now—under shocking page-two headlines in the newspaper. The video feed from tonight's attack had been lurid enough to interrupt the eleven o'-clock news. When the anchorwoman cut to a commercial I reached for the remote and turned off the set.

My feet remained planted in front of the television long after the screen went black. Something was bugging me, something besides the obvious heinousness of the crime. I stood very still, taking an inner inventory and trying to name the feeling. I had a sense of familiarity, as if this rape case had something to do with *me*. Creepy.

I did my best to dismiss the feeling. I buffered the hour between the newscast and bedtime by replacing the hinges on my sagging back door and watching late-night comedy. This didn't work. The case resurfaced in my sleep. The dream began with a vacant-eyed goat standing on a lawn in front of a house with three gables. A gated wood fence surrounded the property. I knew without question that a friend of mine lived in this three-gabled house. When I passed through the gate the dream was no longer just a dream—it was real. I could see through the darkness like a cat. I smelled the wet grass, felt the soles of my shoes sinking into the spongy lawn. I looked up into one of the windows and stopped short when I saw a man's dark form stealing into the bedroom. I knew he carried a knife. My friend screamed, and I jerked awake.

For most psychics a vivid dream life just comes with the territory. Learning to sift the meaningful images from mere subconscious garbage becomes a survival skill. A precognitive dream—that glimpse into an actual future—has an entirely different flavor from a symbolic dream. It's charged with emotion. It's extraordinarily vivid. It has *that feeling*, a feeling that must be experienced and cannot be described. The dream I had Halloween night definitely had *that feeling*.

The next morning I stepped into the shower feeling spooked by what I'd seen. It even crossed my mind to contact the San Diego Police Department. No way, I decided. Unless it's a sure case of impending life or death I don't stick my nose into police business. I've never needed to solicit work, thanks to a continuing stream of enthusiastic referrals. My current caseload was typical. I was dividing my time between investigating an arson case for one of the local deputy DAs and helping a computer software firm locate its onetime brightest star, Gary Warren Niebuhr, a genius who morphed from supernova to black hole overnight, sucking sixteen million dollars into the void. The last thing I needed at the moment was another job.

I turned off the water and stepped out of the shower. As I was toweling off I remembered that the woman in my dream had been a friend.

Not only was I working two time-consuming cases, but I'd just promised my mom I'd help organize an AIDS fund-raiser coming up in January. Taking on something like this rape case would be idiotic time management.

A friend.

I put on my robe and went to the phone. *You're just passing along a tip*, I told myself as I dialed the SDPD. I presented myself as a licensed PI with inside information that could lead to a break in the rape case. After all, if psychic insight doesn't qualify as inside information, what does? Not that I mentioned it to the personable desk sergeant who answered the phone. "Lieutenant Douglas Marcone's in charge of that investigation," he said. "I can put you through."

I thought better of it. I could hardly expect a psychic tip to be taken seriously over the phone. Within the hour I was walking down the sixth-floor hall of the police department, approaching Marcone's open office door. An imposing figure even when seated, the lieutenant was on the phone. When he saw me he hung up and waved me in. "You're the PI?"

I nodded.

"What have you got?"

The lieutenant's question flew past me like a killer serve ball. His expression was polite but unsmiling.

I felt my mouth gape open. "Ah—" An intelligent opener. "I had a dream." Great follow-up.

Marcone's stony face and unbending posture were unnerving me. I took a moment to breathe before continuing. "Let me back up a minute. You must know Dave Franks."

"Dave Franks over in Robbery?"

I nodded while I searched my purse for a card. "Yeah. I helped him close that La Jolla case recently. My name's Elizabeth Chase." I handed him my business card, the one that read *Dr. Elizabeth Chase, Psychic Investigator*.

Marcone gingerly took the card, glanced at it, and raised an eyebrow. "So you had a dream."

"Yes. I saw another rape. It's going to happen in a house with three gables."

His world-weary eyes didn't leave my face. He sat silently, waiting for more.

"There was a lawn, and a fence around the house, and a gate in the fence." I didn't mention the part about the goat. It would have sounded too weird, and I was sounding weird enough as it was.

"Do you know where this house is?"

"No."

"Can you give a description of the rapist?"

I shook my head.

"Could you identify the victim?"

No, but I know she's a friend of mine. "No."

"Do you know *when* this is supposed to happen?"

Again I shook my head.

Marcone continued to sit ramrod straight. "So you're warning us that an unknown perp is going to rape an unknown victim in an unknown neighborhood in a house with three gables."

Put that way, it did sound pretty silly. "With a lawn and a fence with a gate," I added. "Gabled houses aren't all that common in San Diego. I know it's not much, but maybe it's better than nothing."

He looked down and fingered the edges of my stiff blue business card. His eyes came back up. "Thank you, Dr. Chase."

I moved toward the door, assuming my card would hit the trash can the moment I was out of sight. "Thanks for your time, Lieutenant. Hope you catch him soon. Let me know if I can help."

My visit with Marcone met with a resounding two-month silence. I wondered about the case a lot at first but less and less as I was pulled into my work and the distractions of the holiday season. Then, at three thirty on a cold rainy morning in January, I was awakened by the shrill electronic scream of my cordless phone. I put the receiver to my ear and mumbled hello.

"Dr. Chase, this is Lieutenant Marcone, San Diego Police Department. Sorry to call so early."

I scrutinized the glowing digits of my clock radio. "It's not early, Lieutenant. It's the middle of the night." I was half asleep and my words were coming slowly. "What—"

"Listen. We found your three-gabled house. It's at three three two three Montezuma, near the university. I'd appreciate it if you'd come down here. Right away if you can."

2

The ambulance was long gone by the time I arrived at the rape scene. Two patrol cars parked along the curb were the only evidence that there had been any kind of a scene at all. A heavy, unrelenting rainfall had dampened any curiosity that may have lured neighbors out of their warm, dry beds to see what was going on. The street was quiet and dark, sunrise well over an hour away.

I parked behind one of the patrol cars and sat quietly for a moment to get my bearings. Through the downpour I stared at the front-yard fence and the three-gabled house that rose up behind it. In my dream a friend of mine had lived in this house. Yet the address was unfamiliar—I didn't know a soul who lived in this part of town. As the storm pounded the roof of my car I resisted getting out. Not simply because the cold rain would fill my shoes and find its way under the collar of my coat. Something far more chilling urged me to restart the engine and turn around and go home. Fear? Screw that. I got out of the car and moved quickly up the sidewalk. The gate was open. As I splashed up the rain-soaked walkway I checked the front lawn. No goat.

They'd seen me arrive, because the front door swung open as I approached. Backlit against the interior light, Lieutenant Marcone stood in dark silhouette, projecting his commanding presence from thirty paces. That intimidating stance had spooked me at our post-Halloween meeting two months ago. Now it was reassuring.

Marcone put his hand on my arm, pulling me out of the rain and guiding me into the hallway. "Thanks for coming at this hour."

A freckle-faced patrolman and a blond woman stood behind Marcone in the hallway. "This is Officer Billings"—at the sound of his name, the patrolman looked over—"and Detective Powers." Solid in her chinos and cable-knit sweater, the detective smiled and gave me a nod. "This is Elizabeth Chase." We exchanged hellos. I wondered how much Marcone had told them about me. He didn't let on. "We've collected our evidence. Now I guess you collect yours."

I began by circling the living room. This was purely a delay tactic. I knew full well the rape had occurred in the third bedroom at the northeast corner of the house. I'd already seen its dark doorway gaping open like a mouth, had heard its silent screaming. I had no desire to go in there yet. Billings and Powers followed my movements with wary eyes.

I pointed to the rear of the house. "He entered through the sliding glass door in back. Lifted it right out of its tracks. Quietly. No amateur job."

The officers looked at each other, and I saw their expressions change from wariness to surprise. They turned to me with eager expressions.

I continued walking. "He's very cold, conscious, calculating. No drugs or alcohol. He's very clear about what he's doing."

The three followed closely alongside me. "Can you describe him?" Marcone asked.

"I can't see his face. . . . I'm picking up intense vitality—an athlete, maybe steroids, maybe just hyper physical energy. Black pants, black shirt."

Billings's eyes got wide. "How about a name?"

I stood for a moment, hoping for greater powers than I actually possessed. No name came to mind, which was no surprise. "I hate to disappoint you, but I'm not *that* psychic. Names are not my forte. To tell you the truth I sometimes have trouble calling up the names of people I've already been introduced to."

"Pop quiz. What's my name?" The detective on my left didn't smile, but her eyes twinkled at me.

"Powers. But that's an easy name to remember."

A deep dimple appeared in her cheek as she grinned. "It's Dianna from now on."

I returned her smile and went on. "I have an affinity for colors, and sometimes I'm remarkably accurate in seeing numbers." At the mention of color, a scene as vivid as it was ugly played out in my mind. "For example, I'm seeing the bloodstained sheets the techs hauled out of that bedroom." I pointed to let them know I *knew* precisely which bedroom. "Kind of a dusty rose with embroidery along the top. Am I close?"

Lieutenant Marcone was impressed and didn't try to hide the fact. "That's *exactly* what they looked like," he said.

"The victim is a woman of color, a terrific woman." *My friend.*

Marcone shrugged. "Well, I can vouch for the first half of that statement. I don't know her personally."

A bizarre, fleeting impression—*white fingers*—crossed my mind's eye. "There's something about this guy's hands," I began.

Dianna looked encouragingly at me. "Yes?"

But whatever insight had flickered in my mind was now gone. I tried to call it back, but it was like trying to remember a dream—sometimes the harder you force the door to your visions, the more insistently your waking consciousness cements it shut.

I stopped abruptly in front of the bedroom door. Something foreign was forcing the door to my consciousness. The cold feeling I'd fought against in the car came back with a vengeance. In a sudden physical rush the heart-pounding horror of the victim filled me, making my chest tight. Breathing became an effort. My face began to sting as if I'd had a sudden punch to the nose. I struggled to maintain my composure, and for a moment thought I might not. I needed to say something, anything. "You've got a monster on your hands," I finally mustered. It came out as a whisper.

The muscles in Lieutenant Marcone's face were tight and his tone was sad. "We don't need a psychic to tell us that."

The four of us stood sharing the blackness of the moment. I'd just had a glimpse into something darker and uglier than I'd ever seen before, and I was afraid. It occurred to me that I could decline the case and let someone else fight this war. I could stick with finding lost relatives and recovering stolen property, the bread and butter of my practice. I had no moral obligation to find this rapist, just because the police had actually taken me up on my offer. I would not be running away, I would be *choosing to fill my life with more positive experiences.* . . .

This positive-thinking rationalization probably could have

picked up momentum and carried me right along with it if I hadn't heard the sobbing. Low and muffled, it began as the sound of a lone woman crying. Soon I could hear another woman crying, and another, and another, until my mind was filled with a dirge of women's sorrow. I resisted the impulse to cup my hands over my ears.

Marcone could hear none of this, of course. He studied my face, his knitted eyebrows asking silent questions. I was looking past him, past this moment, into an unclear future. What little I was able to make out scared the hell out of me.

I took a deep breath. "You'll need to give me the case file."

He put a hand on my shoulder and gave it a squeeze. "I'll do you better than that. I'll give you the case detectives."

3

"You look like you could use some coffee."

I lifted my head and felt a dent along my cheek where it had been resting against the back of the vinyl sofa. Dianna was breezing toward me through the second-floor reception area of the SDPD, where I'd been slumped since quarter to five that morning waiting for the case detectives to gather for their six fifteen lineup. I'd been too jangled for breakfast after leaving the crime scene, but now the adrenaline was wearing off and I could actually feel the circles that had formed under my eyes. Dianna had managed to change clothes, apply lipstick, and pull her thick blond hair into a ponytail since I'd seen her last. In her smart navy pants and shirt she looked positively vibrant. I smiled weakly at her. "Is there such a thing for a poor soul like me?"

"I guess you've earned a cup. Come on. Follow me."

We walked around the corner to an alcove furnished with a stainless steel coffee machine, a compact refrigerator, and a ridiculously large microwave oven, probably a relic from the seventies. She filled a Styrofoam cup for me. "I was pretty blown away by what you were able to see at the crime scene this morning."

I reached for the cup and nodded my thanks. "Well, it horrified me. I just hope I can help. How long have you been working on this case?"

"They just pulled me over from Domestic Violence a couple weeks ago." She checked her wristwatch. "We'd better hustle. Marcone doesn't like latecomers."

We hurried across the hall and into central line-up, where about a dozen detectives were taking seats around several tables arranged in a U. As we sat down Lieutenant Marcone strode to the front of the room, back straight and head high. All conversation stopped.

"I'm going to start with the bad news." The worry in the lieutenant's eyes underscored that the news was bad indeed. He easily won the undivided attention of his audience. Once again I noted his commanding presence, which now projected clear to the back of the squad room.

He scrutinized the group before him. "As you know, last Friday we thought there was a good chance we'd arrested our serial rapist. We'd hoped we were on our way to closing the case. Early this morning those hopes died. Allow me to read from a report taken by Officer Billings, who was dispatched to three three two three Montezuma at oh three twenty hours regarding a rape/attempted murder.

" 'Victim stated today at oh three hundred hours she was awakened from her sleep by an unidentified man pushing her head into her pillow. The suspect held a knife to her neck and stated, "Keep your head to the side, don't make no noise, and you won't get hurt." Suspect proceeded to pull victim's nightgown over her hips and vaginally rape her.' "

As literary works, police reports lack subtlety. To be of any use at all to prosecutors, the language must be explicit. Although the words Marcone read this morning were harsh, I knew that the reality they described was harsher.

" 'After approximately fifteen minutes, suspect demanded victim to turn over on her stomach. When victim protested, suspect stabbed her in the breast.' "

Again the image of rose-colored embroidered sheets came to me. My heart sank, and a chorus of groans rose up from the assembled detectives. Marcone waved his hand for silence, cleared his throat, and read on.

" 'Victim then turned over onto her stomach and suspect attempted to sodomize her. At that point victim screamed, and suspect stabbed her in the right buttock. Victim screamed again, and the neighbor's dogs began to bark. Suspect then left the bedroom. Victim stated she believes the suspect exited through the back door.' "

Marcone stared hard at the detectives. "I know what you're thinking. Make that I know what you're *hoping:* Maybe it's not the same guy, maybe this is a separate incident. Forget about it." Marcone resumed reading. " 'When asked to describe her assailant, victim stated he was medium height, stocky, and muscular. She could not describe his hair or skin color because he wore a cap and ski mask, as well as . . .' " Marcone looked up and interjected, "Get this, boys and girls—*'doctor's gloves.'* " He frowned. "It's our guy, all right."

This last statement elicited bitter swearing from around the room. I thought back to the image of white fingers I'd picked up at the rape scene. From the end of the table another cop spoke up. "So Lieutenant, if that's the bad news, what's the good news?"

"I didn't say there was any good news. Your assignments continue where they left off, with a vengeance. We're pulling in every resource we have. Getting creative, which brings me to my next agenda item. Now this could be good news, but at this point it's too early to tell. Let's just call it a promising development."

Lieutenant Marcone looked at me and gave me half a wink.

"This morning we've got a new investigator on the case, Dr. Elizabeth Chase." All heads turned to inspect me as Marcone gestured in my direction. I looked across the tables to a circle of curious eyes. "She's a PI with a rather unusual private practice. I'm going to cut to the chase here: Dr. Chase is a psychic." Wearing his stony expression, he appeared oblivious to his own pun. The wordplay didn't go unnoticed by his listeners, though. A few politely muffled snickers emerged from around the tables. Then again, perhaps just the embarrassing connotation of the word *psychic* was sufficient to raise a few chuckles.

"Laugh if you want," Marcone continued, "but there's more to this psychic thing than meets the eye." Another pun, but this time he paused for effect. The laughs he'd been playing for rose up from his audience, and he smiled with satisfaction. Someone had told me the lieutenant was popular with the department, and I could see why. He cared, but he didn't take himself too seriously. The best kind of cop.

"Honestly, folks, Dr. Chase is not some bag lady fortune-teller I dragged up here from Tenth and Market."

I was glad he'd cleared that up. This early in the morning it could be hard to tell.

"She has some impressive credentials. A Ph.D. from Stanford, for one. Psychology, wasn't it, Dr. Chase?"

I nodded. "Also a doctorate specializing in parapsychology, obtained in tandem with work I completed at the Stanford Research Institute." Not that my certified ability to pile it higher and deeper had any bearing on my usefulness here.

"Most important," Marcone said, seeming to read my thoughts, "Chase has closed some damn tough cases in the last couple of years. Five missing persons, four of 'em kids. Three homicides. That big La Jolla robbery case was hers. Last summer she blew the cover on a meth lab in Ramona"—here he paused and smiled—"literally."

A man at the end of the table widened his eyes and asked, "That was you?"

"Yeah," I said, under my breath. A round I'd fired in self-defense during the case in question had resulted in a cloud of toxic waste and the death of two drug dealers. I wasn't particularly proud of it. On the bright side, $80,000 worth of shit wasn't reaching the street every week from *that* hellhole anymore.

Earlier this morning, the lieutenant balked at paying my fee. You'd never guess it from the enthusiasm in his voice now.

"Two months ago Dr. Chase called on me and described this morning's crime scene in significant detail. I can personally attest to the fact that she not only has some very impressive credentials but she also has an amazing talent—"

I cleared my throat. Loudly. "May I interrupt you just a moment?"

"Sure. Go right ahead."

I looked around the room, making as much eye contact as possible. "Before the kind lieutenant here gets carried away, I need to interject a little reality. Yes, I occasionally get psychic insights into my work, but I'm not *that* amazing. During my research years at SRI, I ran across psychics with far more astonishing gifts than I have, believe me. My extrasensory abilities tend to be sporadic. For example, while it's true that two months ago I gave Lieutenant Marcone details about this morning's crime scene, I couldn't give him names or an address. That kind of spotty insight is typical for me.

That's why I think of myself as a licensed private investigator first. The psychic stuff is secondary. Yes, I do use my psi talent. But for the most part I work the same way you guys do. Same old stubborn routines, same old stupid tricks."

A few smiles around the room.

"The main thing is, I'm not out to impress anyone with my so-called psychic prowess. What motivated me to get into this work—well, it's probably similar to what motivates most of you. To protect and serve the citizens of our community."

A hand shot up across the table. "Yes," I answered quickly. I was eager to elaborate, to explain, to *connect*.

The earnest-looking young man wore pale-rimmed glasses. He smiled broadly, radiating two-hundred-watt enthusiasm. I could hardly wait to answer his question. "Please, fire away," I said.

"Do you ever get insights into the results at the Del Mar racetrack?"

Laughter broke out, and the questions started flying from all sides. It was hard to hear with everyone talking at once, but I caught the words "lotto numbers" rising above the din. Twice, at least.

"All right, enough." The lieutenant didn't need to raise his voice much to quiet the group. He grinned and shook his head. "Now that we've impressed Dr. Chase with our collective maturity, let's get down to business. She'll be teaming up with Detective Powers and Detective Dietz. Any leads, evidence, suspect interviews—all matters pertaining to the rape case—are open to Dr. Chase's investigation. Understood?" An affirmative silence filled the air. "Like I said earlier, our primary suspect was in custody at the time of this morning's incident, so he's out. But we have others. Don't we, Powers?"

I joined the group in turning my attention to Dianna, sitting on my left. "Yes, sir," she said, "we do. And how we do."

4

"Let me warn you: This place is a friggin' dump."

With that Dianna swept open a glass-windowed door marked SEX CRIMES. We walked through a room of partitioned-off desks, across a carpet that had seen enough coffee and God-knows-what spills to be long past salvaging. I followed her into a walled-off cubicle at the far end of the room.

"I'm still moving in over here," she said, taking a seat at a desk in front of a computer. "The serial rape case now merits a special task force. Like I said, Marcone pulled me over here from DV. Dietz came over from Robbery a few weeks ago."

Dianna's cubicle had the look of a command headquarters. Like a small mountain range, several stacks of paper spread from the desk and onto a long table along the wall. She pulled a clump of paper-clipped sheets from the peak of one of the paper mountains. "Here are some of those *others* I was talking about," she said, handing me the sheaf.

I began shuffling through a deck of all points bulletins. Each page featured a photograph on the left and pertinent data on the right. Warrant, issue date, charge. A couple of yes/no questions ("Armed and dangerous?"). A section of fill-in-the-blanks to describe the suspect, the crime, the vehicle. From the dates at the top of each page, many of these bulletins were old, archive copies probably.

The suspect photos were depressing. Cold, blank stares. Young men, wasted hopes. Lights on, no one home. At the fourth bulletin I stopped and caught my breath with a gasp. Someone was home behind these black eyes, but nobody I'd ever want to meet. At first glance his gaze appeared direct, but on closer inspection I saw that his eyes were asymmetrical. One pupil stared off over my left shoulder and the other stared down behind my right. One said "fuck you" and the other said "fuck you to death." The date of birth told me I was looking at a thirty-one-year-old, but there was something ancient about the man who glared into the camera. His neck was thick, his shoulders powerful. He managed to intimidate all from the space of a three-by-three-inch head shot. "Good God," I muttered.

I looked up to see Dianna watching me. "The guy's rotating a little off center, wouldn't you say?"

I shook my head. "Off center baloney. This jerk knows exactly where he's coming from. Hell central."

She laughed. "You pegged him. Ah, yes, let's see. Richard Zimmer." She dug down into another paper mountain and pulled out a handful of track-fed computer paper. She held one end and tossed the stack into the air. It fluttered noisily, unfolding accordion-style into a long sheet that extended to the floor.

Dianna pored over the pages. "Here we go: Zimmer, Richard. October 1990, 23152(B) CVC, driving while under the influence. December 1990, 459 PC, burglary. June 1991, 242 PC, battery. September 1993, 11351 H&S, possession with intent. May 1994, 211 PC, robbery, and 245(A)(1) PC, assault with deadly weapon.

"Now, what the paperwork won't tell you is that the last charge was in actuality a brutal rape. The victim lost the partial use of her right arm. Zimmer pinned it behind her during the assault and her shoulder came apart. Oops." Dianna put a disgusted spin on the last word.

I felt my jaw tightening. "How come the paperwork doesn't tell us that?"

"The victim knew Zimmer. She refused to testify. Swore that if we subpoenaed her she'd say it was consensual, that the injury was an accident. She had complete faith that Zimmer would follow through on his death threat to her. She had absolutely no faith that the justice system would lock him up. Hate to say it, but I don't blame her."

I stared at Zimmer's picture again. The black eyes stared back—and beyond.

Dianna picked up a coffee cup and looked warily inside. "Another thing the paperwork doesn't tell you is that Zimmer was a suspect in two rape cases. One got thrown out of court at preliminary. Second time the jury walked him." She bravely swallowed the remains in her cup, made a face, and continued. "We picked him up two nights ago. His van fit the description of a vehicle seen in the neighborhood at the time of the first rape in the series. So many pieces of the puzzle fit with Zimmer—the body type, the brutality. *Damn*." She shook her head. "Anyway, he was the one we had in custody when this morning's rape occurred. Too bad. Guess we'll have to spring him now."

The mere thought of sharing San Diego's streets and sidewalks with this man mortified me. I glanced at the right side of the bulletin to review his warrants. He had a list of vehicle code violations an arm's length long. "Can't you hold him on any of these traffic warrants?"

"For a while, but it's hardly worth precious prison space. The DA would rather wait for us to book him on something he can do real time for. Frankly, I agree."

"Meanwhile he's just out there, grazing on society."

"More or less." The phone rang and Dianna picked it up midring. "Domestic, uh, Sex Crimes. Hey, Dietz, where you been? Uh-huh . . . in a few . . . okay."

She hung up and explained. "That was Dietz, the other task force guy. He's on his way over here now with another suspect. He found a possible peeper near this morning's rape site. Had to chase him down. You know about that, right? That rapists quite often return to the scenes of their crimes?"

A peeper near this morning's rape site sounded so pat. "Yeah, but isn't it unlikely that a rapist would hang around *immediately* after a rape, with police crawling all over the place?"

"Probably. But we're not sure we're dealing with someone rational here. And at this point we're following up on everything. *Everything*. Even hiring psychics." She flashed a quick smile. "Just kidding."

I smiled back. I was used to that sort of kidding. "So what am I looking at here?" I pointed to the western edge of the paper mountain range, to three paper stacks in particular.

"Those are incident reports grouped according to the rapist's MO. This first stack"—she plopped it on my lap—"are the definite for-sures. The rapist in each of these cases was described identically, right down to the latex gloves."

I leafed through the stack, four cases.

"This next stack"—she slid it over my way—"is the maybes. Similar MO, similar description, but no absolute ID." The stack was larger, maybe six or eight cases.

She picked up the third pile and flipped through the files. "This stack is your what-the-hell long shots. Variations on the MO, variations in the description, but enough similarities to make you stop and wonder. Some of these are several years old. You never know, sometimes a long shot turns out to be the solution to the whole case. Like I said, we're following up on everything."

I cocked an eyebrow. "Even, for godsakes, hiring psychics."

She stopped her busywork. "Hey, I think it's a great idea. Seriously." Her eyes—an intense light blue ringed in black—looked directly into mine. "You don't have to convince me of anything, Elizabeth. I believe you are who you say you are. My grandmother could see things, too. When I was sixteen she told me not to go for a ride in my friend's new convertible. I was a wild girl back then, but something in the serious way Gramma said it made me listen. If I hadn't, I wouldn't be here today. The next day the car plowed into a semi, and two of my best friends were decapitated."

I'd heard hundreds of stories like this during my research years at Stanford. "Intriguing, isn't it? At SRI we found a thirty percent significance in our precognition experiments where only five percent was expected statistically. The odds of that happening by chance are something like one in a billion."

"Doesn't surprise me." Dianna refolded Zimmer's computer-generated rap sheet. "I wouldn't know how to explain it, but I have no trouble believing there are people like you who can pick up more channels than someone like me who's wired strictly for network programming."

"I think we all have the potential—" I began, but stopped short when a man appeared in the doorway.

Dianna made introductions. "This is our other partner, Jeff

Dietz. Forget the Jeff part—everybody calls him Dietz." She nodded toward me. "This is Elizabeth Chase, a PI Marcone brought in."

Dietz made a visual impact. His hair was so blond it was nearly white. With his high brow, long nose, and narrow mouth he looked like some latter-day Norse god. He glanced briefly at me, too preoccupied to make chitchat. He spoke to Dianna. "I've got the suspect downstairs. You want to help me prep him for the interview?"

Something unspoken passed between the two of them. "Sure, why not." Dianna put her hand on my shoulder as she walked past on her way out. "Make yourself at home. But if you take any paperwork be sure to leave me photocopies. The copier's over there in the corner. I'd start with these guys." She handed me the computer printout with the names, addresses, and penal code violations of the primary suspects.

In the meantime I'd been reading this morning's report from the rape in the three-gabled house. The image of the victim, Thomasina Wilson, began to haunt me:

> Victim was bleeding heavily from the chest wound and appeared to be going into shock at the time of our arrival. She gave a brief description of the attack, stating several times that her doors had been locked.

"Thanks," I called after her. "But if you don't mind I'll start by talking to the victims."

5

The city was up and humming by the time I walked out of the police station. I glanced at my watch. Two minutes past seven, yet the sky was so gunmetal gray that January 3 had hardly dawned at all. January. Capricorn time of year. Every sign of the zodiac has its pluses and minuses, but I've always found the negatives of Capricorn particularly distasteful: coldness, darkness, rigidity. As I splashed across the street to my car a stiff westerly pushed a heavy rain sideways onto my legs.

This morning's victim, Thomasina Wilson, had been dispatched to Sharp Hospital, a ten-minute drive up 163 from downtown. I suffered a pang in the pit of my stomach as I drove north on a freeway made noisy by the hissing of wet tires. My reaction surprised me. I don't share the same dreadful association many people have with hospitals. For me hospitals are linked with pleasant memories of the joy my father, a neurosurgeon, has always taken in his work. I thought back to 1972, Dad's first CAT scan. I could still see him standing against the white hospital wall, eyes eager and bright as he placed the shiny transparency in my hands. He had invited me to the hospital to show me a picture that would let me "see inside the patient's head." At fifteen I still harbored childlike wishes and had fully expected to witness magic, a view of the dreams inside his patient's mind. When I looked at the CAT scan I became confused. This was just an X-ray image of cell tissue. What could this tell me about his patient's thoughts and hopes? "That's not the inside," I'd said to him, handing back the CAT scan. "That's the *outside* of the inside." I remembered the way Dad had laughed.

No amount of happy reminiscing was dissolving the cold ball that had taken up residence in my stomach. The dread lingered as I pulled into the hospital parking garage and intensified as I traveled up the elevator to Thomasina Wilson's room. The hospital corridors were quiet this morning. Outside the rooms I passed three or four breakfast trays filled with half-eaten plates of poached eggs and untouched bowls of oatmeal. On one an alarming sight: a bloodied napkin, the dark red stain mocking the subdued walls with their pastel paintings. I sought a prosaic explanation. A nose-bleed, perhaps.

I rounded the west wing and saw an African American couple, their faces etched in concern, standing near the entrance to Room 209. They were watching as a nurse tended to her patient. The man and woman turned and stared at me with dazed expressions. "Hello," I said. "How is she?"

"And you are?" The man raised his arm and leaned against the door frame. A protective gesture.

"My name is Elizabeth Chase—"

Before I could finish he nodded eagerly. "The investigator. We got word from the police you might be coming. I'm Robert Wilson, Thomasina's brother." He placed his hand on the woman's arm. "This is my wife, Robin." Robin looked up and nodded an acknowledgment but quickly resumed her vigil.

The nurse made a notation on her clipboard and approached the three of us. "I've just administered a dose of morphine. It's imperative with this kind of injury that the patient be as still as possible, particularly in the first twenty-four hours. She'll probably be asleep in a few minutes." The nurse spoke matter-of-factly, but beneath her surface efficiency I could see she was troubled by the fate that had befallen this patient.

Robert approached Thomasina's bedside, and Robin and I followed him into the small room. Behind the bed a narrow window looked onto the gray parking lot below. Gently, Robert placed a hand on Thomasina's arm and inclined his head toward me. "She's with the police."

Thomasina Wilson's bed had been cranked up so that she was sitting nearly vertical. The position would put less pressure on her chest wound, which was bound by layers of bandaging. The white gauze had been wrapped diagonally across her collarbone, toga style. Against Thomasina's mocha-colored skin the alabaster swath gave her an elegant bearing, as if she were some ancient Ethiopian priestess. Her high cheekbones and proud nose did nothing to contradict the regal image. Looking at her I had a feeling of immediate recognition. I raked my memory for the connection but couldn't make one.

"Hi, I'm Elizabeth."

She looked at me under heavily sedated eyelids. Her wide-set brown eyes narrowed as she studied me. "Where've I seen you before?"

I could feel a grin tugging the corners of my mouth. "I don't know. I was just wondering the same thing."

"We can wait outside," Robert said.

"Your brother and his wife are welcome to stay if you'd like them to," I said.

Thomasina nodded slowly. Robert gave her hand a little squeeze and sat in the chair by the bed.

I held up my slim leather portfolio. "I've read the statement you made to the police immediately following this morning's attack. If you're up to it I'd like to go over it again. It's very important to remember what you can now. A lot of the details of what happened will be lost as time goes by. Even a day can make a big difference."

"I have a good memory." Her voice was determined if a little groggy.

"It's not so much a question of memory. When something this atrocious happens, your mind's first line of defense is repression. Even though you might want to remember, the memories are bound to retraumatize you. Your brain doesn't want that to happen, so it spares you. It may remember the event, but it will bury the details."

Thomasina's eyes were closed again. I thought she might have drifted off and was surprised when she answered. "You're right. I know what happened, but the details are hazy." Her voice was thick with the sedative.

"Let's see if some details come into focus when you tell the story." I pulled out the police report. "The officer who wrote up the incident reported that you were asleep when the attack occurred."

Thomasina nodded. "I get up very early. I'm usually asleep by ten," she said groggily.

"What was the first thing you remember?"

"There was this knife against my neck. But I knew my doors were locked. I didn't think it could be real."

"So at first you thought you were having a nightmare?"

Thomasina nodded.

"When did you know it wasn't a nightmare?"

"I couldn't move my head. He had my head shoved into the pillow, and I couldn't move it."

"Did he say anything at that point?"

Thomasina screwed up her face, concentrating. "Something about . . . some kind of a threat like I'd get cut if I moved. I don't remember the exact words."

But she'd remembered them this morning when the police had first interviewed her. "Did he say, 'Keep your head to the side, don't make no noise, and you won't get hurt'?" I asked.

"Yeah, that's it. That's what he said."

Already the details were getting hazy for Thomasina. The morphine wasn't helping. I leaned a little closer to her ear. "Did you have any sense that you might possibly know this man?"

She shook her head.

"Did you see anything? Can you describe him at all?"

"My room was pitch-dark. It was the middle of the night. I couldn't see him."

The small hospital room was silent. Over the public address system someone summoned a Dr. Clarkson.

"If you can't tell me what he looked like, can you tell me"—how could I put this?—"could you tell me what he *felt* like?"

When the question registered in her slowed-down mind, Thomasina let out a feeble laugh. "Yeah. I can tell you what he felt like. He felt like a dog from hell." She let her eyes close and her head rolled to the side. I noticed a series of contusions along her neck, red welts rising out of her smooth brown skin. I didn't remember reading about those in the incident report. I made a note on my legal pad.

As I scribbled, the oppressive feeling I'd had in Thomasina's house early this morning came over me again. Again I felt the heart-pounding horror. This time I also experienced the sense of being pinned under a great weight, utterly unable to move. I closed my eyes and searched for visual details, praying to see something helpful. I found nothing but blackness.

The feeling faded and I opened my eyes. I watched Thomasina. For now, that part of her horror was over. The muscles in her jaw were slack from the drug. She appeared to be drifting off to sleep.

Unexpectedly, her eyes popped open and she spoke. "He blocked my face thrust."

"He what?"

Thomasina's head rose from the pillow, and her eyes focused on mine. "That son of a bitch blocked my face thrust. I have karate training. I got one of my hands free and had a perfect opening to poke his eyes. He blocked me and had me in a wrist hold so fast you wouldn't believe it. He's a pro. He's been trained." For a moment her liquid brown irises shone with crystalline intensity. Then the morphine haze clouded them over, and her lids dropped again.

I turned to Thomasina's brother and his wife. "Looks like I'll have to come back later." I pulled out a business card. "I'd like her to have this. Could I leave it with you?"

Robert Wilson glared back at me. Given what he'd just heard from his sister, I didn't take his angry face personally. When he answered, his voice was civil. "Certainly."

"Hey. You." The patient lifted a hand off the blanket, pointing a long, slender finger in my direction. "Where've I've seen you before?" She was having trouble keeping her eyelids open. "I *know* I've seen you before." Her hand dropped back onto the blanket, and the room became silent. The blanket rose and fell with Thomasina's labored breathing. Soon she was asleep, leaving me to wonder. *Where indeed?*

6

It had been a tough morning, and the weather wasn't helping any. I headed out of the hospital parking complex, turned on my wind-shield wipers, and made my way toward the interstate trying to think bright thoughts. That's about the time my pager went off. I pushed the button and recognized the SDPD prefix. The follow-ing four digits were unfamiliar—Dianna's extension, no doubt. I dialed from my cellular phone as I rounded the rain-soaked on-ramp into slow southbound traffic.

"Sex Crimes. Powers."

"Hi, Dianna. It's Elizabeth."

"Well, hello. You busy? Sounds like you're calling from a car phone."

"Indeed. I'm at one with the rush-hour crowd headed south on Five, approaching Genessee. Just paid this morning's victim a visit."

"How is she?"

"Mercifully stoned but not fit for interviewing. I'll call on her later. What's up on your end?"

"I was calling to invite you to a couple of suspect interviews. First we're gonna talk to the guy Dietz dragged in this morning. He's got some similar priors. Thought you might want to sit in, tune in, whatever it is you do. You'll definitely want to stick around for the second interview. Turns out our earlier suspect was *not* in custody when this morning's rape occurred. Paperwork mix-up. So you'll get a chance to meet him after all."

I flashed back to the mug shot of the man with the skewed black eyes. "Oh, no. Not the one from Hell central. What was his name? Zipper?"

Dianna cracked up. "*Zimmer*. But I like your name for him better—Zipper. That's perfect. Memorable. You'll find out soon enough that after a while all these jokers begin to sound alike."

"Like they all went to the same charm school or something?"

"Yeah. SOB University."

I smiled. "So when do I meet these gentlemen?"

"Around eleven. You can join up with me and Dietz a few minutes before the hour at the elevator bank in the main lobby. We'll take you down."

Take me down. It sounded ominous. "Okeydoke," I said with mock cheer. "Looking forward."

Suspect interviews at eleven. Who knows how long they'd last. I suddenly remembered that it was Monday, and I had a lunch meeting on the books that I would have to rearrange. Which made me think of food, an idea that was beginning to appeal. As I dialed my car phone I kept my eyes open for a place to eat a decent breakfast.

She answered on the first ring. "Good morning." That voice. Clear and strong, musical without sounding silly. My mom.

"Your erratic daughter strikes again. We're going to have to reschedule our brainstorming session today." Mom was this year's chairperson for the largest AIDS fund-raiser in San Diego. As the committee's volunteer-at-large I'd mailed hundreds of letters in the last few weeks. Two days ago I'd agreed to fill a sudden hole in the events subcommittee but had yet to settle on any concrete money-making ideas. Mom and I had been planning to nail those down today over lunch.

"And what pressing matter takes precedence over lunch with your mother?" She was joking. Partly, anyway.

"The San Diego police called me in on a rape case."

"Oh, dear. Well, that is pressing. When do you think you'll be free? We're just eight days away from the big night."

"How about now? I've got the better part of two hours, and I can be all yours."

"You're in San Diego?" There was a pause while she thought it over. "Hmm. The newsletter *is* ready. I suppose I could meet with you now, then stop at the printer and kill two birds with one stone, to use a sadistic cliché." Raising cockatiels was one of Mom's hobbies. Her other "hobby," publishing an investor newsletter, was occupying more and more of her time these days. Her investor base had grown from five thousand to twenty-five thousand in the last year. These days she found it made financial sense to have the newsletter printed at a commercial press downtown.

"Perfect," I said. "Let's meet at the Grant." A historic hotel with fancy trappings and mediocre fare, but the ghosts were friendly.

Mom made a tsking noise. "But honey, the food's so lousy."

"Yes, but it's halfway between your printer and the police department. Remember, location—"

"I know," she sighed. "Location, location."

My scrambled eggs *looked* pretty, sitting on a china plate amid crystal stemware and polished silverware, but tasted as if they'd been chilled before serving. I'd been pushing them around with the corner of my toast for the last few minutes when Mom said, "Why don't you just give up on those and have a muffin?" She extended the basket my way.

I picked a cranberry muffin out of the linen-lined basket and flagged the waiter for a coffee warm-up. "I don't know how much of a storm my brain can muster at this point. I've been up since three thirty this morning." I'd filled Mom in on the basics of the rape case but hadn't wanted to discuss the details. She hadn't pressed, bless her.

"You don't even need to brainstorm. I've done all the brainstorming for you." The woman sitting across the table—Mom to me, Suzanne Sarah Chase to a growing army of admirers—looked invincible, capable of anything. As always, she had tied her long graying hair in a knot on top of her head Aunt Bea style, but with her red and gold silk Nehru jacket and pants she looked anything but matronly.

"Let me guess. You want me to emcee the charity auction."

She shook her head. "A little less traditional than that."

"Hmm. You want me to round up bachelors to be auctioned off?" This particular charity event would be patronized largely by San Diego's upper crust, an older crowd with a preponderance of well-to-do females.

"No," she said, buttering a muffin. "Although that could be lucrative."

"I give up. What's your brilliant idea for my part in filling the coffers?"

"I thought you might set up a table and read astrological charts."

For six years I had studied under two of the world's finest astrologers, and I'm always amazed by the accuracy of my chart readings. But astrology is something I pursue privately and discreetly. Mom's astrologer-at-the-charity-ball idea brought to mind a ridiculous image of myself in gypsy attire, crystal ball hovering nearby. I screwed up my face in distaste. "Oh God, Mom, no. No way."

She held up placating hands. "Hear me out. We could charge five hundred for each reading—"

"Five hundred!"

"For this crowd, darling, that's comparable to you and me buying a tube of toothpaste. Anyway, I figure you can do four readings an hour, over a four-hour evening that's eight thousand dollars. Eight thousand dollars would pay utility bills for a *lot* of AIDS patients, Elizabeth. And look at it this way: The donors would actually be getting something of *value* for their contribution, as opposed to yet another material object or some awkward evening on the town with an eligible stranger."

She was making sense. Mom was good at that. "Well . . ."

She reached across the table and squeezed my arm. "Thanks, honey. I just love the way I can count on you."

7

Mom had insisted on handling our breakfast tab so that I wouldn't be late. After checking in at the front desk I reached the SDPD elevator bank a few minutes early. So I really had no choice but to eavesdrop shamelessly on a couple of officers discussing how schedule changes had messed up their sex lives.

"Have you tried counseling?"

"Counseling? I need time in *bed*, buddy, not on the couch."

When Dianna came around the corner I was almost disappointed to see her. "Well, *we're* here on time," she said. Together we looked up at the clock above the elevator. Just then the doors dinged open to reveal a towheaded Dietz, standing cranelike on one leg, left foot and broad shoulders resting against the rear of the car.

He smiled. "Going down?"

The elevator descended slowly into the underground level and stopped with a bump. After an agonizing delay they parted again. Dietz stepped off first. Dianna and I followed him across the hallway and through an exit door into a vast, darkened garage.

I felt nervous and unprepared. "Suppose one of these suspects we're about to interview is our rapist. Won't a police interview tip him off? Wouldn't it be better to do a little surveillance on these guys?"

Dianna slowed her step. "Surveillance would be ideal. But surveillance work takes a lot of resources and a lot of time. Two months ago our guy went from rape to rape and cut. This morning he graduated from rape and cut to rape and stab. Time is a luxury we can't afford."

We walked the length of the garage in silence, our footsteps echoing back to us. The air down here was damp, and my lungs began to complain. An area contained by chain-link fencing came into view. "This is our prisoner control section," Dietz said.

Three black chairs made of industrial-strength plastic were secured to the cement floor. The seats were equipped with unforgiving restraints—woe unto the excessively resistant suspect. A sign on the wall read, DO NOT LEAVE 10-16s UNATTENDED. In one of the chairs a grizzled man bound by a single handcuff dozed peacefully. Nearby a uniformed officer sat reading a magazine.

We headed toward a door that led back into the building. A sign near the entrance read, CHECK YOUR WEAPONS. Dianna pulled a Ruger P85 from her belt, and Dietz opened his jacket and removed a Sig Sauer nine-millimeter from his shoulder holster. He glanced at me. "Are you armed?"

I opened my coat and felt for the bulge on my inside pocket. I pulled the piece out and offered it to Dietz. He glared at my outstretched hand. "That's a *pen*."

"Mightier than the sword."

Dianna chuckled. Dietz gave me a sidelong scowl and thrust the trusty Waterman back into my hand. "I don't think so, Chase."

"Oh, all right, have it your way." I pulled my own nine-millimeter—a Glock—from my purse and handed it to him, barrel to the floor. Dietz opened a wall locker beside the door and placed our weapons inside.

In the building we walked down a short hallway and into a small room badly in need of fresh paint. Black scuff marks marred the dirty white walls as if people had been climbing them for real. A few folding metal chairs surrounded a cheap laminated table. A tiny, thick-paned window in the door looked back out to the hallway. Dietz pulled out a chair for me. "Make yourself comfortable," he said.

I eyed the cramped quarters. "I'm not sure that's going to be possible. Especially when our company gets here. Sometimes this business of 'tuning in' can get downright unbearable."

"What do you mean?" Dianna asked, taking a chair.

"Sociopaths tend to leave physical as well as psychic impressions on me." I settled into the cold metal chair. "As a psychic guinea pig back at Stanford I did a series of interviews with convicted felons. One guy left me with some nasty asthma symptoms that took weeks to clear up. Later I found out he was a serial murderer, really into suffocation."

Dietz sat at the end of the table. "So what exactly is it that you do? Can't say as I've ever met a psychic investigator before. You like a human Geiger counter, or what?"

I wrapped my arms around my torso. "That's not a bad analogy. A Geiger counter detects the presence and intensity of various radiations. My ability to 'tune in,' as you call it, works much the same way. I feel presences as differing radiations, vibrations, if you will. Sometimes I can actually *see* what people are thinking."

Dietz frowned.

"I'm particularly good at numbers, for some reason. If a person thinks of a number, six times out of ten I can see it in my mind's eye. When I was a kid my parents used to trot me out at cocktail parties to amuse their friends. That old parlor game was the inspiration for some of my later research work at Stanford."

Dietz looked at me through narrowed eyes.

"Seriously."

He stroked the stubble on his chin with his thumb. "So how do you explain all this? As a scientist, I mean."

"Every thought is an electrochemical reaction, a physical reality, in the brain. That's a known fact. My own theory is that each thought has a corresponding wavelength, although we haven't yet developed the technology to measure these wavelengths. That doesn't mean they don't exist. Some people call them 'thought forms.' Anyway, psychics—people like me—have some kind of internal Geiger counter, to use your analogy, that picks up on and reads these thought-generated wavelengths. Sometimes."

"But not always?"

"Heck no. That was another phase of my research at Stanford, trying to figure out why extrasensory abilities are so damn sporadic. Even the most gifted psychics draw blanks or downright misread much of the time. The best explanation I could come up with has something to do with compatibility of vibratory rates. In other words, my brain recognizes certain people and situations the way some computer programs recognize certain files and not others."

"I'm not a computer person," Dianna said, "but I think I get what you're saying. Like putting your ATM card into different machines around the city. Some work, some don't."

"Yeah, there you go."

Dietz shook his head. "Sorry. Too way-out for me. No offense, but I'm not a believer."

"No offense taken," I replied. "Reasonable minds can differ."

He stared challengingly at me. "So, can you read the number in my mind?"

I looked into the ice-blue eyes, at the pale lashes that rimmed them. The eyes told me nothing—I felt about as receptive as an unplugged television set. "Frankly, you're difficult to read."

Dietz sat up straighter and smiled. He was obviously proud of his insusceptibility. "Can't read the thought form I'm beaming your way, huh?"

I pushed past my initial block, but whatever I was picking up was scrambled. I'd almost get something, but I couldn't quite *see* it. Videotape editors sometimes superimpose fuzzy squares on faces when they're trying to conceal identities on camera. Frustrating as hell to the viewer. Trying to read Dietz was a lot like that. I shook my head. "No, I can't read you."

An amused dimple appeared in his cheek. "Hmm. Maybe if you close your eyes."

But I didn't want to close my eyes. Not in this tiny interrogation room. Not in this cold underground place where the sun never reached. Something down here was giving me the willies.

8

A sudden knocking interrupted our conversation. The three of us looked up to see a smiling face framed in the door's small square window. It was Billings, the officer I'd met early this morning at Thomasina's house. He stepped into the tiny room and handed some paperwork to Dianna. "I'll be bringing our suspect over in a minute." While Dianna and Dietz read the paperwork he turned his freckled face toward me and began chatting. "We arrested a psychic once, you know."

My brows went up. "You're kidding."

Some people might have thought Billings's nose was a couple sizes too big for his face. I thought it was cute. "No kidding," he went on. "This midget who claimed he could channel. Weird thing was he escaped from jail."

I frowned. "Wait a minute—"

"Then we had a small medium at large." He gave me a mischievous grin and left the room.

Dietz looked up. "Rick's a compulsive jokester. May take some getting used to." He handed me the paperwork. "We've already seen this. Like I said, the guy's got a history. Look it over if you want."

I read with interest about the man Dietz had picked up near the rape site this morning. Robert "Bobby" Morgan. Born in Kentucky, high school dropout, moved west through a series of states and odd jobs. Served six months for a burglary conviction in 1979. Charged with sexual battery and aggravated assault in 1987, served four of an eight-year sentence. Bobby's pathetic life story on half a page.

I handed the paperwork to Dianna. "So what exactly are we trying to accomplish here? A full confession, or what?"

She shook her head. "We can always hope. More likely what we'll get from a guy like Morgan is a pack of lies, some of which could be incriminating. The majority of these SOBU graduates are remarkably stupid."

Officer Billings reappeared at the doorway. The man he escorted into the room hardly cut an imposing figure. Bobby Morgan was not much taller than me. Beneath a blue mechanic's uniform he had a dense build, more muscle than lard, but his body language was apologetic, not aggressive. His face also seemed to apologize for his receding hairline and outdated sideburns. I intuitively knew he had some kind of health problem, sick kidneys. I was beginning to feel sorry for the guy until his eyes locked onto mine. No apologies there. He smiled at me, revealing a well-worn set of graying teeth.

Dianna pointed Morgan to the chair directly across from mine. Bobby Morgan sat down, clasped his hands across his stomach, and patiently waited for the interview to begin.

Dietz began by reading Miranda. As he rattled through the right-to-remain-silent routine I focused in on Morgan. My hope was to catch some thought forms. There didn't appear to be a whole lot of action in that regard. As I tuned in more I did notice an underlying tension in the room, a negative presence. Hardly unusual, given the circumstances.

"Knowing these rights, are you willing to answer my questions?" Dietz spoke in a lifeless monotone.

Morgan grunted an equally monotonous "Yep."

"Why'd you run when I wanted to talk to you this morning?"

"I told ya. I wasn't runnin' from you, I was runnin' for the bus. I just got a new job that requires me to be to work on time. I didn't want to be late."

Dianna jumped in. "What job's that, Mr. Morgan?"

"The auto works down on Kettner."

Dietz fired off the next question. "What time do you start work there?"

" 'S'posed to be there by eight o'clock Tuesday through Saturday," Morgan shot back.

"Then what are you doing all the way over on Montezuma at six in the morning, if you have a job on Kettner and don't start work until eight? Don't lie to us, Morgan. We've got several witnesses who put you at the scene, on that very block." Dietz's voice was sharp and unforgiving. He bored into Morgan with an unrelenting stare.

Morgan blinked defiantly back at Dietz. "I told you. I was headed for the bus. Right now I'm relying on public transportation, as my license has been removed." He spoke with the unconvincing formality of an uneducated man trying to disguise that fact.

Meanwhile, Dianna had been scribbling on a yellow pad. She looked over at me and tapped her pencil on the note. I read surreptitiously: *Bus story prob'ly true. D got him in on traffic warrants.*

Dietz continued to press Morgan. "A six o'clock bus to get to an eight o'clock job? Come on. You expect us to believe that?"

"I got to transfer to the forty-one bus to go 'cross town. Next one that direction cuts it too short. The six o'clock goes a little too early, but it gives me time to stop at Coco's for breakfast before I go in."

Dietz hammered away with several more questions. Morgan fielded them in a defenseless, casual manner. He was either a remarkably practiced liar or an innocent man. I couldn't tell which. The only thing I felt certain of was that Bobby Morgan had problems.

Dietz finally ran out of steam. "Dr. Chase, you got anything to add here?"

"Yes, if I may. Could you two leave Mr. Morgan and me alone for my portion of the interview?" This was pure theater. The room was monitored and bugged. Any ex-con worth his salt would know that. Still, I could expect more candor one-on-one. Dietz and Dianna nodded and rose, squeezing past the table on their way out.

When the door closed I looked deep into Morgan's eyes. There wasn't much going on in there. "You were convicted and served four years for sexual battery and assault with a deadly weapon back in 1987. Would you be willing to talk to me about that now?"

Morgan unfolded his hands and leaned forward in his chair. "I already done my time for that."

"Yes, you have. And you can't be punished for discussing that crime now. I'm just trying to understand more about it." All that was true. It was also true that anything Morgan revealed that connected him to the rapes under investigation would be used against him in a heartbeat. If he had five minutes' worth of memory he'd understand that.

I continued to watch Morgan carefully, trying to match him with my psychic impressions of the intensely physical, calculating intruder I'd picked up on when the police escorted me through Thomasina Wilson's house this morning. It was difficult to picture this laid-back man countering Thomasina's karate move with a swift, unrelenting wrist hold. People can change dramatically, though, when their demons are let loose. I braced myself to see what I might find in Morgan's sexually twisted mind.

He scratched idly at one of his sideburns. "So what is it that you want to know?"

"Why don't you just tell me how the 1987 incident happened."

Morgan made a what-the-heck face. "Okay, I guess I can do that. Well, let's see. The thing occurred on a weekend. I'd been fightin' with my woman and was out drinking with a couple of buddies. I happened to meet a lady in the bar and started associating with her. This led to other things, and soon we was taking a ride in my car.

"After a ways I told her that I would like to do it with her. She refused me. One thing led to another and before you knew it, her clothes were off and this thing occurred."

"What thing?"

"As the lawyers say, 'forceful intercourse,' " he replied nonchalantly.

"Did you use a weapon?"

"I had a hunting knife in the car there," he answered vaguely.

"A hunting knife. Was it some old, dull thing you had in the trunk? Or was it a decent knife?"

He nodded vigorously. "Oh, it was a fine knife, all right. I know how to sharpen a hunting knife. If I'd touched that knife to any portion of her body, it would have laid her open."

The pride shining in Morgan's face was sickening. God forbid I insult his knife-sharpening skills. I willed the muscles in my face to remain impassive.

"Did you intend to use it on her?"

"I suppose if she had made trouble, yes, I would have used it. But I just held it there, and she didn't scream or nothing. She didn't put up much of a struggle at all."

"So you raped her, then?"

"In a manner of speaking, yes, I suppose I did." Morgan scooted up in his chair a bit. "I don't consider myself a rapist, as far as that's concerned." His graying eyebrows came together, as if he were pondering life's deepest question. "You see, I look at myself as being a lover of women. Now at first she objected and such, but on account of certain clues I had—her not having stockings on and such things—I know I was giving her what she wanted. But as far as the law's concerned, well now, that's a different interpretation."

"Apparently the law didn't consider you a rapist, either." I heard the bitterness in my voice and made an effort to tone it down. "You were charged with sexual battery."

He nodded thoughtfully, as if appreciating this new angle on his criminal career.

"Would you rape again?"

Bobby Morgan thrust his hands deep into his pockets and pondered for several moments. "At this point right here I would have to say that I don't believe it will happen again. But if things should happen such that there are the right combinations of troubles and tensions . . ." His voice trailed off.

"Then what?"

He shrugged noncommittally. "It might happen again."

I don't know which appalled me more, his complete lack of responsibility or his supreme stupidity in making an admission like that during a police interview. The shock must have shown in my face, because he went on to explain himself. "What I'm saying is, under certain circumstances it could happen again, possibly. If the circumstances was all there. Do you understand what I'm sayin'?" He seemed determined for me to comprehend.

"I hear what you're saying, Mr. Morgan." I was doing my best to keep my mask in place. Apparently my disgust was still obvious, because he shook his head and made a "sheesh" sound under his breath, as if I were the biggest fool he'd suffered all week.

"Well then, I guess that will be all." I took a deep breath and heaved a long sigh of relief that the interview was over. But the relief didn't last long. It disappeared the moment I looked through the door's tiny square window. Staring through the thick-paned glass was a familiar pair of skewed black eyes.

9

The room was too damn small. I came to this conclusion the moment I realized I'd be sharing it with Richard Zimmer. The scuff-marked walls made perfect sense to me now. I might be scaling them soon myself.

The door opened, and Dianna popped her head in. "You about done in here? The next interviewee is ready." Behind Dianna, Dietz stood smiling. He was having a good old time.

My heart kicked into overdrive. "Just a sec." I turned back to Bobby Morgan. "Do me a favor?"

"Yes ma'am?"

I looked him in the eye. What the hell, no harm trying. "Don't rape any more women."

"No ma'am."

Lying bastard. He stood up, shoulders slumping, and turned toward Dianna, who escorted him out. His blue pants bagged in the back. As Mr. Morgan shuffled through the door I indulged in the gratifying fantasy of giving his sorry ass a kick.

I called out to Dietz. "Hey, could you come in here a minute? I need to talk with you."

Dietz stepped through the doorway and stared at me. "You look a little worried. What's the matter? Did Morgan pull some weird shit on you?"

I shook my head. "No, I'm okay."

Dietz pushed the door shut, looking concerned. "What's up? You afraid of Zimmer?"

"Under different circumstances I'd be terrified of him. Right now I'm just afraid I don't know what we're expecting to gain by interviewing him. He's got a rap sheet that could carpet a runway, so I'm sure he knows how to play this game better than I do. The man looks nasty, but he doesn't look dumb."

"No, he's not dumb. Under ordinary circumstances Zimmer's pretty tight-lipped. But these aren't the usual circumstances. Today we have the beautiful Dr. Elizabeth Chase to unhinge that jaw of his." He popped his knuckles and grinned.

I thought about Zimmer pulling his girlfriend's shoulder apart and shuddered. "Let's not talk about the Zipper unhinging any more joints."

Dietz pulled out a chair and sat down. He leaned close enough that I could feel his hot breath on my ear. It didn't smell so great. "I think you're tougher than you let on," he whispered. He looked right through me with his pale blue eyes, found my tough self, and smiled at her.

His last move startled me. *We'll see*, I thought.

Dietz smiled reassuringly. "Remember, we're not expecting a confession here. What Dianna and I are hoping to do is confront him with the case. Let him know it's tight, that we're onto him. All we're really looking for are incriminating lies, bullshit details that could come back to haunt him. What you're looking for, I'm not sure."

I wasn't entirely sure myself, a fact I didn't advertise. "I still don't get the game plan here. If you let him know you're onto him, won't he run or lay low or otherwise make it impossible to catch him?"

Dietz shrugged. "Yeah, he might. But think about it. These attacks have escalated from every few months to every two months. From surface cutting to serious stabbing. This is a murder just waiting to happen. If Zimmer's the guy, our interview might slow him down. Nothing wrong with that, is there?"

A rush of cold air entered the room as the door swung open. I surrounded myself with a cocoon of white light and pushed my chair as far back against the wall as it would go. Dianna stepped through the doorway. Zimmer followed closely behind.

In all fairness I have to say that the Zipper took a bad photograph. The hideous creature from the APB mug shot was not the man who walked through the door and lowered himself gracefully into a seat across the table from me. Zimmer was buffed out all right, but he didn't wear his muscles like a clumsy suit of armor as so many weight lifters do. In person his asymmetrical black eyes, set off by thick black eyebrows, were more intriguing than unsettling.

He smiled, a brief flash of ultrawhite teeth under a thick but neatly trimmed mustache. "Hello," he said politely.

I didn't reply. An urgent message was hammering in my gut. Something was very wrong here. Dietz, drumming the table with his fingers on my right, was distracting me. I took a deep breath, hoping to clear my mind. I tried to picture a perfectly still mountain lake, an image sometimes conducive to insightful reflections. What came up were gray high seas on a stormy day, restless, choppy waves as far as my inner eye could see. Great.

Dianna sat down and slapped a stack of paper onto the table. I recognized the computer printout of Richard Zimmer's formidable rap sheet. She flipped through the pages and began in a congenial tone: "I wish to advise you that you have the right to remain silent. If you give up the right to remain silent, anything you do say can and will be used in court against you. . . ."

Zimmer caught my eye. He extended his hand toward Dianna and pushed the mute button on an imaginary remote control. Or perhaps he was detonating an imaginary bomb.

". . . You have a right to speak with an attorney of your choice before questioning and to have the attorney present during questioning—"

Zimmer broke in. "Excuse me, ma'am. I got a question: What do I do if my lawyer is up to his neck in paperwork?"

Dianna glanced at Dietz, who shook his head.

Zimmer delivered the punch line. "Pile on more paperwork, obviously."

No one laughed but Zimmer.

Dianna got Zimmer's consent and began with the easy questions, an old ploy to get the suspect's tongue loosened. What is your birthday? Where were you born? Where do you live? Where do you work?

To this last question Richard Zimmer replied, "I gave the answers to all these same questions to that other cop, what's his name? Billings. Last Saturday. Don't you guys talk to each other, or what?"

Dianna answered by repeating the question: "Where do you work?"

"I own my own contracting business."

"How long have you been in business?"

"Since summer of ninety-two."

"You were operating this same business in March of last year?"

"Yes."

"Do you recall what you were doing on the night of March twentieth?"

Zimmer's mustache twitched as he suppressed a smile. "Do you recall what *you* were doing on March twenty?" he asked reasonably. "That was ten months ago."

"A simple yes or no will do, Mr. Zimmer."

"No."

"Do you recognize this woman?" Dianna tossed an eight-by-ten glossy across the table to Zimmer. His hinky eyes lingered on the image of a blond woman in her twenties. When they came back up to meet Dianna's, Zimmer's eyes were unreadable. "No."

"How about June ninth?"

"Six nine?" Zimmer asked, smiling over at me.

"The ninth of June, Mr. Zimmer. Summer vacation, perhaps?"

"Again, I would have to check my diary."

"You keep a diary?"

Zimmer rolled his eyes. "That was a joke, Detective."

Dianna slid another photograph across the table. I caught a glimpse of a woman with curly brown hair and very full lips. Zimmer reached across the table for the photograph. The third finger on his left hand was missing, severed just below the knuckle. "No idea," he said, looking up.

"Maybe you recall what you were doing on Halloween night. Trick-or-treating in your costume, perhaps?"

"I'm wearing it now."

The three of us took a visual inventory of Zimmer's outfit, an unremarkable ensemble of casual pants and a knit shirt open at the collar. When he saw us looking, Zimmer smiled, an eerie movement that crept across his face like something spilled. "The costume's under my clothes, of course."

Again no one laughed.

Zimmer shook his head. "God, you people have no sense of humor."

Dianna slid a third photograph over to Zimmer. It was a full-color profile of a Hispanic beauty whose loveliness had been destroyed by a savage knife wound. The blade had torn through her cheek to the edge of her mouth, leaving gums and teeth exposed to the camera. "Perhaps she'll jog your memory."

Again Zimmer stared at the photograph. I could feel him drinking in the violent image. A man with a thirst. When he looked up his black eyes were cold and remote. "That's just absolutely horrible," he said.

"Officer Billings brought you in for questioning on Saturday. You were detained for possession of a controlled substance. When were you released?"

"They let me go late Sunday afternoon."

"So where were you on Sunday night?"

"Taking a long walk on the beach. Enjoying my freedom."

"You sure you weren't enjoying her?" Dianna slid a fourth picture across the table. I recognized Thomasina Wilson, her features rigid with trauma, the muscles in her face not yet relaxed by morphine.

"Never seen her before." He smiled. "Looks like she's having a bad day though, doesn't it?"

Dianna shot him a withering look, but Zimmer kept on smiling. She turned to me. "Do you have anything to add, Dr. Chase?"

I nodded.

"Dr. Chase is a . . .. psychologist, helping us interview today. She'll be asking just a few more questions."

"A psychologist? What fun. So, are you gonna play with my head?" He leered at me when he spoke, making it obvious he was referring to his *little* head.

People often hide their innermost selves behind external subjects—politics, the weather, the dire state of the world. Humor, particularly sarcastic humor, can be another mask. I wanted to see Zimmer talk about himself. "I'd like to find out a little about your criminal record," I said, looking directly into his indirect eyes.

He nodded at me and started humming "Getting to Know You."

"Don't you think the comedy schtick is a little inappropriate under the circumstances?" I asked.

His humming stopped abruptly. "Look, I'm an innocent man who's being inconvenienced. I'm being cooperative. Do I have to be morbid, too?"

"Let's review the record. Tell me about this Health & Safety Code violation from 1990."

"Ah, yes. Under the influence. When I relax, I prefer to smoke the natural herb, rather than destroy my liver with alcohol. According to the unenlightened laws of this state, that makes me a criminal." Anger flickered in his black eyes.

"Then three months later, December, possession with intent to sell?"

"Ludicrous. Tell me, when you buy a pound of that socially sanctioned drug, caffeinated coffee, do you have any intention of selling it? Yet my pound of pot automatically throws me in league with the drug lords. The State of California should be renamed the State of Paranoia. It's pathetic, really." His tirade was filled with contempt.

"Burglary?"

He threw back his head and laughed. "Oh, God. It's almost funny to me now. When your girlfriend loves you she can't give you enough. Televisions, stereos, video cameras. When she's mad at you all the sudden they're hers again, and somehow you've *stolen* them."

"Assault?"

"That's what they call it when the same girlfriend goes ballistic on you, and all you meant to do was defend yourself." Palms up, hurt puppy eyes, Zimmer obviously relished playing the part of the innocent accused.

"Assault with a deadly weapon?"

Again his eyes rolled. "Deadly weapon. Did you know that your bedroom lamp is a deadly weapon? That whole thing was a misunderstanding. She was hysterical. I was trying to calm her down, keep her from hurting herself. She panicked and got a little muscle strain." His tone was so sincere I might have believed it myself.

"The victim was treated at Mercy Hospital for a dislocated shoulder, Mr. Zimmer. Describing the injury, a doctor wrote that 'the elbow and shoulder were ripped apart like a chicken wing.' Off the record your 'girlfriend' later told acquaintances that you had forcibly raped her."

He gestured emphatically with his three-fingered hand. "Exactly, *later*. When she'd had time to make up a dramatic story. She admitted herself that whole thing was an accident. By the time the cops got there she'd calmed down and didn't even want to make a report. Only reason there's anything in my record at all is because of the ridiculous domestic violence laws. Mandatory reporting and all. Probably a good idea for some situations, but in a case like mine it was absurd."

I waited silently to see if he might modify this story, perhaps add a postscript that admitted to some weensy bit of accountability in any of these events. It was a long wait.

Finally I broke the silence. "What happened to your finger?"

"I'm embarrassed to tell you."

"After all we've shared?"

My joke elicited a smug smile, as if he were pleased that I'd come down to his level. "This"—he gave me his half-mast finger—"is very symbolic. My own dog bit this finger off. I tell ya, I don't get no respect!" His Rodney Dangerfield was perfect.

Richard Zimmer had told me enough. Even if the facts fit his whitewashed version of the story, this was a man filled with rage. That he pretended to be so carefree demonstrated a profound and dangerous repression.

"I'll be frank with you, Mr. Zimmer. Your record clearly shows a pattern of escalating violence. Where do you think this is headed?"

"I really can't say, Dr. Chase." Anyone could see the hostility boiling under his smirk. His tone was pure sarcasm. "I try to live one day at a time, you know?"

The black eyes fixed on me, but didn't. They were no longer intriguing.

10

"So you really believe Zimmer's responsible for all the rapes?"

Dietz, Dianna, and I were walking back out the way we'd come in. I had almost asked them if they thought he was guilty, but I rephrased my question before it left my lips. Zimmer was obviously guilty of a truckload of lawless indiscretions. The question was, which ones?

Dietz opened the hallway door, and Dianna and I stepped through. "Hard to tell. Let's say he's as good a guess as any right now. Morgan's alibis hold together awfully well, especially considering the guy's no rocket scientist."

We stopped at the locker near the exit to the underground garage. Dietz opened it and pulled out his Sig, then handed Dianna her Ruger and turned my Glock over to me.

I placed the gun back in my purse. "So. Finding a rapist in a city this size is like locating the proverbial needle in the haystack, isn't it?"

"I wish it were that simple." Dianna checked her weapon before replacing it in her holster. "At least with the haystack scenario you're fairly sure the needle's in there somewhere. We don't even know if we're looking in the right haystack. How do we even look for this guy? We can't go through mug books, we have no face ID. We have no fingerprints, no witnesses, nothing."

"But Zimmer's your best suspect because—"

Dietz started walking. "Because he's an asshole, because he's got a sex crime history, because a van fitting the description of his vehicle was reported in the neighborhood at the time of the first rape in the series."

"Zimmer's van was parked in Hillcrest the night of the March twentieth rape?"

"Someone saw a white van there earlier that day," Dianna explained.

We walked in silence for a while through the darkened garage, back past the prisoner control area. The man who had been handcuffed to the chair was now gone. This time I noticed that the chain-link fencing extended along the entire back wall of the garage. Dark forms and shadows loomed beyond the fence. "What's back there?" I asked.

Dietz looked over. "Stuff that's too large to be stored in the evidence room. Vehicles impounded from crime scenes, mostly. See? There's that congresswoman's Lincoln that was bombed awhile back. It'll stay back there until the DA doesn't need it anymore. Stuff like that."

I edged closer. It looked like the world's creepiest used-car lot. "Back to this morning," I said. "Say Zimmer's the one. What's stopping you from getting a semen sample and making the DNA match?"

Dianna sighed. "Apart from the monumental legal hurdles, there's no DNA to match."

"I don't understand. We're talking rape here. Do you mean to tell me the man's not leaving physical evidence at the scenes, so to speak?"

Dietz glanced back at me. "We have some clothing fiber. Very inconclusive. That's about it."

I stopped in my tracks. "Are you telling me there's no . . . *biological* evidence?"

Dianna stopped alongside me. "Let's put it this way: The gloves on his hands are not the only pieces of latex this guy wears." She watched my face as I figured that one out.

"Whoa." *Cold, conscious, calculating.* "How about pubic hair?" I asked.

"We expect he's one clean-shaven dude."

Very calculating. I let it all sink in. "No positive ID, no physical evidence. Unless you walk in on him he'll be impossible to catch— let alone prosecute."

"Yeah," Dietz said, "but we've hired this really good psychic."

"Smart move," I replied.

We continued walking. The cavernous garage seemed even more ominous after brushing elbows with the likes of Morgan and Zimmer. The perpetual darkness down here left me with a strange sense of timelessness. It was never morning, never afternoon, never night. Just dark. I was relieved when we approached the elevator, brightly lit with oversized outdoor lightbulbs.

"So what do you think? About Zimmer, I mean." Dianna looked expectantly at me.

"He's an asshole with a sex crime history. There were definitely evil vibes in that interview room. Don't ask me that next question, because the answer is I don't know yet. Even if I did, you're going to need a lot more evidence than what I can give you at this point. Bad vibes hardly constitute probable cause."

The elevator dinged, as if my last point had been right on target.

11

That cranberry muffin I'd eaten at the Grant Hotel had held me for about forty minutes. I'd pretty much been starving ever since. Fortunately, the first reported incident involving the rapist with latex gloves had occurred in the same neighborhood as one of my favorite restaurants, so at least I could get a good meal before investigating the crime scene. The City Deli was a western outpost of New York Jewish delicatessen heaven with booths roomy enough to accommodate both paperwork and a generous bowl of matzo ball soup.

The nearest parking space was two blocks away, so I was damp but not soaking by the time I reached the door. I took a booth by the window and spread my map of San Diego out across the Formica tabletop. I sent a hint to the waiter by turning my coffee cup upright and settled down to work. Using a felt-tip pen I marked the four "definite-for-sure" attacks by the gloved rapist, noting the dates, victim names, and salient details on a separate piece of paper.

The first victim, Annie Drummond, had been attacked here in Hillcrest on March 20, the first day of spring. *In like a lion*, I thought grimly, circling the spot on my map. In San Diego, Hillcrest is synonymous with the gay community. Blocks filled with chichi coffeehouses, hip boutiques, retro diners, and independent bookstores center around a venerable movie theater featuring the finer offerings of maverick filmmakers. Parking is scarce, and walking is the preferred mode of travel. Same-sex couples, fashionably dressed, stroll the busy sidewalks until fashionably late hours. In short, Hillcrest is the kind of place a girl would never expect to be raped.

The second victim, Sandy Devereaux, had been raped in June, three months later, at her home in University Heights, just east of Hillcrest. I made another small oval on the map.

The third victim, Marisa Sanchez—the woman whose bloodied nightgown had made Halloween's eleven o'clock news—had been attacked farther east, in Kensington. Again I circled the spot.

This morning's victim, Thomasina Wilson, had been raped in her home near San Diego State University. As I circled the address, an image of the three-gabled house appeared in my mind. I tried to head off what I knew was coming next but could not close my inner eyes against the memory of Thomasina's bloodstained sheets.

Plotted on the map, the sites formed an obvious pattern. All four rapes had occurred along the canyon rim above the Mission Valley freeway. Looking down at the map I saw the oval pen marks as an ominous trail of footprints heading east along the freeway.

"Getting better acquainted with the World's Finest City I see." The waiter smiled down at the map.

I gave him a strained smile. "You could say that." He filled my cup, and I ordered the matzo ball soup. While I waited for my meal I pulled the "maybe" file from my briefcase. There were seven cases here, some going back two years. None of the victims had described latex gloves, but all had been raped in the middle of the night by an intruder.

I was using a blue pencil to circle the "maybe" incidents on my map when the waiter brought my soup. Fresh and perfectly seasoned, it smelled sublime as always, especially on a day as wet and cold as this one. The waiter refilled my coffee. "I know a great little place if you're looking for a house to rent," he said brightly.

"Thanks, but I'm happy where I am."

"Well, that's good. I certainly wouldn't want you living out *there*." He pointed to the smattering of blue circles on the southeastern edge of the city map. The "maybes" did seem to be clumped into the rough side of town.

I pushed the whole business aside and concentrated on my meal. When I was through I tried to brace myself to face the rain again. Dessert suddenly became a necessity. I opted for a slice of pure and simple New York cheesecake. Something about the satisfying, sensual experience of eating it inspired me to connect with Tom McGowan, an officer with the Escondido Police Department. While he wasn't exactly my "other" at this point, McGowan had been playing an increasingly significant role in my life in the months since we'd met. The prospect of rearranging my comfortably eccentric existence to accommodate a man had been scaring me a bit, but never enough to offset the pleasure of his company. And so far my eccentricity hadn't scared him off, either. I called his office from a pay phone near the restrooms.

He answered on the second ring. "Sergeant McGowan."

"Detective Chase."

"Oh, hi. I was just thinking about you. It's lunchtime, let's go grab a bite."

I smiled as I pictured McGowan's big hand wrapped around the receiver, his lips smiling against the mouthpiece. "Too late. I just ate. Besides, I got hauled downtown by the San Diego police."

McGowan made a tsking sound. "They gave you one phone call and I'm it, huh? Didn't I tell you to stay out of trouble?"

Now I could picture his entire face—deep dimples at the corners of his smile, big brown eyes twinkling. "Why should I mind you?"

"No good reason." There was a pause during which a palpable warmth crossed the wires. "So what are you doing down there anyway?" he asked.

"The SDPD finally took me up on my offer to assist in that serial rape case."

I'd told McGowan about visiting Lieutenant Marcone after my dream of the three-gabled house. McGowan was hardly surprised when I hadn't heard back from the SDPD. He sounded surprised now. "What do you think prompted that?"

"Maybe the vicious stab wounds on this morning's victim had something to do with it."

He groaned. "Ugh. I hate working rape cases. That particular brand of emotional pain the victims go through unglues me. And I'm not even a sensitive. How're you holding up?"

"So far so good."

"Why don't I come by tonight? We'll go out for dinner. Rain be damned."

"Sounds good to me."

"Who are you working with down there?"

"Lieutenant Marcone brought me in, but he's got a bunch of people on the case. I'm working with, let's see, a cop named Rick Billings and a couple of detectives named Dietz and Powers."

"Dianna Powers?"

"Yeah. You know her?"

"Yeah. She's good people. We worked together on a countywide DV task force about a year ago." I heard him blow out a breath. "People around here were talking about that rape this morning. Sounded bad."

"It wasn't pretty. Hey, Tom?"

"Yeah?"

"You're more sensitive than you think. I keep telling you that."

"I've got another call," he said abruptly. "Not to be insensitive. See you tonight."

"See ya."

Next I tried to call the first rape victim, Annie Drummond, but her number was no longer in service. I left money on my table and prepared to brave the rain back to my car, making a mental note to buy an umbrella. I'd managed to live most of my life in San Diego without owning one. This year was another story.

I drove west on University, made a right turn against the red at Fourth, then drove north all the way to the canyon rim. In the 1920s this neighborhood, two miles from downtown, had been suburbia, a quiet street lined with pepper trees, bungalows, and a Victorian or two. Today multistory condominiums dominated the area, but the occasional quaint house survived between the highrises. Annie Drummond's address, 4212, turned out to be just such a dwelling, a small white bungalow with wood-sashed windows, green wooden shutters, a matching green porch, and a red brick chimney.

I squeezed my Mustang into a space along the curb about a half block from the house. The rain had let up to a temperamental, sporadic splattering. With a grimace I left the warmth of my car and jogged down the cement sidewalk. As I turned up Annie Drummond's walkway a gust of wet wind came from behind and practically pushed me up the wide green steps onto the covered porch. I took a moment to rewrap my coat and get my bearings before pushing the stiff little black button protruding from the old-fashioned doorbell.

I thought I heard chiming inside but opened the screen and knocked on the door just in case. The inside shutters were closed, so it was hard to tell if any lights were on or if anyone was home. My senses of sound and hearing stymied, I tuned in with my other sense, the sixth one.

I saw the interior—a living room with gleaming hardwood floors. Eyes closed, I saw a brick fireplace flanked by built-in bookshelves enclosed in panes of beveled glass. I got the impression of the occupant's valiant attempt to create order and beauty in an otherwise lonely life. Beyond the living room I vaguely made out a short hallway, bedrooms off to either side. At the end of the hallway, a bathroom. Original porcelain fixtures.

Something made me nervous, and the picture faded. All that talk in Dianna's office about rapists returning to the scene of the crime was getting to me, no doubt. I turned around. The neighborhood was quiet, save for the rain spattering the pavement in bursts. The day was dark enough that a few lights shone through the windows of the houses and condos across the street. I turned back toward the house. Then I saw it.

In my mind now, back inside. In the bedroom off to the right, a woman asleep. A man approaching from the hallway, stepping slowly on the wooden floor, careful to keep his footfall quiet. Nearing the bed. Standing over the bed for a long time, watching the rise and fall of the sheets as the woman breathes, dreaming. Now extending a gloved hand toward her throat, now pinning her chest to the bed with his knee—

"Don't move!"

I did the exact opposite. I spun around and found myself staring down the barrel of a gun.

12

I recognized the gun's manufacturer—Lego—but the red, yellow, and white blocks had been fashioned into a model I couldn't readily identify. Something between a Saturday night special and a twenty-two was my guess. My captor was blond, about four foot two, fifty-five pounds. A kindergarten graduate from the intelligent gleam in his eye.

"Okay, relax, I'm a good guy." I smiled hopefully at him, but he didn't lower his weapon. "Do you know where Annie Drummond is?" I asked. Perhaps name-dropping would let him know I belonged here, more or less.

"She moved away after the robber," he said.

The robber.

"Are you a friend of hers?" I asked.

"Uh-huh. Are you?"

"Kind of. I'd like to be. My name's Elizabeth. What's yours?"

"Sean." Dropping the toy gun to his side now.

"Nice to meet you, Sean. So, do you know where Annie moved to?"

"She moved to her parents' house."

"Know where they live?"

He shook his head.

"So you heard about the robber, huh?"

He nodded.

"Pretty scary, isn't it?"

He shrugged, as if being scared had never occurred to him. Tough kid.

"Do you know anything else about what happened?"

He shoved the Lego gun into his right pants pocket and said, "Yeah, I know *all* about what happened." His voice was surprisingly low for a six-year-old's.

"So tell me."

"A robber broke in the back door of Annie's house and scared her with a knife. He took so much of her stuff that she had to move into her parents' house. He didn't take the birds, though."

"Annie had birds?"

"Fred and Barney. They were really kind of my birds, too. I named 'em and stuff."

I wondered what other little white lies, besides this business of a robber, had been put into Sean's impressionable mind by protective, well-meaning adults. He probably wouldn't be my most reliable source. "So did they catch the robber?"

"Nope."

"Is it kind of scary, knowing there could be a robber around here?"

"Kind of. But I'm going to catch him if I can. I'm keeping a lookout on Annie's old house. From my bedroom window, see?" He pointed across the yard to a window on the side of the house next door. "That's how I caught *you*," he added.

Very tough kid. Showed promise in law enforcement.

"Okay, Sean, but be careful, will you? Even cops have backup, you know. Does anyone know you're out here?" I looked over to Sean's house and saw a woman's face peering from the front window.

"I can take care of myself," he said.

I began a reassuring wave to the woman in the window, but at that moment the door before me opened. A tall brunette in a raincoat, preoccupied with the task of opening her umbrella, began to step out onto the porch. She stopped short when she saw us and inhaled dramatically with a high-pitched gasp. Then her eyes fell on Sean and registered a friend. She put her hand to her chest, relaxed a bit, and said, "You two nearly scared me half to death."

"I rang the bell and knocked—" I began.

"I couldn't hear you over the radio. Listen, I'm late for work. Whatever it is you want, sorry." She was direct but not unfriendly. Her eyes were warm, and her apologetic smile was genuine. She held her black umbrella aloft and moved toward the street.

I followed her down the steps and into the rain, which had started up steadily again. Sean followed us both. I turned to the boy and said, "Sean, I need to talk to this lady alone. It's very important. Okay?" He nodded and headed toward home.

"I know you can't right now"—I was jogging to catch up to the woman, raising my voice against the rainfall—"but I would like to talk to you at your convenience about the rape that occurred at this address in March of last year. I'm a private investigator." I handed her one of my cards.

She stopped, ran her eyes over the card, and then over to me. "Psychic. That's different." She resumed her determined walk to the car. "Look, I've already been interviewed by the police. I don't know anything. I moved in after that all happened, after that poor girl moved out."

"Brave of you," I said.

"Hey, what are the chances of lightning striking in the same spot twice?" She said it half laughing, her black umbrella floating above her like a dark cloud.

"Actually, there have been some studies on the very question of lightning striking twice in the same place. Statistically, the probability is something like one in ten to the tenth power. From a scientist's point of view, that's not the outer limits of unlikelihood." The woman gave me an incredulous look, and for a second I felt like a nerd. "The point is, we're not talking about lightning here," I finished.

She shook her head, clearly amused. "Statistical probability, huh? You're a hoot. I promise I don't know a thing that could help you. You'd be a kick to talk to, though. Wish I could, but I'm already running late. I work up in Orange County." She rolled her eyes. "I know, the commute's insane. At DigiCom. Give me a call up there, or leave me a voice mail if I'm not in. You're getting wet."

Her last remark had been an understatement. I brushed rain out of my eyes. "What's your name?" I asked.

"Oh, sorry." She opened her car door. "Forgot you didn't know me. Cheryl. Cheryl Arendt." She slid inside, shut the door, and waved good-bye through the window. Then rolled it down with a parting comment. "You wouldn't believe how much the landlord discounted my rent."

"Yes I would." I said it to the rain. Cheryl had already pulled away.

I climbed back into my Mustang with a sigh. This was the kind of thing I'd been talking about when I told the case detectives I worked the same old boring routines they did. I groped in the backseat for my gym bag, hoping to find a towel. My coat had done a decent job of keeping my body dry, but my hair was drenched. I pulled a wrinkled length of terry cloth from a tangle of wadded-up sweats, wrapped my head, and rubbed. In the rearview I brushed my wet hair straight back off my face, aiming for a snazzy European look. I was pretty sure I missed.

I picked up the March 20 police report off the car seat. Once again I read the description of the crime. Annie had been awakened at approximately three thirty in the morning by a man's latex-gloved hand shoving her face into the pillow. Her rapist had pinned her chest to the bed with his knee and had threatened to slice her if she resisted in any way. She was attacked twice during her hour-long ordeal. Annie had obviously been in shock during her police interview, answering questions but offering little on her own other than, "I didn't fight back," repeated over and over again like a mantra. There wasn't a space for an alternate home address, but the address and phone number of Annie's employer, the First National Bank on Broadway, had been penned on the form.

I called First National from my car phone and spoke with Joyce Hendricks, the bank manager. Annie Drummond had left the bank eight months ago. Ms. Hendricks didn't come right out and say it, but I gathered that what had begun as a "medical" leave of absence for Annie had turned into a formal termination. As far as she knew, Annie was still living with her parents. When I reminded her that I was working with the SDPD, she gave me the parents' address in Clairemont.

"Good luck, Ms. Chase," she said before hanging up. "You know," Annie's old boss added slowly, choosing her words with caution, "we all hope that Annie is getting . . . better by now. We'd all like her to be her old self again."

Something told me that Annie Drummond wouldn't be her old self again for a long, long time. Maybe ever.

13

Always a bit of a thrill, passing the peephole test. There I stand on a stranger's doorstep, unbidden, ringing the bell with no assurance of entry. I'm completely at the mercy of the occupant behind the closed door. It's true that I probably don't cut a threatening picture. I'm physically fit and of decent height but by no means powerfully built. A cosmetologist once described my features as "open and honest." I'd like to think those qualities apply to my character as well. But whatever image I project to a householder, the best-case scenario would be that I'm some nice lady raising money for a worthy charity. Worst-case scenario, I'm an ax murderer. I suppose private investigator falls somewhere between the two.

The peephole at 1963 Norwalk in Clairemont darkened. I waited several long moments while the occupant sized me up, my features this morning apparently not open and honest enough to gain immediate trust. I smiled wanly at my unseen judge, the way I sometimes smile for the invisible security guards who monitor the discreet closed-circuit television cameras at ATMs and department stores. The simpering smile worked. The door swung open.

"You here from Ford Motor Credit?"

Ah, I'd been mistaken for a bill collector. That meant I looked more like an ax murderer than a do-gooder today. The man continued to size me up and I sized him right back. Late fifties, early sixties. Very fit for any age. Five eleven. Grecian Formula dark hair. The appearance of youth belied only by his polyester no-iron pants and shirt.

"No, I'm not a creditor." Behind me the rain intensified, and I raised my voice to be heard above the downpour. "I'm a private detective working with the San Diego Police Department regarding Annie Drummond's case." I handed him my card.

He couldn't read very well without glasses, otherwise he would have commented on, or at least raised an eyebrow over, the line that read *Psychic Investigator*. As it was he looked at the card briefly, slumped a bit, and waved me forward. "Come on in."

I stepped onto an immaculate faux marble hall floor and hoped the gritty sensation under my soles didn't look as bad as it felt. Beyond the hallway I could see a sunken living room decorated entirely in tones of white and silver. The house felt chilled, as if the two of us had just returned from a vacation and the heat had been off for days.

"Can I take your coat?" he offered.

I shivered at the thought. "That's okay. I don't intend to take much of your time. I wondered if I might—"

Before I could finish the sentence he leaned toward the living room and yelled, "Ja-ane!" Giving the name two drawn-out syllables. Then he turned to me and said in a speaking voice, "You talk to my wife here."

A woman wearing thick tomato red sweats and white athletic shoes approached from the back of the house. Her smooth-skinned face, framed by a lovely head of well-cut gray hair, silently questioned her husband. He pointed to me. "She's working with the police about Annie's case."

I extended my hand to her. "Hi. I'm Elizabeth."

The woman's soft, slender fingers were freezing, but her shake was firm. "How do you do. I'm Annie's mother, Jane Drummond. Have you met Roger?"

I glanced in his direction and smiled. "Sort of unofficially, yes. Hi, Roger."

Roger Drummond nodded without smiling.

"I was just saying that I had hoped I could talk to your daughter, Annie, if she's here." The Drummonds exchanged a ponderous glance, and an awkward silence followed.

Roger finally responded. "Annie tends to take a lot of naps." He kept his eyes on his wife as he spoke, as if she'd been the one asking. "Why don't the two of you talk and I'll see if I can go rouse her." He marched out of the room and disappeared into a back hallway.

"Well, come in and sit down," Jane said. "We haven't heard much from the police these last couple of months. Beginning to think they'd given up."

I followed Jane Drummond down two white carpeted steps and took a seat with her on an alabaster sofa. The living room had no visible dust and even less color. In her red sweats Mrs. Drummond was the solitary bright spot, a cardinal in the snow. "No," I said, "the police certainly haven't given up." I slid my fingers under my thighs to warm them and tried to be discreet about it. "The investigation is intensifying. That's why I'm here. I'm hoping to get some more information from Annie, anything the police might have missed."

She took a deep breath, as if on the verge of making a bold statement. I could practically hear her suppress the thought. I watched her eyes shift as she ventured into more comfortable territory. "Can I get you anything?"

My heart's desire was to ask for a blanket, preferably an electric one. "Anything hot would be very nice."

"I'll get us some tea." She looked up expectantly as her husband reentered the room. There was a changing of the guard as Jane Drummond rose to make tea and Roger sat down to make conversation.

"Annie'll be out in a few minutes." He forced a smile. "That girl can really lay around." He tried to pass it off as an amusing tattle but I heard the accusation in his voice, felt his embarrassment. I didn't know if the sexual innuendo was intentional but it was clear he believed his daughter was a lagger. I would wager Annie's sleeping pattern had more to do with depression than laziness.

"What Annie's been through must be hard on you, as her father."

He waved that comment away. "Oh, I wouldn't make too much of that. I'm not the type who expects life to be a bowl of cherries. Don't waste my life whining about things."

The standard denial. I could have predicted it. I heard a voice inside my head start to give Roger Drummond a discourse on the distinction between genuine grief and whining. I reminded myself that I was an uninvited guest here, in search of evidence. Edifying the victim's family was not the purpose of my visit. It was an effort but I kept my mouth shut.

A strained silence gaped between us. Roger eventually filled it. "I told Annie that was no neighborhood to live in."

The voice in my head clamored, this time eager to clue this man in on the fact that Annie's former community, Hillcrest, had one of the lowest rates of rape in the entire city of San Diego. Again I censored myself. "Oh?" I answered mildly.

"Hate to say it, but I'm not all that surprised such a thing happened. Kids these days are so careless. If you were to see some of the clothes she pranced around in you wouldn't wonder that what happened, happened." Apparently Annie didn't share her father's taste in clothing. Taking in Roger Drummond's pea green polyester slacks, I figured that for Annie this was probably a good thing.

"It's my understanding that your daughter was attacked in her own bed, Mr. Drummond, in the middle of the night. Surely what she was wearing at that point was irrelevant?"

He sat back in his chair and folded a pair of Jack Lalane arms across his chest. Shook his head of dyed black hair with a long-suffering look that told me I'd missed his point. "You gotta look at the big picture." He spoke patiently, as if to a child. "I love my daughter, but I have to be honest and tell you she's exactly the kind of girl this thing happens to."

His speech was interrupted by Jane, who came in carrying three steaming teacups lined up on a beautiful tray of carved pine.

"I made Earl Grey for all of us. I hope you like it." She smiled a little too intensely.

I reached for my cup as soon as the pinewood tray hit the table, grateful to find a warm spot in this chilly place. "Earl Grey is my favorite, thank you. And what a lovely tea tray."

She smiled proudly. "Annie made this. She's a very talented woodworker."

"Anyways," Annie's father continued, "I never could talk any sense into that girl of ours. She insisted on living alone in that place."

I blew across the top of my cup. Trying to cool my temper, not the tea. In his short-winded diatribe Roger Drummond had managed, however indirectly, to blame the rape on his daughter three times.

"Before she moved in there we had a place all lined up for her here in Clairemont, didn't we, Jane? Not far from our house here, as a matter of fact."

"But I didn't want to live with my alcoholic aunt and I didn't want to drive through rush-hour traffic to work every day." The three of us swiveled our heads toward the hallway, where a young woman stood leaning against the door frame.

14

"Annie." Jane Drummond addressed her daughter with a smile, but her eyes were sad.

Annie was an attractive girl in that exciting but treacherous decade, her twenties. She'd been blessed with shiny blond hair and her mother's smooth skin. She wore apricot leggings and a matching T-shirt that reached to midthigh. The clothes fit snugly, as if they'd been purchased about ten pounds ago. Annie's eyes met mine. "Hi." Her voice was barely audible, her smile barely discernible.

"Hi." I smiled back. I turned to her parents. "May we talk alone?"

Jane gathered up the tea tray. "Sure, you two go right ahead." She motioned her husband toward the door with a tilt of her head.

Roger picked up his cup and stood, placing a hand on my shoulder. "Good luck to ya." Looking up at him I was treated to a view of his luxuriant nose hair. He gave me a pat between my shoulder blades. "Best to do what you can, I suppose." He glared at his daughter as she moved into the room and he and his wife moved out.

Annie took a seat beside me on the sofa. "You don't look like a cop." Her eyes were a warm shade of brown, but wary.

"I'm not. I'm an investigator, well, here." I reached into my coat pocket and handed her a card.

She scrutinized the type. "So what's this supposed to mean?"

"Bottom line is, the police are trying really hard to find the asshole who raped you. They hired me to help. I'm going to do my best to get this guy too, and I need your cooperation."

The wariness in her eyes was replaced by a glimmer of hope. The glimmer died quickly. "Why should I talk to you?"

A fair question. I had to give it some thought before answering. "If you mean why should you assist in the investigation: Your help could save a life. Lives. If you mean why should you talk to me in particular: I've had some success cracking cases where the police have been stymied. And by the way, I'm a pretty good listener. I practiced psychotherapy for a while before I became an investigator."

"So what do you want from me?"

"I want you to tell me what happened. Tell me everything you remember. Even if you don't think it's relevant."

Annie shifted in her seat and looked toward the back hallway. When she was certain of our privacy she began.

"Okay." She swallowed, then took a deep breath and sighed. "It was a Saturday night. I'd been up refinishing a table in the living room—I remember I was wearing *overalls*. I started getting ready for bed around eleven o'clock, brushing my teeth, washing my face, all that. I was too tired to take a shower. I just took off the overalls and got into bed in my T-shirt and undies."

Annie paused to pull open a narrow drawer in the low table in front of us. She retrieved a pack of Marlboros and a cheap plastic lighter. "So I got into bed and went to sleep. Then, the next thing I know—" Her voice broke. She looked down and stroked the clear plastic on the pack of cigarettes in her hand, visibly struggling to keep the tears at bay. In a minute she found her voice again. "Mind if we move into the garage? I can't smoke in here, and frankly, I need to."

"Let's go," I said.

The garage was hardly any colder than the house, and its casual ambiance was a lot warmer. Annie lit her cigarette as soon as the door closed behind us. I hopped onto the long workbench lining the wall and dangled my legs. "Anyway," she went on, exhaling smoke and leaning against a purple Ford Ranger, "after I fell asleep the next thing I knew some guy was shoving my head into the pillow and saying, 'Just keep your head to the side, don't make no noise, and I won't have to cut you.'" She pulled hard on another drag of the cigarette and stared at me challengingly, waiting for my reaction.

"How terrifying," I said softly.

She blew the smoke out with a long sigh and hardened her face with a determined jaw. For a long time she stared at the burning cigarette between her fingers, watching the ash grow. She tried to raise it for another drag, but her hand was shaking. Her lips began to tremble. Grief pulled down the corners of her mouth, and her tough expression dissolved into pure pain:

I got down from the workbench, walked over, removed the cigarette from her fingers, and put my arms around her. Her body shook with muffled sobs. "I'm so sorry, Annie," I said gently into her ear. "You didn't deserve this to happen to you."

She cried for perhaps five minutes. I stroked her silky hair and did my best to make my arms a safe place. Every now and then she took a breath as if to say something, but her tears had been held back for too long and the force of them was stronger than any pretense. At last she bucked herself up and pulled away from me. Her eyes pleaded to be understood. "I didn't fight back!" she sobbed. "I couldn't scream. I couldn't move. I was paralyzed. I just, just—"

"Annie," I said firmly, "you're alive. If you had struggled, there was a chance you could have been killed. You didn't do anything wrong. *He* did."

She snuffed her running nose. "But I always thought if something like that happened I wouldn't let it, I'd—"

I put my hands on her shoulders. "Annie, look at me." Her eyes, marbled with red and brimming with tears, met mine. "Early this morning a woman was stabbed in her chest and in her buttocks because she tried to resist a rapist who matches the description you gave the police." I watched her pupils dilate in horror. "I'm not telling you this to frighten you. I'm telling you this so that you'll stop blaming yourself for not fighting back. You undoubtedly saved yourself brutal bodily injury."

"Did he kill her?" A whisper.

"No. She's going to make it."

Annie bit her upper lip and for several seconds stood silently staring at the floor. When she looked up at me her eyes had filled with tears again. "I know this sounds stupid, but sometimes in my heart I wonder if it was even really rape." Her voice was high and strained. "I mean, I've read that if the woman doesn't struggle or scream, or . . ." She searched out and found the pack of Marlboros on the hood of the truck. She scooped it up and regained control of her voice. "In my head I know it was rape, I mean the guy broke into my house and all, but deep inside—do you understand?—I wonder."

If she'd been listening to her father she was probably convinced that she'd seduced the guy. "Annie, do you know how the law defines rape?"

She wiped her nose with the back of her hand and shook her head.

"According to Section 261 of *The California Penal Code*, rape is sexual intercourse accomplished *against a person's will by means of force or fear*. Now, look deep inside and tell me. Did it happen against your will?"

She nodded.

"Did he use force?"

She looked at me and nodded again.

"Did he use fear of immediate bodily injury?"

Annie continued to nod, the realization at last dawning in her eyes. "Oh, my God," she said. "Thank you. I wish I'd known that before."

A gust of wind threw a sheet of rain against the outside of the garage door. In a momentary audial hallucination I heard the pellets of rain as a shower of bullets. Too many movies. I hopped back up onto the workbench and drew my knees up to my chin, wrapping my coat around my legs. "Okay, I have a clear picture of the fear part," I said to Annie. "Now tell me about the *force* the rapist used. All I've got on your case is a bare-bones physical description of the guy—stocky, muscular, ski mask, latex gloves. I need to have an idea of who he *is*, how he *behaves*. Can you help me with that?"

"I'll try."

"You left off where he told you if you didn't make noise he wouldn't have to cut you. What did his voice sound like?"

Annie shook her head. "I don't know—just, you know, a man's voice. Nothing unusual about it, no accent or anything."

"Low register? High register?"

Annie looked ashamed. "I don't remember."

"That's okay. Don't worry about it. Go on. After he threatened you, then what?"

She sighed again, and I could feel that she was forcing her mind into places she'd spent a great deal of energy running away from. Her eyelids crinkled as she shut them tightly, concentrating. "Okay, his leg was pushing down on me, like this." She demonstrated by placing her bent knee on a sawhorse standing near the workbench. "He took his leg off and told me . . . told me to . . . ."

"I know this is hard, Annie. You're doing great."

"He told me to take off my underwear."

"And so you did that and then he raped you?"

She nodded silently, fresh tears rolling down her cheeks.

"Was it completely dark in your bedroom?"

She shook her head. "There was moonlight coming through the windows."

"So your eyes were open during the rape?"

She let out a painful laugh. "Open! I remember they started to hurt after a while. I finally figured out I'd been so scared I hadn't even *blinked*. My eyeballs were so dry they ached."

My eyes hurt just thinking about it. I blinked involuntarily. "Did he say anything else during the rape?"

She thought for several moments. During the silence I felt a blackness welling up around her, could almost see it. "I know he said other things," she finally answered, "but I can't remember. Something about how he'd been watching me, the way I walked." She knit her brows, struggling to bring it back. "He raped me twice."

"Twice? You mean he climaxed, then attacked you again?"

Annie put her hand over her eyes, as if she didn't want to see the images she was remembering. "No. I don't know that he ever climaxed. But he did it twice. It seemed to go on forever. So I know there was more, I just can't really remember."

Her account made sense. Rapists often do not ejaculate, a fact that surprises people. A rapist lusts for domination and control. He's desperate for release from feelings of powerlessness. The pressure comes from his sick head, not his groin.

"Have you ever been hypnotized, Annie?"

"No." She looked at me quizzically. "Why?"

"I'm thinking it might be less traumatic for you and a lot more productive for both of us if I finish this interview with you under hypnosis. Would you agree to doing that?"

"I guess so."

Annie had plans—she didn't specify—for the next day, so we set our hypnosis session for Wednesday afternoon. She bit her lip. "Can we do it at your place?"

"Sure." I scribbled directions on a piece of paper and handed it over. "It's the two-story house on the corner of Juniper and Tenth. Just look for the only structure that was built a hundred years ago."

She fidgeted with the edges of the paper. "This hypnosis stuff isn't dangerous or anything, is it?"

"No. In fact, it could be healing for you. I get the impression you don't have a tremendous amount of support."

"Oh, no," she said, correcting me with a shaking head. "My parents have been great. They're being so patient with me. I'm not exactly the perfect daughter right now."

"And what would a perfect daughter be that you're not?"

"She'd get it together already. She'd have a job, for one thing. And pay her bills. And not be *fat*." She spit the word out of her mouth. Her self-loathing and shame were palpable, and it hurt me to hear her.

"Have you seen a counselor, Annie?"

"Oh, right." She banged her hand against the Ranger. "This puppy's about to get repo'd because I've already been through the two-thousand-dollar loan Mom and Dad gave me. Like I have money for therapy."

"California has a crime victim's assistance program. Your counseling would be subsidized."

"Public assistance? If my dad found out he'd hit the roof. 'Mooching off the government gravy train.' I'd never hear the end of it. Forget it."

"Why does your dad have to find out?"

She didn't have an immediate answer for that one.

"Here." I retrieved the piece of paper and wrote down the Women's Resource Center rape crisis hot line number. Then I handed the paper back to her. "Call them. They're very nice. Really. And if you need money, I'd like to hire you to do some woodwork for me. I hear you're good, and I'm in dire need of a bookcase."

A squawking noise came from the back of the garage, behind the truck. For the first time I noticed a tall birdcage. "Hey," I called out. "Fred and Barney."

Annie was awed. "Oh my God, you *are* psychic. You know their names!"

I laughed. "In this instance, merely well informed. Your friend Sean in Hillcrest told me about your birds."

Annie and I walked over to visit her feathered friends. She got a nostalgic look in her eye. "I miss Sean." She put her nose against the cage. "Hey, you two, what's up?" she cooed. "I worry about these guys, out here in the cold. They can't come inside. Dad says no pets in the house."

"Even birds?" In truth it was nearly as cold inside as out here, but I didn't say so to Annie.

She hooked a shank of blond hair behind her ear and frowned at me. "He reminded me of somebody, but I don't know who."

He. The rapist. I felt my eyes widening. "Did you discuss this with the police?"

"No. I just thought of it now, talking to you."

"Who, Annie? Who'd he remind you of?"

She slid her finger along the birdcage, thinking. "I don't know. I can't . . . can't make the connection."

I waited, but she remained silent. "That's okay. We'll go into this at our session on Wednesday. In the meantime, if anything comes to you, call me." I'd already given her my business card, but I left her with an extra just in case.

15

I tossed my guck-covered shoes inside the door. Unlike the Drummonds I live in a not-so-immaculate farmhouse that's had more than a century to accumulate character. The grit on my shoes wasn't going to ruin these floorboards.

It felt like years since I'd been home. I'd just put in an eleven-hour workday and it was only three thirty in the afternoon. The discarded footwear was promptly inspected by my cat, Whitman, named for his fondness for leaves of grass. He took one sniff and backed away. "What's the matter, sir, did I step in something distasteful?" He lifted his little masked face toward mine, then came forward and rubbed my legs as if to say that however bad my shoes smelled, I was still okay.

I punched my message machine and listened while I fixed myself a cup of chamomile tea. Mom had called to say thanks again for agreeing to read charts at the fund-raiser. She already had six customers lined up. Tom had called to confirm our dinner date at seven thirty, "unless of course something comes up—I'm on call tonight." And Mark Clemmens, my client at MicroLight, had called for a progress report on my search for Gary Warren Niebuhr. In the last two months I had wrapped up my arson case, and fairly easily at that, since the arsonist had left an earring at the scene. The whereabouts of Mr. Niebuhr, however, remained a mystery.

I pulled out the Niebuhr case file and sat down with my tea to go over it again. I'd run through the usual gamut of sources: Social Security, IRS, National Personal Records Center, DMV, courthouse, licensing boards, city directory. All dead ends, which didn't surprise me in the least. Niebuhr was a computer wizard, after all. Not only would he cover all these tracks, but he'd probably plant a decoy in the system just to toy with slow-witted bureaucrats and plodding investigators. I did not intend to plod. Someone as ingenious as Niebuhr could be impossible to catch, an idea that excited me. If I were going to find him it would have to be through unconventional means, a road less traveled. I fished in the file for his picture, which I'd cut from the MicroLight annual report. Wearing a cool baggy suit, long sideburns, and clear-framed specs, this was one hip nerd. His eyes danced behind his glasses, his grin was pure imp. I peered closer, then got out my magnifying glass. Sure enough, that was a Mickey Mouse tie he had on.

I leaned Niebuhr's photo against a crystal-filled granite geode on my coffee table, then lit a candle and sat on the sofa. I stared at the picture, inviting a psychic connection to the man. What was he doing right now? What was he looking at right now? Where was he . . . right now?

Bells, bells, bells, bells! Someone was leaning, repeatedly, on my doorbell. "Shit," I said, getting up to answer. I peered into the peephole and saw a familiar sun-bleached head. It was Toby, the sixteen-year-old high school student who lived across the street. The kid lived to surf and rode the waves year-round. Competitively, which cost money. He was always selling something. Occasionally I hired him to do odd jobs and odious chores. Windows, for example. I opened the door. "Hi, Toby. What's happenin', dude? You still peddling candy bars?"

He flashed me a bumpy white smile—his parents had gifted him with cosmetically correct white braces. "No, but I'm still trying to make money. Got any work for me?"

"Sorry, Tob. Not right now. But I'll keep you in mind if something comes up."

"Okay, thanks. See ya." He shoved his hands in the pockets of his baggy jeans and spun around to go.

"Bye." I closed the door and went back to the sofa to try tuning in to Niebuhr again. I focused on the photograph but couldn't shake the feeling that the man was mocking me. To get around that I closed my eyes, intending to fall more deeply into meditation. Instead I fell asleep.

16

I had already slipped into my sable cashmere sweater dress and was just adding the finishing touches to an earthy shade of lipstick when the phone rang. Even before I picked up the receiver I knew that it was McGowan, that he'd been called out on another SWAT detail, that our dinner would have to be postponed.

Sometimes being psychic is a real drag.

I picked up the phone and skipped the hello part. "It's okay, don't apologize, I knew what I was getting into when I started dating a cop. I mean it, not one word."

Except for cellular static there was only silence on the end of the line. Could I have misread this one? Maybe it wasn't even McGowan. "Hello?"

"You said, 'Not one word.' " It was him.

"Okay, I'll let you have one word."

"Just one?"

"Yeah. Just one."

He was calling from the road, I heard highway noise. "Then that word will be *later*. Something's come up . . . for to . . . think about . . ."

The call was cutting out. I raised my voice, trying to compensate for the spotty connection. "Just let yourself in, whatever time you're done." McGowan was completely gone. I hoped he'd heard me.

After my nap this afternoon I'd done an hour of invigorating yoga. Sleeping now would be impossible. The long night stretched out before me like so many miles of lonesome highway. Since dinner with McGowan was out, I heated a can of lentil soup and contemplated my options for the evening. There were about a dozen books I'd been meaning to read. Trade journals to catch up on. But I didn't want to read. An anxiety had been brewing inside me all day, and until now I hadn't realized how much I'd been looking forward to one of my honey's famous bear hugs. He's six foot six, two fifty. A lot of bear to hug.

Anxiety. What did I used to prescribe to my therapy clients who suffered from that dreaded postmodern malaise, free-floating anxiety? "The best remedy for anxiety is *action*," I'd tell them. Mobilized by my own pep talk, I walked across the living room and picked up the case file. I'd culled only the most compelling documents from Dianna's office, but the paperwork still managed to fill my entire briefcase. Incident reports, suspect mug shots, rap sheets, interview transcripts. Once again Richard Zimmer stared out at me from his photo. It was time to turn the tables and give *him* a good, hard look.

The transcript from today's interview with the Zipper was not yet available, but that hadn't been his first audition with the police. I reviewed a statement taken earlier in the year, this one related to the burglary. All those items his girlfriend had "given" him. Zimmer's vital stats were outlined on the cover sheet. Date of birth: January 13, 1963. Hair: black. Eyes: black. Complexion: light. Weight: 195. Height: 5'11". Farther down the stack was another sheet, this one related to the assault with deadly weapon. The victim, his alleged girlfriend, was a Belinda Crews. I wrote her phone number on my calendar as a reminder to give her a call tomorrow.

The address listed for Zimmer was 5516 El Cerrito, near San Diego State University. If I were to call on him now it would be a good thirty-mile drive from my cozy home in Escondido. Through pouring rain. I thought about it for a half second and came to a decision. The cashmere dress would have to go.

I changed into a pair of sweats topped with a lightweight Gortex warm-up. I shoved my hair up under a baseball cap and pulled on my trusty combat boots. I wasn't planning a social visit.

It was a poor evening for surveillance. If anything, nightfall had increased the amount of rain pouring from the sky. I could make out maybe four cars ahead of me driving south on Interstate 15. The occasional fog pocket didn't help any. Forty minutes and God knows how many beats of my lame windshield wipers later I pulled into the Zipper's neighborhood. His place was dark—no vehicles in the driveway or out front. I circled around the block and parked at the opposite end of Zimmer's street. As rain pounded the roof of my car, I thought back to the wee hours of this morning, when I had sat outside Thomasina Wilson's house, fighting an urge to flee from this case.

It didn't seem so bad now. I reminded myself about the darkness I'd seen ahead, even before I'd offered my services to Lieutenant Marcone. It had loomed in the future like some ominous force on the horizon. How fast was it traveling? When would it arrive? Even that didn't seem so bad, now. Perhaps this was like going through the five stages of coming to terms with cancer or death: denial, anger, bargaining, depression, acceptance. I was just contemplating which stage I might have reached when Zimmer's van appeared at the far end of the street.

It was a white Dodge, one of those windowless jobs. License number 2MG654, which matched the one I'd seen earlier on his police report. Nothing supersneaky going on there. Black lettering along the side of the van announced EZ Home Improvement. He pulled in and parked in the driveway. The door opened, and Zimmer ran through the rain into the house. I saw a couple of lights go on but was too far away to see much else. I wondered if I could move my car closer without being noticed and decided not to chance it. I pulled the handle gently and slid out. The rain was much colder than what we usually get in California. A few degrees lower and it would be snow.

The house—an uninspired rectangular structure—featured a large picture window that faced the street. I could see Zimmer inside, puttering in and out of the living room. The unmistakable glow of a television went on. Zimmer approached the set, carrying something black, a videotape, probably. Yes. He leaned over and slipped it into the VCR, stepped back, and futzed with the remote a minute, then walked to the window and pulled the blinds shut. End of show for investigator standing in near-freezing rain.

I walked around the van to see if there might be a side window into the front room. Without warning a floodlight drenched the driveway. I must have tripped a motion detector. I was certain my shivering body couldn't be generating enough warmth to trip a heat detector. I slipped back behind the van and waited, keeping my eye on a neighboring hedge should further retreat become necessary. After a minute the floodlight went off.

I stood there in the relentless rain for another minute or so. Whatever Zimmer was doing in there, he wasn't out hunting down another victim, terrorizing her . . . or worse. Meanwhile, I was risking pneumonia. My teeth had actually started chattering. When a ferocious barking started up behind the backyard fence, Zimmer's missing finger—the one his own dog had bitten off—flashed to mind. It was all the incentive I needed to get going. Just as I moved for the street, something on the side of the van caught my eye.

It wasn't the world's slickest paint job by any measure. The lettering on the van was muddy, amateurish. I took a closer look. EZ Home Improvement was painted in black, with a black and blue hammer logo on the left. But under the word *Improvement* some red lettering was showing through the white background. I remembered an art world word for this ghost image phenomenon: *pentimento*.

The barking got louder, and something heavy threw its weight against the fence separating the driveway from Zimmer's yard. I pulled a penlight from the pocket of my Gortex jacket and shined a beam from about eight inches against the side of the van. Through the white topcoat I made out the pale red letters: py Lock & Safe. I stood there a moment, consciously committing the letters to memory. It wasn't much, but it was enough to give me the feeling that the entire trip hadn't been a waste.

The back door opened, and Zimmer screamed at his dog to shut up. I trotted down the street the long way back to my car. By the time I got to it I was drenched. I kept the heat on full blast the entire drive home and finished thawing by stepping into a scorching bath, scented with plumeria in my wishful attempt to invoke the tropics. Steam was still rising from my damp rosy flesh when I slipped between the sheets. Warm at last, I fell into a fitful sleep.

I woke from a restless dream to sheer terror. I hadn't heard him come in. My eyes popped open to see him standing in black silhouette by the bedside. I froze. My heart began to thump wildly.

"Elizabeth, it's me."

McGowan. The five-alarm fire that had begun burning in my chest came under control.

"Mind if I turn on the light? I need to see to get out of all this stuff."

SWAT officers do outfit themselves. Kevlar vests and thigh pads are just the beginning of it. I breathed again, even managed a response. "Lights on to undress by? By all means flip the switch."

The lamp on the bedside table clicked on, and McGowan stood before me in a wet camouflage jumpsuit. He tossed his protective gear in the corner and smiled down at me. "Gee, do you think you have enough blankets? Good grief." I'd piled on two comforters and an unzipped sleeping bag for good measure. He leaned down to kiss me, stopped just short of my lips, and smiled. "On chilly nights, you know, you could do like some people and wear pajamas."

"Never." McGowan ran his hand along my face, down my neck. "So," I said, "fun night?"

His hand continued roaming. "Don't want to talk about it right now. Hey, what's this?" McGowan's fingers had stopped at my shoulder, where he was squinting at something.

"What's what?"

"You've got some kind of a, I don't know, a patch of red skin here."

I jumped out of bed and looked at the back of my shoulder in the dresser mirror. Sure enough, a smattering of red spots, shaped something like a bite mark, stood out. "Probably psoriasis. I'm not surprised. All part and parcel of being a sensitive. I've told you how I get physical symptoms from sociopaths."

"What sociopath?"

I dabbed at the red skin. It stung to the touch. "I'm not sure yet. I encountered at least two people today who made my skin crawl."

McGowan scowled at the wound. "Wish I could make it better."

I grabbed him by the front of his cammies and pulled him onto the bed. "Ah, but you can."

He rolled onto his back and pulled me onto his chest. After a long kiss, he examined my shoulder again and pouted his lower lip. "It looks like it hurts."

"It does, a little bit." I smiled. "But don't worry about it. This is a good sign. It means I'm getting somewhere."

17

Dr. Rebecca Goode, Thomasina Wilson's attending physician at Sharp Hospital, examined me through her large tortoise-shell eyeglasses. "Have a look at these. They were taken with a laproscopic camera. It's called magnification photography."

We were standing in a narrow room near the second-floor nurses' station reviewing Thomasina's post-rape photographs. It was an unpleasant job at any hour, more so this early in the morning. On first glance the images looked like close-ups of somebody's pink, wet gums. "What am I looking at here?" I asked.

"Microtrauma. When there's no sexual response from the victim—none of the psychological or physical stimulation associated with voluntary intercourse—this is what you get. Wounding to the soft tissue in the vaginal region."

I squinted my eyes and took a closer look. Sure enough, a pattern of crisscrossed lacerations covered the tissue, as if some miniature slasher had been set loose.

"Sex is a"—I searched for a descriptive euphemism—"a physically dynamic act: Wouldn't you see this with normal intercourse?"

"Absolutely not. Forced intercourse always leaves wounding like this, voluntary intercourse doesn't. Photographs like these come in handy when the defense cries consensual sex."

"Given Thomasina's stab wounds, I'm sure that won't be an issue in this case."

Dr. Goode looked at me sideways, rolled her eyes, shook her

head. "When it comes to a rape case, you can never be too sure. I could tell you some tales."

"If your tales involve overbooked courtrooms, sleazy defense attorneys, and rapists going free, I'll pass. Such tales would give me nightmares."

"Yes, they probably would. Anyway, the microscopic wounds you see here on the patient's vaginal tissue are similar to lacerations on the macro level. Here." She pulled several more photos from a large white envelope. "Take a look at Thomasina's chest wound. See how the tissue is pulled sideways from the top epidermal layer? That shows that force was applied from the side, like this." She gestured convincingly.

For a minute the reality of it got to me and I squeezed my eyes shut. "Poor baby."

"*Strong* baby," came Dr. Goode's forceful reply. "The blade tore the pectoral tissue but didn't penetrate the chest cavity, partly because her muscle is so tough. Same scenario with the gluteus wound." She flopped a close-up onto the counter. "This was more of a straight stab, but the penetration is less than you would expect with a blade that wide."

I averted my eyes. The room was lined with shelves and locking overhead cabinets. Medical supplies were neatly arranged along two long countertops. A box dispensing thin rubber gloves caught my eye. White latex, the same kind the rapist wore. It looked like a common box of Kleenex.

I took a deep breath and got back to the nasty business at hand. "What about her neck contusions?"

Dr. Goode pulled more photos from the envelope and spread them across the shelf. I recognized Thomasina's elegant neck. "These were taken with the others, shortly after she was admitted." She pointed to a pair of snapshots. "These were taken twelve hours later. I think you can see what's happening a little better here." In the second set, the tentative marks near her throat had ripened into dark purple splotches.

"These look like thumbprints." I pointed to two large bruises on either side of Thomasina's trachea. "But do you know exactly which fingers these marks relate to?" I pulled the photos showing the back sides of Thomasina's neck out of the group. Two distinct bruises appeared along each side of her neck. Something that might have been an additional bruise appeared farther back on her left side.

"In strangulation cases the bruises actually appear in the spaces *between* the fingers," Dr. Goode said matter-of-factly.

"So these marks, two bruises on each side, were actually made by three fingers?" Zimmer was missing the middle finger on his left hand. This could be a detail linking him to the crime.

"Three or four. It depends on whether the attacker's fingers were pulled together as they wrapped around her neck. The fingers are just used for leverage in a strangulation, anyway. It's the thumbs that do the real damage."

"So you couldn't say, looking at these photographs, whether Thomasina's attacker had three or four fingers?"

Dr. Goode shook her head. "No, I'd hesitate to say for sure. You'll have to check with a forensic pathologist on that one." Rats.

"Do you think I could speak with Thomasina this morning?" It had now been more than twenty-four hours since Thomasina's life-threatening ordeal. I felt an urgency to retrieve what memories remained before they sank into her quicksand of repression.

Dr. Goode gathered up the photos and returned them to the envelope. "Sure, you can interview her right now. She's an incredible patient. Walking, I'll have you know. Insists it's the best thing to minimize stiffness from the wounds. And of course she's right."

Finding the patient was something of a goose chase. I finally caught up with her as I rounded the far corner of the hallway, where she appeared to be walking laps. She was making steady progress, only occasionally leaning on a single crutch under her left armpit. "Unbelievable," I said, as much to myself as to her.

Thomasina pivoted on the crutch, her bright brown eyes lighting at the sight of me. "Use it or lose it, that's what I say. Hello again."

I shook my head in disbelief as I caught up to her. "Attitude like that, you're not in danger of losing much. Can you possibly feel as good as you look?"

She leaned onto her crutch and smiled. "The damn cuts hurt like hell, but I think my body's going to be okay. My mind, I don't know. I feel like I've lost my wits."

The sense of familiarity with this woman was eerie. We were talking like old friends, taking up where we'd last left off. "Well, as my grandmother Merry used to say, 'She who doesn't lose her wits over certain things, has no wits to lose.' "

Thomasina stared at me while she considered that last statement. "And this is one of those things, huh?"

"Aggravated rape? Yeah, I'd say so. You're allowed to go stark raving nuts over this one."

She resumed walking, barely using the crutch. Thomasina Wilson sure didn't look like a woman who was losing her wits. She turned around with a dead-serious expression. "I want to kill him," she said flatly.

Didn't *sound* like she was losing her wits, either.

"Is there a place we can talk privately?" I asked.

"I've got a roommate now, but I know a place. Listen, I'm a lot less stoned than the last time you saw me, but I still don't remember a whole lot."

"Don't worry about it. If it's all right with you I'd rather interview you under hypnosis anyway. No pain, more gain."

"Hypnosis, huh? That stuff really works?"

"It can. With the right subject."

She stopped walking and turned to me. "If it has a chance of helping you find the bastard, I'll try anything."

I followed her out to a courtyard filled with indoor-outdoor furniture. On a nice day the area would be popular with patients. Today anything out-of-doors looked uninviting. For the most part the rain had stopped, but the clouds hadn't budged and the dark sky was growing more threatening as the morning wore on. I was beginning to feel ripped off. This was the southwesternmost corner of the country, damn it. The weather wasn't supposed to betray us this way. It seemed I hadn't taken off my coat in weeks.

Thomasina settled sideways onto a chaise, favoring her wounded haunch. I sat down next to her on one of the patio chairs and shivered. "You sure you don't want me to run in and scare up a blanket for you?" I asked.

"Nah, I'm fine. If you're worried that I'll be too chilly, why don't you just give me a hypnotic suggestion that I'm warm and comfortable?"

No question about it, this woman had her wits about her. "Okay, then, close your eyes." Thomasina's lids dropped, her thick black lashes locking together. I pulled a small tape recorder from my purse and pushed the record button. "That's it, Thomasina, just relax. Now, take a deep breath. Again. And again." I could see from her peaceful expression that she was putting up little if any resistance to my suggestions. "Now, surround yourself with a brilliant aura of bright, white light. You are perfectly safe within this light, perfectly cozy and warm." Thomasina was cooperating splendidly—I could actually see the light shield she built up around herself. "You will feel neither the physical nor psychological pain of the experience you had early yesterday morning." Thomasina breathed in the suggestion. Her face was beatific.

"All right. We are back in your bedroom on the morning of the rape. What's the first thing you notice that tells you something's wrong?"

"I feel the edge of a knife on my neck. It's cold."

At that the temperature on the patio seemed to drop several degrees. Perhaps it was only in my mind. "What else is happening?"

"I can't move. He's got me pinned to the bed. He's saying something. 'Keep your head to the side, don't make no noise, and you won't get hurt.' He keeps repeating this."

"Can you describe his voice?"

"It's just a man's voice. I don't know, nothing special about it."

"Okay. Again, Thomasina, let me remind you that you are watching this like a movie. You will not feel any pain or fear as you review this event. What's happening now?"

"He's jerking my nightgown over my hips. I'm trying to kick him, but he has my legs trapped under his body weight. He feels so heavy. It's impossible to move."

"That's good, Thomasina. You're describing what you feel very well. Can you tell me if you see anything? Please describe what you see."

"I see stars."

"Stars?"

"He has his hands around my neck and I'm starting to see stars."

"Thomasina, can you feel each finger on your neck?"

"I feel his thumbs cutting off my windpipe . . . I feel his fingers around the back of my neck."

"How many fingers can you feel?" Very often subjects under hypnosis can recall minute details of past events that never registered with them consciously.

"I feel all of them. He's using both hands. They feel slick, rubbery. He's wearing rubber gloves."

"You feel both thumbs and all his fingers?" Again I was thinking of Zimmer.

"Yes, all of them."

It was very quiet on the patio. I realized that Thomasina had stopped breathing. "Take a deep breath. That's good. Remember, you're watching all of this from a distance. You are completely safe. Can you see anything else?"

"It's dark. His head is there above me like some horrible mask. I just see the shape of a head."

"Can you describe the shape?"

"It's just a head."

"Eyes? Ears? Hairstyle?"

"It's just a head, looming there."

"Okay. What happens next?"

"He's between my legs now. Very brutal. I can feel the rubber. He's panting. I can smell his nasty sweat."

My stomach was beginning to churn. "Okay, that's enough, Thomasina. Let's move on to the next event. What is the next important thing that happens?"

"After a time he says, 'Get over now, get over on your stomach.' I say no, and . . ."

"Remember that you feel no pain now. You're safe."

"I see him come out with the knife. The blade is fat at the top, I can see it shine by the light of the window."

"Remember, you do not feel any pain."

"I know I've been stabbed, but I don't feel it. I move my left arm up to block, I'm coming at his eyes with my right fingers. He's got both my wrists now and he's flipping me over. He moves so *fast*. I feel what he's planning to do back there. I let out a scream, loud as I can."

"You do not feel any pain."

"No, I do not feel pain. I just hear the dogs next door, barking, barking like crazy."

"Do you see him leaving your bedroom?"

"I don't know. My head's in the pillow."

"Look up at the doorway, Thomasina. Can you see him leaving?"

She paused for some time, her eyebrows pulled together. "I'm looking at the doorway. He's coming through again. I can see him better now."

"What can you see?"

"I see his bulky neck, I think I make out his eyes. Yes, he has crazy eyes. He's a frightening sight. We're struggling now. He has both hands on my neck. I feel something gritty under my thighs, like sand."

"You feel sand?"

"Yes. Now we're on the floor."

"You're on the floor?" This was not consistent with the police report.

"Yes. Now I see the stars again. It's starting to get black. It's all black now. I can't see anything else. I can't see or hear anything now."

"Do you know if he's still in the room?"

"Yes."

"He's still in the room?"

"Yes."

"What is he doing?"

"He's deciding what to do."

"What does he do?"

The muscles in Thomasina's face twitched, then twisted in pain. A low moan escaped from her lips.

"You feel no pain, Thomasina."

Her chest rose and fell in quick succession as she began to hyperventilate. Her moaning escalated to short bursts of screaming. I had to bring her out of it, and quickly.

"At the count of five you will wake up. One, two, three, four, five."

When Thomasina's eyes popped open they were filled with terror.

18

Even on a lousy day the view from the La Valencia Hotel is inspiring. I stood at the lobby's west end, a wall of floor-to-ceiling windows, looking at what is arguably San Diego's prettiest patch of coastline. Just outside the windows the high rock cliffs of La Jolla drop spectacularly into the ocean. During low tide I had often seen sea lions gather here to sunbathe on rock formations jutting straight up from the sea. Not today, though. Today the view held only taupe-colored sandstone cliffs. Then water, water, everywhere, all the way to the gray horizon.

Thomasina's hypnosis session had troubled me. Her memory of the events of early yesterday morning didn't appear to be reliable. I needed to bounce my growing concerns off someone with a good head on his shoulders. Who better than a neurologist? Dad was just ending his rounds at Scripps Hospital in La Jolla when I'd called. I would have been happy for his time on the phone, but he'd suggested we meet for lunch at the La Valencia. Something about seizing the opportunity to appreciate his beautiful daughter in a setting worthy of her. He does lay it on thick sometimes. Naturally, I do nothing to discourage this.

I'd arrived early. I wandered back toward the entrance and studied the nearby wall of black-and-white photos. Mostly long-dead patrons, movie stars from the thirties who had come here to escape Los Angeles, a rat race even sixty years ago. Charlie Chaplin, Vivien Leigh, Clark Gable, Carole Lombard. Ardent admirers of the hotel. I wondered if the allure of the La Valencia might be enough to attract their spirits still.

I could feel a presence now, coming up behind me. "Hi, Dad," I said, turning around.

He beamed at me and gave me a quick hug. "Mind if we eat on the patio?"

I turned toward the window and warily eyed the gray skies and churning ocean.

"Humor me. I've been gulping stale hospital air all morning. They have space heaters out there."

Our waiter obliged us. As we walked onto the patio I was surprised to see we weren't the only outdoor patrons. A few feet over a group of five conversed animatedly in German over the catch of the day.

"Thanks for coming, Dad."

He pulled out my chair for me. "I hope I can help. This is about the serial rape case?" I had told him about my visit to Marcone back in October and on the phone today had brought him up to date on my involvement in the investigation.

I nodded and sat down. "Yes. So far this is the closest I've come to experiencing what it must be like to be blind. There is no evidence. The rapist wears gloves and a mask, so the victims can't identify him. He leaves no traces—no semen, no fingerprints. No nothing."

"Just heartache and destruction."

"Yes, he does leave that."

A waitress came along, filling our water glasses and placing a dish of lemon slices on the table. Dad waited for her to step away before speaking. "You're not having any luck psychically either, then?" My father has often questioned my career move from psychologist to psychic investigator, but he's seen too much evidence over the years to question my psychic ability.

"Haven't had any clear insights yet. Since the only eyewitnesses are the victims themselves, my thinking is to get inside the minds of these women, help them unearth memories that will lead to the rapist. They may not have seen his face, but surely some of them must have seen *something*. Anyway, I hypnotized the most recent victim, and the strangest thing happened."

Dad didn't say anything, but his intense gaze urged me to go on.

"The first part of our session went along fine. The victim reported events pretty much as she'd reported them after the crime. But later in the session she said she saw herself struggling on the floor, which wasn't consistent with what she'd told the police. Also, she began hyperventilating when she reviewed the stabbing—I mean really freaking out."

The waitress brought our menus and I took a drink of water. "I had to bring her out of the trance quickly. When I asked her what had happened she told me she'd seen the rapist stabbing her 'over and over and over and over.' In actuality, she was stabbed only twice, once in the chest and once in her backside, after he flipped her over."

Dad squeezed a slice of lemon and stirred it into his water. "So the seeming inaccuracy of the victim's memory under hypnosis is what's disturbing you?"

"Exactly. I know evidence obtained via hypnosis can't be used in court, but I was hoping it would lead to a break in the case for me. Now I'm not so sure. If these details are inaccurate, then what weight can I give to the other details? His 'husky neck' or 'crazy eyes,' for instance? One of the things I was hoping to nail down was the number of fingers the guy had. The police department's number-one suspect is missing a finger. This victim clearly remembers that her rapist had all of his fingers—he spent some time choking her with them. But if she could be wrong about significant facts like struggling on the floor and the number of times he stabbed her, how can I trust that she's not wrong about details like the number of fingers the rapist had?"

He opened a packet of sugar and stirred that into his water too. "You're wandering into a blind alley with this stuff."

"What do you mean, blind alley?"

"Science is only beginning to understand how memory operates. People used to assume that the mind was like a video camera, recording—and therefore capable of accurately playing back—everything it sees. Now we know that's not the case. The mind not only omits but sometimes even *changes* important details. Especially under stress."

"How's that?"

"You want the Mr. Wizard answer?"

"I want the Dr. Wizard answer."

He put his spoon down and looked at me. "All right. At the moment of a traumatic event—a rape, for example—the brain undergoes intense biochemical changes. It perceives a life-threatening event and releases emergency neurotransmitters: epinephrine and norepinephrine to mobilize the body and enhance alertness, serotonin and endorphins to serve as painkillers."

I thought back to the life-threatening crisis I'd experienced when I blew up a meth lab last year. Vividly remembered the surreal impressions of my serotonin-soaked brain. "So the victim's mind is flooded by naturally produced chemicals that alter her consciousness."

"Right. Now you're going to ask me what this has to do with inaccurate memory."

"Right."

"The straight answer is, no one's sure. False memory syndrome has a name, but no one knows much about it yet. Many compelling cases have been documented. Witnesses swear by erroneous identifications and are shocked when proved wrong. A woman recently was one hundred percent certain she'd identified her mugger in a line-up. She simply couldn't believe that the guy she picked was a police decoy. Especially when someone's life is being threatened, the mind distorts, symbolizes, even fabricates memories of the event. The corresponding neurological theories are still in their infancy." With that he took a drink.

Oh, boy, I thought. A budding new field—the chemistry of terror. "So how would you explain what my victim 'recalled' under hypnosis?"

"There are those who would argue that her memories are symbolic of an earlier trauma that she's repressed from her conscious mind. I don't buy that, though. I would hypothesize that the life-threatening nature of her rape triggered excessive levels of endorphins in her brain, which resulted in temporary amnesia and faulty memory. That'd be my best guess. But my best guess is not what's important here."

"What's important here?"

"The police department didn't hire you to analyze the victim's brain chemistry, Elizabeth. They hired you because of your psychic gift. What do you think—no, what do you *perceive* is going on here?"

My heart swelled. This was the first time I'd heard my father discuss my calling with genuine acceptance. "Well?" he prodded.

I stared out across the Pacific. The sea today was gray and agitated, appearing, in fact, exactly as it had in my visualization in the interview room yesterday. Restless, choppy waves as far as the eye could see. "I don't know, Dad. Nothing's clear at this point."

Rain started to fall on the patio. Dad held out a palm and I saw a drop splash on the pad of his thumb. He stood. "Okay, I give. Let's go find a table inside."

The Germans, too, had had enough California sunshine, or lack of it. As we followed them into the restaurant I wondered how many memories of my life were real and how many were illusion and distortion.

19

The brisk sea air smelled fine. I breathed it in as I walked back to my Mustang, parked at a metered space along the ocean cliff. Maybe ocean air would clear my thoughts. I leaned against the car and watched the churning gray waves. Given what Dad had just told me about false memory syndrome, hypnotizing the victims could be a total waste of time. Yet the solution to this case would come through the victims—this was something I just *knew*. From a psychic point of view it was the *only* thing I knew about this case.

I stared at the steel-colored ocean as if the tide might somehow bring answers to the surface. How lovely if the identity of the rapist—and all the evidence to convict him—would come to me in some blinding flash of truth. Such episodes make for great television, but real extrasensory perception rarely works that way. It comes when it comes, reveals what it wants to reveal. I spent ten postgraduate years trying to control my gift—document it, direct it, channel it. Meanwhile, it laughed at me, played hide-and-seek with me. Waited until I didn't even believe in it anymore, then dropped unassailable proof in my lap. I chuckle at those New Age promotion hounds who promise the development of psychic powers during a weekend seminar in the mountains. I wish it were that simple. At the moment I had no clear sense who was committing these horrid crimes.

Fortunately I'm not a one-piston engine. When my right brain isn't firing, I have the left one to fall back on. I had leads to follow up.

I started with Belinda Crews, the woman who had lost partial use of her right arm during her "misunderstanding" with Richard Zimmer. I would have preferred dropping in on her but unfortunately didn't have her address. I found the number I'd written on my calendar and dialed it from my car phone as I pulled onto Coast Boulevard. After six rings I heard a woman's sullen hello.

"Is this Belinda Crews?"

"Who wants to know?" Her voice cut me no slack.

"My name is Elizabeth Chase. I'm working with the San Diego Police Department on a special task force and I could use your help. Mind if I ask you a few questions?"

"Like what?"

"Last year you pressed charges against Richard Zimmer for assault with a deadly weapon. Your injuries were quite extensive, more extensive than what is implied by Mr. Zimmer's record. I understand that you were raped."

"That's not what I reported."

Five cars ahead of me the light turned yellow. Three cars slipped through legally, two ran the red, and I pulled to a stop. "I know that's not what you reported. But that's what happened, isn't it?"

"I don't want to talk about it. Besides, what's it to you?"

"Someone is raping and terrorizing women around San Diego. There is some evidence to suggest that it could be Mr. Zimmer."

Silence.

I cleared my throat. "Look, I've met him. I know what kind of guy he is."

"Well, if you know so much about Richard Zimmer, you'll sure as hell know why I'm not going to go talking to the cops about him."

I spoke gently but insistently. "Woman to woman here, okay? This guy beat you, he raped you, he tore your shoulder apart, and he stole from you. I for one am angry that he's getting away with it. That he can inflict the kind of injuries you suffered, serve a token sentence, and then walk right back into society is a crime in itself. I want to bust this guy, and I need your help."

The light had turned green, and the woman behind me was already tapping her horn. My engine roared as I pushed the accelerator. There was a hush on the phone, and for a moment I thought I'd lost Belinda Crews. "Belinda?"

When she spoke her voice sounded angry, but I heard the fear behind the anger. "Look, lady, do me a favor. Leave me alone."

With that she hung up.

Zimmer. What a creep. The pentimento lettering I'd seen on his van last night kept nagging me: py Lock & Safe. I doodled in my head, trying to fill in the missing letters. Spy Lock & Safe? Sloppy Lock & Safe? Happy? Sleepy? Grumpy?

I pulled into a gas station phone booth to consult the Yellow Pages. No help there. I then got the bright idea to call my friend Deb, who works in the business department for the City of San Diego. A couple of keystrokes searching by name of principal owner—Zimmer—and she was able to locate Zimmer's former company. "It was called Zippy Lock & Safe," she said.

Zippity-do-dah.

"That operation went out of business two years ago," Deb continued, "but Richard Zimmer is up-to-date on his building and electrical permits. Looks like he's operating legitimately as EZ Home Improvement."

I wrote it down, thanked her, and pulled the phone booth door all the way shut. The rain had stopped, but the wind was picking up and it was getting nasty. The whole Zimmer business got me curious as to what qualifications a person needed to legally tamper with locks around town. A few more phone calls turned up that locksmiths in the State of California are licensed through Sacramento's Department of Security and Investigative Services, the same outfit that licenses private investigators like me. I learned from a clerk at the DSIS that if I wanted to become a locksmith all I had to do was fill out an application and provide a set of fingerprints. My paperwork would filter through a few in/out baskets on its way to the Department of Justice, where my prints would be run through the computerized CAL-ID system.

I thanked her very much and hung up. Zimmer's prints probably collided in cyberspace with some of his penal code violations. The fallout from that crash must have forced him to redirect his career from locksmith to carpenter. Bottom line: License or no license, Zimmer still knew how to pick a lock.

I sensed messages on my machine at home and picked them up remotely. There were two. McGowan had called to remind me about a standing date to have dinner at his place tonight. Something about a "six months since we met" anniversary. Six months. So far so good, I thought. That hadn't lulled me into complacency just yet, though. I'd been around long enough to know that people change with the seasons of their lives. McGowan and I simply hadn't hit any rough weather yet. The second call was a surprising message from Annie Drummond. "I remember now who the rapist reminded me of. It's kind of weird, but for some reason he reminded me of Kevin Knutsen, the security guy at the bank where I used to work. But Kevin's all right, I mean, I'm sure it can't be him."

I wasn't so sure. I went back to my car and slipped behind the wheel just as my pager went off.

20

"I say we pay this guy a visit. You up for a social call?"

I was surprised how quickly Dianna Powers jumped on Annie's bank security guard lead. "The victim says she's sure he can't be the guy," I cautioned. "This may be nothing."

"In police work, everything may be nothing, and victims are rarely sure about anything. I was paging you to have you come in and look at suspect photos, but I'm climbing the walls around here and you just gave me a valid excuse to get out. Meet me at the elevator bank. We'll take a black-and-white."

I was ready to let someone else drive.

About twenty minutes later the SDPD elevator deposited Dianna and me into the underground garage. We had just a short walk through the echoey dark to her cruiser. Dianna's car was fully loaded—toggle switches for the roof lights and spotlights, mobile computer, two-way radio, and a twelve-gauge shotgun mounted on the rear of the cab. Something smelled good as I slid into the front seat. Real good, not that chemical car deodorizer smell. "What's the fragrance?" I asked.

She pulled a bundle of potpourri out of a cubbyhole in the dash. "Smells better than that other crap. Some of the guests I chauffeur in the backseat there smell pretty ripe. This is my defense. The guys give me hell about it, ask me when I'm going to put up wallpaper and hang drapes, that kind of thing."

We circled upward through the garage. Dianna slowed and waved to the officer manning a small booth at the exit. He waved back, and we burst from the black underground into the brightness of a downtown city street. Even on an overcast day the contrast was an affront to the eyeballs. Dianna reached for her sunglasses. "So you're a real psychic. You probably get a lot of grief about that, huh? People thinking you're weird and stuff."

I laughed. "Oh, yeah. Someone recently asked me if I was an amateur psychic like the ones on Dionne Warwick's phone line or if I was a professional psychic like the ones Jackie Stallone personally trains."

"How do you respond to harassment like that?"

"I tell them I've been professionally trained by Jackie Stallone, of course."

I didn't know if Dianna was ever going to stop chuckling, so I just broke in on her. "So how long have you been a police officer?"

"I can't believe this, but seventeen years next month. Lord, I'm getting old."

I was seeing her smiling face in unforgiving daylight. "No you're not. So how long have you known Tom McGowan?"

"Couple of years, I guess. We were on a task force together. You know McGowan?"

"Quite well." Dianna didn't look like she'd shock easily, so I dove right in. "In the biblical sense, even."

She leaned her head down and looked at me over the top of her dark glasses. Gave me the *Oh, really?* expression. Then returned her concentration to the traffic. "So you're dating a cop."

"Afraid so."

She smiled and maneuvered into the left lane. "Can you keep a secret?"

"Of course."

"A few years ago, before I met my husband, I dated a cop."

This didn't strike me as a particularly earth-shattering confession. "So?"

"So his name was Jeff Dietz."

"Oh." New information. I remembered the unspoken something I'd seen pass between them. "Hmm. What happened with that?"

We stopped at a red light. Dianna tapped her beautifully manicured hands on the steering wheel. "It ended kind of badly, actually. Not Dietz's fault, really. He was separated from his wife at the time, and things were a real mess for him personally. It just wasn't the right time for him to be starting a relationship."

"So he went back to his wife."

"No, she eventually divorced him. Royally. Poor guy."

"But by that time you'd met your husband."

The light changed and Dianna stepped on the gas. "You got it."

"So what's it like working with him now?"

She shrugged. "This is the first time we've ever really worked together on a case. But it's fine. No hard feelings. He's very professional. Respects privacy—his own and others'."

I watched the buildings passing by. "Thanks for enlightening me. I thought I was sensing something with you two."

"I guess you would. Boy, being psychic must come in handy when it comes to picking friends and lovers."

Big sigh. "I wish. Unfortunately, when I'm personally involved is when my insights are most inaccurate, or nonexistent. It's as if once I have a personal attachment to someone or a vested interest in something, all my human desires and projections interfere with the channel. I'm very fallible that way."

"Like a surgeon not being able to operate on himself?"

"Something like that. Although I recently heard about a doctor who successfully performed his own vasectomy."

She shot me a look. "No!"

"Really."

First National Bank was just a few blocks from the police station. I was delighted when we parked in the red zone out front. Cops get away with all manner of flagrant traffic violations and it never fails to thrill me. We walked through a massive front entrance door into a deep green marble lobby. The quiet interior glowed with the reflection of tastefully mounted halogen lighting. A man in a dark green uniform sat at a matching green marble booth, his eyes riveted to a closed-circuit television. He didn't look up until we were practically on top of him. When he saw Dianna's badge he sat up straighter.

"We're looking for a Mr. Knutsen," she said.

"Yes, ma'am." He consulted the directory on his desk, running his finger slowly down the alphabetical listing of personnel. "Knutsen, Knutsen," he said under his breath. Suddenly he looked up. "Oh, you must mean me."

I couldn't look at Dianna or I'd burst out laughing. Fortunately she took the ball. "Mind if we ask you a few questions, Mr. Knutsen?"

He was beaming now, proud as punch to be of service. "Not at all, ma'am. Go right ahead." His thin brown hair clung to his head as if each strand were charged with static electricity.

"You're employed as a security guard at the bank here, is that correct?"

"Well, I'm not really a guard, but I man the front door here. Tell people what floor to go to and things." He gave us a gap-toothed grin.

"And how long have you worked here?"

"Three years, ma'am."

I threw a question out of left field. "Do you know Annie Drummond?"

His face, so attentive until now, slowly melted into an expression of dumb worry. He looked at Dianna. "Oh, no! Officer, you're not coming to tell me something else terrible has happened to Annie now, are you? Oh, no." He looked like he might cry.

"No, Mr. Knutsen," Dianna assured him, "Annie's doing fine. We just wanted to know if you knew her, is all."

"Oh, yes, ma'am, I certainly did. She worked for Mrs. Hendricks, and she was a nice girl, a very nice girl to me."

Dianna held the door open for me as we walked out of the building. "Not the sharpest tool in the shed, is he?"

I cracked up. "But sweet. Let's test your psychic powers, Dianna. Does that man lead a secret life as a knife-wielding serial rapist?"

"Put it this way. If he does he's the best damn actor on earth."

"Which is doubtful. Kevin Knutsen has the aura of a guy who'd rather put a bug outside than step on it. But what might it be about him that reminded Annie of her attacker? Body type?"

She unlocked my car door. "I don't know. He was medium height and stocky. I'd peg him about age thirty-eight, five-ten, two hundred pounds or so, very few of them muscle. What else?"

I waited for her to get in the car before answering. "He could have used some grooming tips. Other than that I don't know. I wouldn't waste too much time investigating Mr. Knutsen. Richard Zimmer, on the other hand . . ."

A low laugh rumbled in Dianna's throat as she pulled onto Fifth Avenue. "Zimmer I'm onto."

"You too, huh? I happen to know that he used to run a locksmithing business, which seems to me a very handy occupation for someone who's into breaking and entering. It might be worthwhile for one of us to find out who in the victims' neighborhoods had locksmithing work done. And when. And by whom."

"I can put Rick Billings on that. *You* might be interested to know that I found out Mr. Zimmer's maiden name was Shapiro, but he changed that identity when a child pornography rap became attached to it."

Something between a groan and a cough escaped my lips. "Oh, man. His dog bit off the wrong body part, that's all I can say."

21

Technically, Dianna and I were going against the flow of rush-hour traffic on our way back downtown. However, cars come out of nowhere to clog the streets and freeways at 4:30 P.M. in San Diego. To say that traffic *flows* in any direction at this hour is a bald lie. The trip from First National to the SDPD took twice as long as it should have. After a timeless hell of accelerate/brake, accelerate/brake, accelerate/brake, my nerves were jangling like cheap bracelets.

"I'm going to go round up Lieutenant Marcone and Rick Billings," Dianna said, hanging a left at the elevator. "This is a good time to compare notes."

I hung a right and was soon pushing through the door of the Sex Crimes department. I nearly slammed into Jeff Dietz. Luckily he saw me coming and stopped short. "Whoa."

"Sorry," I said. There'd been no impact, but instantly my head hurt. My shoulders were tight, and the muscles in my neck felt like Silly Putty just before it snaps. I put my hand to my forehead. "I need to sit down."

Dietz escorted me to his desk. I took a seat and shook a pair of aspirin tablets out of the emergency bottle I kept in my purse. I didn't ask for water, just popped them into my mouth and let the drug dissolve under my tongue. The headache was that bad.

"You okay?" he asked.

I nodded and rested my head against the soft wall of his carpeted cubicle. "Traffic headache." My eyes wandered over to the pictures in brass frames on his desk: a sailboat at sea, a gleaming red and chrome motorcycle. I pointed to the photos and made small talk. "Those your toys?"

He leaned back in his chair. "The Harley's mine. Heritage Softtail Classic. A great ride. Pretty, huh?"

I'm not really into motorcycles, but I bobbed my head up and down, appreciating the handiwork on the chopper's studded seat and saddlebags. If these were sweepstakes prizes I'd definitely pick the boat, with its sleek lines and white sail glowing in the sun. "The boat's pretty too."

He picked up the photo of the sailboat. "Kind of a cash drain, but I like to spend time with the ocean. Get away from things. People. Traffic." He smiled sympathetically at me.

At the mention of ocean a vision of the restless waves I'd seen in La Jolla today came back to me, along with the clueless feeling I'd had staring at the gray sea. "So what about these photos Dianna wanted me to look at?"

Dietz gave me a quizzical look. "What, the Peeping Tom photos? They're over on her desk. You sure you're up to it right now?"

"Yeah, I'll be fine. Peeping Toms, huh? Not to sound stupid, but aren't those guys generally pretty harmless?"

Dietz spoke over his shoulder as we walked to Dianna's cubicle. "They start out harmless. Lot of times they don't end up that way. These guys, for example."

Three photos were lined up in front of the computer monitor. I put my head down to get a better look. "So where'd these come from?"

"We sent some information bulletins to other departments around the area. Got a pretty good response. Most of the names that came in we were able to eliminate right off. Guys who are now living out of state or who're locked up, serving time. These are the leftovers."

"So these men I'm looking at are registered sex offenders, then."

"Yeah."

This wasn't easy. I was picking up negative energy all over the place. Hardly surprising. All of these men had committed crimes against women or children. The pertinent questions were: Which crimes? When?

I was bent over the desk gazing at the photos—in truth, my eyes were unfocused and my mind had started to wander—when I suddenly saw an image of a woman. She seemed to be associated with the man in the middle photograph. I picked it up. "I'm seeing a woman connected to this man. Is one of our victims a blonde, very thin, with dark circles around her eyes? I'm getting a name. . . . Terry? Tara, Terry, something like that."

Dietz's complexion blanched.

"What is it?" I asked.

He turned toward the door, and I looked to see Lieutenant Marcone and Rick Billings walking in. Dianna was following up the rear with a box of files. She pushed some papers aside and set the box on the table along the wall. "Have you picked out our rapist yet?" she asked.

Dietz, looking haunted, pointed to me. "She sees a skinny blond woman with dark circles around her eyes associated with Kramer. Thinks her name is Terry."

"Wow." Rick Billings looked stunned.

Dianna and Lieutenant Marcone exchanged an approving glance. "Not bad," she said, pulling some papers from her desk. "You got the name wrong, though. Her name's Torrie. The suspect's wife." She handed the papers to me. On top, an incident report. Domestic violence. Attached, photos of Torrie Kramer, taken after her husband had beaten her. Both of the eyes in her bony face had been blackened.

I looked at the three suspects again, then thought about the rapist whose presence I'd glimpsed through Thomasina's and Annie's eyes. *Conscious, cognizant, calculating.* I felt nothing from two of the photographs. I picked up the middle photograph. "This is Kramer?" They nodded.

The man in the picture had a low forehead and wide-set eyes that the camera had captured in a startled expression. I sensed an unconscious, disorganized anger. The kind of guy who might put a fist through a door over burned toast. Not cognizant and certainly not calculating. Unless he was *so* calculating he was fooling even me.

"I don't know. Kramer's got problems—all of these guys do—but I doubt that any one of them is our rapist. Of course I could be wrong. I'm just telling you my first impression, but it's usually accurate."

"Speaking of lousy first impressions," Dianna said to Lieutenant Marcone, "we've got more information on Zimmer. He's got a child porn rap on an aka, and Elizabeth discovered he used to be a locksmith." She turned to Billings. "Might be worthwhile for you to check the target neighborhoods and see who had locks worked on, who did the work, and when."

He nodded. "Right, locks. Could be the *key* to the whole case."

A smile tugged at the corners of Lieutenant Marcone's lips as he turned to me. "You'll get used to him," he said under his breath.

Dietz shook his head. "I'm not so sure we should get too excited about the locksmithing theory."

I pulled my map of San Diego out of my purse and began to unfold it. "Why not? Seems to me it would be a great front for a rapist."

"You have to understand something about victims. They feel embarrassed, they feel guilty about not locking their doors. Easier on their pride to report that their places have been burgled. A lot of them probably just left their windows open."

As if that were a crime. I spread my map onto the desk, pointing to the areas I'd circled in black pen. "Check this out: All four of the definite-for-sure rapes—the ones by the rapist with the latex gloves—happened along the Mission Valley canyon rim."

Lieutenant Marcone leaned forward and scrutinized my map. "We're aware of that. We've got increased patrol working the areas adjacent to the canyon."

Dietz pointed to the areas circled in blue pencil at the southeastern corner of the city. "What are these? Your long-shot cases?"

"Those are the maybes. The assailant had a similar MO, but no latex gloves were reported."

He smiled. "That's southeast San Diego. There's a lot of maybes in that area. That could be an endless job, narrowing those down." It was true that Southeast wasn't the best part of town.

"Not as endless as tracking down the latex gloves. There are thousands of suppliers of latex gloves in this city. Anyone can buy them at the local drugstore."

Lieutenant Marcone nodded. "Unfortunately, we know that too. I think the best use of time at this point would be for you"— he pointed to me—"to get out into the target neighborhoods and do some investigating there." He turned to the others. "When can we pull a surveillance together?"

"I'm off duty tomorrow and Thursday," Dianna said.

"I'm working patrol tonight, but I can be back by swing shift tomorrow," said Billings.

"What about you, Dietz?"

Dietz cracked his knuckles. "I can go out with Billings tomorrow."

"Good," the lieutenant said. "Tomorrow I want you and Billings to take Dr. Chase along."

22

I pulled up under the big eucalyptus in front of McGowan's house and cut the engine. Then heard the music. Rock and roll, pumping out across what could loosely be called his yard. A field of rye grass sloped down to the edge of the driveway where a lawn might ordinarily be. Here and there in the tall grass January wildflowers bloomed, spots of blue and gold captured in the illumination of my high beams. I turned off the lights and got out of the car. The sun had set during my drive over. Stars were beginning to show through broken-up clouds in the young night sky. The air was chilly, but for now the rain had cleared out.

Nero, McGowan's Rhodesian ridgeback, must have recognized the sound of my car door slamming. I could hear him whimpering anxiously from inside as I came up the walk. The kitchen door swung open, and there stood McGowan wearing a kelly green apron over his jeans. He was holding Nero by the collar with one hand and clutching a spatula with the other. Elvis crooned from within: "Everybody let's rock."

I leaned in for a hug, but McGowan swept me into the house, his hips twisting to the music. I was happy to see him but wasn't up for twisting just yet. Nero was beside himself with joy and did my dancing for me. McGowan felt my resistance. He didn't take offense. He let me go, grabbed a kitchen stool, and swirled it across the floor, singing the whole way: "If you can't find a partner use a wooden chair." Let's rock.

He put the stool down and walked back to me. "Glad you could make it. Rough day?"

It must have showed in my face. I surveyed the dish he was preparing in a pan on the stove: navratan korma, my favorite vegetarian Indian curry. Lined up on the counter were tandoori chicken, a basket of garlic naan bread, a colorful tray of chutney, and assorted condiments. "Rough *week*," I answered. "But this feast ought to revive me." I had to raise my voice over the music. "Better turn that down. Your neighbors are going to complain." This was a joke. His only neighbors for a half mile were the cows at the farm up the road.

We ate by candlelight and Elvis, turned down low. McGowan was finishing a second piece of chicken when he stated, "I'm going to be unavailable for the next couple of days."

I was piling more chutney onto my vegetable korma. "I think I can live without you for a day or two." I smiled and looked up at him.

His magnificent brown eyes were staring somberly at me. "I mean really unavailable. By phone, even."

"Is this something I should be concerned about?"

He put down his chicken and took just a moment longer to answer than I would have liked. "No."

"You going to tell me what this is all about?"

He dabbed at his mouth with the corner of his napkin. "Later. It's work-related stuff."

"Okay."

A mood came over me. When Tom brought out the coffee, he caught me staring into the candle flames. He set down our cups and rubbed my shoulders. "You okay? You're not taking what we talked about personally, are you?"

I reached for the cream and sugar. My sigh was so heavy it surprised even me. "It's not that. It's this *week*. And it's only Tuesday. Witnesses who've been raped, beaten, stabbed. It's horrible."

"Welcome to law enforcement."

I stirred my coffee long after the sugar had dissolved. "There's no physical evidence from the rapes—no hair, semen, fingerprints, nothin'. The only blood collected was from the victims' stab wounds. I hypnotized one of these women, hoping she'd remember useful details. Thomasina—a really cool lady, you'd like her—had such a severe reaction that she went into full-bore respiratory distress. The other victim I interviewed is on the road to severe depression. I have lots of victims still to see. Too many. I've started following up several suspects, but I'm not sure about any of them. Guess I'm feeling inadequate."

McGowan dropped his hands to my arms and gave my biceps a squeeze. "You're doing great."

"No evidence, no hunches. Yeah, I'm doing fabulously."

He sat back down and took a sip of coffee. "I think it's something like only sixteen percent of rapes that are even reported. I'm sure this guy didn't start carving women from the get-go. He probably had a long string of practice rapes before they got bloody. I'll bet there are lots of other cases you could look into, other leads to follow."

I leaned back in my chair, exasperated. "I know. Dianna gave me a whole stack of maybes. It's overwhelming. I feel like I'm in over my head."

"Nonsense. Nothing a little cake can't fix." With that he hopped out of his chair and disappeared into the kitchen. McGowan is remarkably agile for a guy his size.

"You got *cake*?" I loved this man.

He returned carrying a silver tray piled high with a concoction that looked sweet and white and wonderful, topped by glowing candles. "Of course I got cake. It's a special occasion. Six whole months."

The sentimental fool. He was as silly as I was. "Candles even. Who gets to blow?"

He placed the tray between us and sat down. "Both of us."

I wished fervently that the rapist would be caught before anyone was killed and blew like hell. The candle on the right corner flickered tenaciously, but in the end I was able to snuff it. It felt like a minor victory.

My knife sank smoothly into the white chocolate mousse cake. When I'd cut two large slices, McGowan pushed a very fancy foil-wrapped package toward my plate. "Guess," he said.

I picked up the gift and held it in my hands. "What's this for?"

"Never mind. Just go on, guess."

But guessing wouldn't be fair. I could already see what was inside the box.

McGowan read it in my face. "Don't tell me you know what it is."

I didn't say anything.

"You *know?*"

I nodded. "It's beautiful, Tom. I'm speechless."

"Goll dang it. For once in my life I take the trouble to wrap a present and for what?" He wasn't really mad. By the huge grin on his face I'd say he was downright tickled. "All right. Let's hear it. What's in the box?"

"A necklace—gorgeous—a delicate strand of clear crystal beads and in the middle an incredible little violet gem, tanzanite? Oh, it's charming."

McGowan shook his head in amazement.

I was having a hard time letting it sink in that he'd given me such a treasure. He must have hocked one of his guns for this. "Oh, Tom, this is so wonderful. Thank you so much! But—"

"But nothing. This is for not letting me buy you a decent Christmas present. Besides, I saw it and just *knew* you should have it."

"Tanzanite is so precious and unusual—how perfect." I got up and squeezed his neck, then planted a grateful kiss on his cheek.

"What else would I get for such a precious and unusual woman? Now, are you ever going to open the box?"

After opening the box I stood in front of the hallway mirror to admire the necklace. McGowan stood behind me, looking very pleased. "Got an idea," he said.

"What's that?"

"Let's get out of town this weekend. Even if it's only for Sunday brunch up the coast. I think we're both working too hard."

"Sounds good to me."

With that he pulled me into the living room, and we slow danced while Elvis sang of wise men and fools. It was the ideal ending to a memorable meal. Romanced out, we settled on the sofa in the den to watch old episodes of *The X-Files* on videotape. I lay in front of McGowan, leaning my back against the warm, comfortable bulk of his chest, hanging on to the big arms he'd wrapped around me. The sensual comfort of our position was highly conducive to blissful dozing. I closed my eyes and started to drift, still aware of the voices on television but no longer listening to what they were saying. At some point I slipped into a trance state.

I had no warning. One minute I was safe in McGowan's arms. The next I was in a darkened house, witness to a real-life nightmare.

A woman, groping in the darkness. I floated above and watched her futile attempt to turn on the lights. Her bedside lamp would not go on. She darted through the room to the wall switch—nothing. I *knew*—the way you just know in dreams—that electricity to the house had been cut off. The woman turned around and I saw her terrified face, recognized it. It was Cheryl Arendt, the tall brunette who had moved into the Hillcrest bungalow after Annie Drummond's rape. Now I recognized the house. I watched as she ran across the hall to the door, trying desperately to escape. The knob turned but the door would not open. Someone had bolted it shut from the *outside*.

In the kitchen now, I read the mind of an intruder with cold intentions. He was fully aware of the panic he had ignited in the woman's pounding heart. *Conscious, cognizant, calculating.* Then I knew with certainty that this was no dream. What I was seeing was reality. Was it happening now? I tried to call out to Cheryl in the bedroom, but I couldn't make any noise. I struggled to help her, I had to reach her—

"Elizabeth. Elizabeth. Elizabeth, wake up." McGowan's voice was insistent, worried.

For a moment I didn't know where I was, didn't remember where I'd been.

"Are you all right? You were moaning." McGowan was holding me upright, peering into my face. His features were filled with concern.

Then I remembered and bolted off the sofa.

23

"I have to get down there." I moved quickly through McGowan's house, hunting down my purse and coat.

"Get down where? What are you talking about?" He followed closely behind on my flight into the kitchen.

"I just saw another break-in. It's *him*, I'm sure of it. The rapist."

McGowan has learned to roll with my strange abilities. "Where?"

I scooped up my keys from the kitchen table. "The Hillcrest house. Same place one of the earlier victims was attacked."

He caught up with me at the door. "I'm going with you. Let's take my cruiser."

I didn't argue. As we headed toward the freeway I used McGowan's car phone to call the SDPD dispatcher and report a break-in at 4212 Fourth Avenue. "Please send a car right away."

At 11:30 P.M. traffic was light. McGowan kept up a steady eighty-five/ninety, taking advantage of police car privileges. Flashbacks from my trance preoccupied me on the ride down. "I was in the kitchen," I told McGowan, "and it was like I could read the intentions of the intruder."

"Could you see him at all?"

"No, not that I can remember. He'd cut off electricity to the house, so it was completely black. For some reason, though, I could see the terror on Cheryl's face—that's the woman who lives there now. But the whole experience was dark, murky." I stared at the stream of headlights on the opposite side of the freeway. Their glow billowed cloudlike in my vision. "I'm feeling a little strange," I said.

McGowan kept his eyes on the lanes ahead of him. "I had to call your name several times before you came to. You were really out there."

Part of me was still out there. People surrender themselves to sleep every night without giving it a thought. Many don't dream; most who do don't believe they really "go" anywhere. I'd had enough verified experience to know that the other side is as real as any mundane point in space. But *where* that dimension is, *what* it is, and why it leaks through to me and not most others were questions to which I didn't have answers.

We exited the freeway at Washington and turned north onto Fourth. The cruiser rolled at a crawl up the 4200 block. I saw a light on at the house where the little boy, Sean, lived. The bungalow next door was completely dark. The blacked-out house appeared exactly as I'd seen it a half hour ago, from thirty miles away. Not so much as a porch or night-light on. There wasn't a patrol car in sight.

"What happened to our backup?" I wondered out loud.

McGowan parked on the same side of the street and slightly north of the bungalow. "Maybe they've already checked it out and everything's fine. Then again, the place looks pitch-dark. If you're right about the rest of it, I guess I'd better not just walk up and knock on the door." He eyed the layout while he checked his .45, then popped his car door open. "I'm going around the back from the far side of the house."

"Then I'll cover this side."

He looked at me hard. "Elizabeth—"

I already had my car door open. "It's okay. I've got my gun."

He didn't pursue the argument, just reached over and pulled his Kevlar vest from the backseat. "Put this on."

I got out of the car and put on the bulletproof vest. On me it was so overlarge it was comical. Then, again, there wasn't anything funny about taking a live round or having a knife plunged into your chest. I pulled the fasteners as tight as they would go, then chambered the first round in my Glock and held the gun at my side. A biting cold wind was the only thing traveling up the street.

Silently we moved up the sidewalk to the bungalow. McGowan slipped behind the shrubs along the far side of the house so quickly he seemed to vanish in thin air. I crept along the edge of the lawn on the north side of the house. The grass was wet. I was reminded of the dream that had prompted my involvement in the case. The vacant-eyed goat made a quick visit to my memory.

Halfway to the back of the house I felt goose bumps rising along my arms and up the back of my neck. They were unrelated to the cold. The bedroom window came into view. It was too dark to see anything inside. There was no screaming, no sound at all. I stopped ten feet from the window. Something hideous was about to happen in there. *Was* happening in there. Where was McGowan?

I stood motionless. Where had I had this feeling before, of horror behind closed doors? A childhood memory: standing outside a large wooden building on the rural side of town. Having this same awful sense of something terrible happening inside. What's in that building? I'd asked my father. "That's a meat packing company," he'd said. "Where cows are butchered."

I stood beside the house for perhaps a minute before the tension became unbearable. I kept seeing Cheryl's terrified face. I wanted to shoot my gun into the air but couldn't, of course, in the city. In a panic I reached for something, anything, to throw at the window. My groping hands found a good-sized rock near the fence alongside the house. I hurled it at the window and ducked.

The sounds came simultaneously: shattering glass, screaming, footsteps. I froze for a beat, then ran around to the back of the house in time to hear the scraping sound of someone heavy climbing up and over the backyard fence.

24

"Elizabeth!"

I recognized McGowan's hulking form standing on the opposite side of the backyard. Recognized his voice. "It's me."

"Someone just went over the back fence."

"I know. Can't do anything about that now. Come here and watch the kid a minute. I'm going inside."

The kid? Sure enough, my eyes made out the shape of a child standing next to McGowan. I stumbled a couple of times hurrying toward them in the darkness. By the time I reached the boy, McGowan had already gone inside to check on Cheryl. "Sean, it's Elizabeth. Remember me?"

He nodded. The six-year-old bravado was gone. This time he was scared.

"Let's get you back home."

Sean's mother was beginning to calm down. I had brandished my PI badge and explained three times now who I was and what I was doing on her front step with her own son at this hour of the night. "There's a police officer next door now," I explained. "He'll be here any minute."

I heard footsteps behind me and turned to see McGowan coming up the walkway with Cheryl Arendt. He spoke to Sean's mother. "I'm Sergeant McGowan, a police officer. Sorry to disturb you, but there's been a break-in next door. Could we use your phone please?" He wasn't wearing his uniform, but he wore the bearing of a cop. She didn't hesitate to step aside and let us in.

McGowan went to the kitchen to make the call. Sean's mother led the rest of us into the living room. Cheryl, wearing pajamas and a robe, took a seat on the sofa. Her hair was a disheveled tangle framing a pale face devoid of makeup. Her feet, too, were bare. A considerably different image from the woman I'd met rushing off to her high-tech job outfitted with career pumps, a London Fog raincoat, and a black umbrella. I sat on an adjacent chair and smiled weakly at her. "Hello again."

She didn't seem to register who I was.

Sean sat down on an ottoman. For the first time I noticed the boy was wearing only blue pajamas, a Star Trek insignia embroidered above the left breast. "What were you doing over there, Sean?" I asked.

He looked hesitantly at his mom. He squirmed in his seat as if the excitement of the last half hour were bottled up inside him. Then the words came tumbling out. "I saw the man go in the house next door and I—"

"Slow down, Sean, slow down. How did you happen to see the man go into the house?"

"I was spying. I always do that. Mom thinks I'm in bed. I could see this, like, *shape* along the side of the house." He made a vague gesture with his hands.

"What kind of a shape? Could you see what it looked like?"

"I don't know, it was really dark. At first I thought it was a dog or something. I watched it for a long time. Then it moved onto the kitchen porch of Cheryl's house, and I could tell it was a man. I couldn't see very good from my bedroom window, so I went into the bathroom to watch from there. You can see next door better from the bathroom. Anyways, that's when I saw the man on the kitchen steps, trying to get in."

Sean's mother looked mortified. "What did you do then?" I prompted.

He glanced at his mom. "I got my gun and ran outside."

His harmless plastic Lego gun. "Sean, that was very dangerous."

He looked again at his mother, who stared at him with worried eyes. "I know, but I'm okay. I was being careful so the robber wouldn't see me." His mother and I exchanged grateful glances.

"When I got next door the robber wasn't there anymore," Sean continued. "I knew he'd gone inside because the kitchen door was open. I started to run then. To tell my mom to call the police—for backup." He looked proud.

I had to smile. He was adorable. McGowan came into the room and stood by the doorway to listen.

"Then all of a sudden this big man, *that* guy"—Sean pointed to McGowan—"had a hold of me and just about scared me to death! Until he told me he *was* the police."

"Here, sport." McGowan tossed something across the room. Sean caught it with both hands. The Lego gun.

His mother stepped to his side, put her hands on his shoulders. "Quite a son you have there," I said.

"He's actually in big trouble right now. But thanks."

Sean looked contrite. "I'm not supposed to be outside after dark."

Cheryl had been watching Sean tell his story and occasionally staring over at me. A sudden recognition lit her eyes. "Now I remember you. You're the psychic."

I nodded. "What happened over there tonight?"

She sat on the very edge of the chair and rubbed her face with her hands. "Oh, God." Sean got down from the ottoman and quietly went to sit beside her on the sofa. "I don't know what woke me," Cheryl went on. "But all of a sudden I was awake, and I had this weird feeling something was wrong."

"This was about what time?"

"I don't know. Now that I think about it, that's the first thing I noticed that was wrong—I couldn't see what time it was. I have an electric clock on my bedside table, you know, the kind with numbers that glow in the dark? I couldn't see it. I reached over and tried to turn on my bedside lamp, but the light didn't work. I remember I was thinking, *Okay, don't panic, just lie here and wake up a minute*. When I was sure I was awake I got out of bed to turn on the wall light. That didn't work either. I thought, *The electricity's just gone out. No big deal*. I have a flashlight in my dresser and I was getting up to get it when . . ." She ran her fingers through her hair. "I heard dishes breaking in the kitchen."

I was taking mental notes furiously and wished I had my tape recorder. "Then what?"

"When I heard the breaking glass I *did* panic. All I could think was, *I gotta get out of here*. There are three doors in my house—front door, kitchen door, and a door off the second bedroom. I went as quietly as I could to the bedroom door." She picked up the sash of her robe and began pulling and twisting it in her hands. "When I reached the door I tried to turn the knob. But the knob didn't catch, it just kept spinning around and around. I tried forcing the door, but it was stuck. I was trapped." Her voice was shaking. She continued to fidget with the tie on her robe.

"And then?"

"I saw someone coming into the room. That's when the rock came flying through the window."

"That was me," I explained to McGowan. I turned to Cheryl. "After the rock went through the window, then what?"

"Whoever it was turned and ran out of the room. Then I just sat there shaking until he"—her eyes darted toward McGowan—"came in." She returned her attention to twisting her sash.

I shifted gears and put myself in Cheryl's shoes. "Are you going to be okay tonight? Do you have a friend or relative to stay with?"

Cheryl looked dazed. She obviously hadn't thought about that yet. "I don't know. I can't go back over there."

"Of course not. You want me to go over and gather up some things for you?"

She nodded slowly. Then looked up at me with somber eyes. "I guess that place wasn't such a bargain after all."

It was hard to know what to say.

"A patrol officer should be here to take a report in just a few minutes," McGowan said. "If they come here, tell them we're next door."

McGowan and I started for the door. "Hey wait," Cheryl called. "How did *you* know to come?"

"Tell you later," I said.

As McGowan and I were walking back over to the darkened house a police car pulled up to the curb. The car door opened, and a patrolman started up the walk. I recognized his profile from thirty paces. "Hey, Billings. I called this thing in ages ago. Where the hell have you been?"

"Dr. Chase? What are you doing here?"

"I'll explain that later. When did you get the call?"

"About an hour ago. They sent me to a break-in at four one two Fourth, which turned out to be a false alarm."

I rolled my eyes. "That wasn't a false alarm. They gave you the wrong address. I called in four *two* one two Fourth Avenue."

Billings shook his head. "Oh, jeez. We've got a dispatcher or two who're just a few Froot Loops shy of a bowl, if you know what I mean. Is everything okay here?"

I nodded. "Yeah, you can get a statement from the almost-victim. She's next door expecting you."

"Who's your friend?"

"Tom McGowan, Escondido PD." Tom and Rick shook hands.

Billings went to get his statement, and McGowan and I continued toward the bungalow. I stood on the wide front steps and tried to tune in with my inner eye. Again a murkiness surrounded my vision, the way ocean water clouds after a squid has released its ink.

I shined my flashlight at the front door. "Hey, look at this." Just under the doorknob a hasp had been mounted, securing the door to the frame. McGowan's flashlight beam joined mine, light bouncing off the steel hasp.

"Looks like somebody was trying to lock this door from the outside," he said. "That's odd. There aren't any screws. How's it staying on there?"

Careful not to smudge any prints, I slid my fingernail under the edges. The hasp was secured firmly to the wood. "Quick-drying industrial-strength glue maybe? That would be faster and quieter than bolting the door shut." It wouldn't stop a battering ram or a few well-aimed bullets, but it would trap an unarmed woman in her own home. I shuddered at how terribly premeditated this intruder was. *Calculating.*

"Let's go through the back way." McGowan bobbed the flashlight beam ahead of us as we walked around the house. Halfway along the south wall we found the open circuit breaker box. McGowan poked his flashlight inside. "Somebody threw the switches all right."

We continued on to the kitchen porch and stepped through the open door. McGowan used the end of his flashlight to flip the on switch. Nothing. Our flashlight beams danced around the kitchen. Expensive looking crystal stemware lay shattered in the corner by the refrigerator. "What do you think this was all about?" McGowan asked as he spotlighted the broken glassware.

"He smashed it intentionally. He wanted the noise to frighten her." The place was giving me a serious case of heebie-jeebies. "Come with me while I get her things." We walked to the back of the house. I ducked into the bathroom to grab Cheryl's toothbrush and cosmetic bag, then found her bedroom and hastily gathered up a few items from her dresser and closet.

McGowan was across the hall examining the other bedroom. "Come have a look at this door," he called.

McGowan was handling the doorknob with a tissue, taking care not to smudge any prints. Just as Cheryl had described, the knob spun futilely, and the door wouldn't budge. "Same deal as the front door," he said. We walked out of and around the house to inspect the bedroom door from the outside. Here too a steel hasp had been glued on the door and the frame, effectively locking it from the outside.

I stared at the lock and shuddered. "Wonder where Richard Zimmer might be about now."

25

Lightning *had* struck in the same place twice. The second attempt on the Hillcrest house made it clear that the other victims—the ones we knew about—had to be warned. The rapist was systematic. It wasn't unthinkable that he'd work through his list. As soon as I'd made my first cup of coffee the next morning I pulled files and worked through my list of the definite-for-sure victims' names, addresses, and current whereabouts:

1. Annie Drummond. 4212 Fourth Avenue, Hillcrest. Now living with parents in Clairemont—probably safe.

2. Sandy Devereaux. 1620 Arizona, University Heights. Status unknown.

3. Marisa Sanchez. 2026 Canterbury, Kensington. Status unknown.

4. Thomasina Wilson. 3323 Montezuma, near SD State. Now in Sharp Hospital—when does she check out?

I popped a bagel into the toaster and called the SDPD from the phone in the kitchen. I knew Dianna would be out so I tried Dietz's line and got dumped into voice mail. Same with Billings. The guys probably wouldn't be in until our surveillance, which wouldn't start until three this afternoon. I made one more call, to Lieutenant Marcone.

"Top of the morning to you, Lieutenant. I wanted to make sure you were aware of the incident at the Hillcrest house last night."

"Yes, but how were you aware of it? I hear you were already on the scene when they called it in."

"I saw it happening, just like before. Only this time I saw it right before it happened. Also, I'd visited that house during my investigation, so I knew where it was."

"Well, it's a good thing." I heard him take a swallow of coffee. "Technically, you know, it was just a break-in. We probably would have connected it to the rape case anyway. We've got people checking incident reports daily looking for just that kind of activity. Break-ins, suspicious loiterers, anything that could be related."

"Did a tech get out to the house? The intruder tampered with the doors and broke some glass. Of course if it's our guy he was probably wearing gloves, but you never know when you'll get a lucky break."

"Yes. We dusted and photographed the place."

"You know, then, that the doors were secured shut from the outside."

"I know. It's the first time we've seen that." There was an anxious tone in Marcone's voice that I hadn't heard before.

"What do you think prompted him to start that? Locking the doors from the outside, I mean." I heard the ding of my toaster telling me my bagel was ready.

"It's a variation on a common pattern. If I had to sum it up I'd call it 'kicks just keep getting harder to find.' Unfortunately, it's typical for the violence to escalate in these cases. He's getting off on the terror he's putting into his victims. He didn't start out cutting the lights, you'll notice. That's been a recent development. Now he's on to locking doors. It's not a good trend."

"You've seen this before?"

"Not this exactly, but I once helped put away a guy who was similarly twisted. Back in Chicago." Marcone let some steam pass through his lips. "Old Sal. Sal the Sadist."

"Someone who started out mildly and—"

"And ended up putting his victims in front of a mirror so he could watch their terrified reactions to having their breasts cut open."

"Oh, Jesus."

"He began his career standing outside bedroom windows and watching women undress. By the time the people of the State of Illinois retired him, he had raped at least twenty-five women and taken eight lives." There was silence on the line. I think the lieutenant and I were saying the same prayer: *Please God, not here in San Diego.* "What are you working on now?" he asked.

"I've been interviewing victims. I thought I'd go down our list and warn these women what's going on, so they can take extra precautions. Wanted to make sure I wouldn't be duplicating task force efforts."

"Good idea. We're short today. We could use your help."

I pulled some cream cheese and marmalade from the fridge. "Why do you think he went back to one of the earlier crime scenes last night?"

"I'm not sure. It was risky. Again, I think he's looking for kicks. The other victims certainly need to be warned, though."

"A job I'm happy to do."

"Think you'll be able to wrap it up by three? Don't forget you're going out with Dietz and Billings this evening."

I felt a cat massaging my ankles. "How could I forget? So is anybody keeping track of a certain locksmith by the name of Mr. Richard Zimmer?"

"Believe me, we're on him. Just a minute." On Marcone's end I heard muffled voices. On my end, I reached down and scratched under Whitman's neck, a daily ritual he'd been missing lately. Then Marcone was back. "Sorry, I have to wrap this up. Hope you're able to pick up our sadist with that extrasensory radar of yours."

"I'll do my best."

My toasted bagel was cold by the time I got off the phone. I ate it anyway. It was already eight thirty, and I needed to make the most of what time I had this morning. My next call was to Annie Drummond. Her father answered. "Annie? Still asleep. You expect to talk to her this early in the morning?" He seemed quite amused by this.

"Could you just tell her something's come up and I'll have to postpone our meeting until tomorrow morning at ten o'clock?"

"Yeah, sure."

I hung up, hoping but not confident that Roger Drummond would follow through.

Sandy Devereaux had been the second victim of the rapist with the latex-gloved hands. I looked through her folder. The first item was an incident report dated June 9, 1993: It read, in part:

On 6/9/93, 12:31 A.M. Victim, a white female, age 31, was in her bed. Victim woke up when she heard a noise in the hallway. She looked up to see a man (Suspect) coming through her bedroom door. Suspect pinned her to the bed with his full weight, held a knife to her throat, and threatened to cut it unless she did as she was told. Victim was forced to remove her nightgown. Suspect taped victim's mouth with electrical adhesive tape and cut two circle-shaped lacerations on her chest. Victim was then forced to have sexual intercourse.

Clipped into the file behind the narrative was a photo of Sandy's chest. Granted, I tend to read things into Rorschach tests that most people don't see. However, I think it would be fair to say that anyone could make a picture out of the circle-shaped lacerations across Sandy Devereaux's breastbone. They looked exactly like bull's-eyes.

Behind the chest photo was a head shot, and I recognized Sandy from the photos Dietz and Dianna had shown to Richard Zimmer. Curly brown hair, very full lips, eyes filled with tragedy.

Sandy's phone number was listed next to her University Heights address. I dialed and got that annoying three-tone off-key chord that precedes the message: "The number you have reached is no longer in service. . . ."

I returned to the incident report to see if anyone was listed as next of kin. "John Huff, Friend" was penned in at 555-4411, but when I dialed the number I got a recording listing show times at the Golden Circle cinema.

There was no choice but to drive out to the house. I got dressed, gathered my papers, and once again headed south.

The house in University Heights was modest but pleasant. The exterior walls gleamed with a fresh coat of paint. Bright orange zinnias and yellow marigolds filled the flower beds. The neighbors had kids—a tricycle stood in the adjacent yard. I rang the bell and through a crack in the front window heard the sound of morning television. Buzzer, applause, laughter. A game show. The door opened, and I was greeted by a man wearing a Chinese silk robe and slippers.

"Hi. Is Sandy Devereaux home?"

"Sandy who?"

"There was a woman living at this address in June. Her name was Sandy. Is she no longer at this address?"

"No. We bought the house last August." Another man, this one clad in flannel pj's, came toward us down the stairs.

"Are you aware that a crime was committed here last June?"

The men looked at each other, concerned but not paranoid. "No. That was before we moved in. What crime?"

"A rape."

They shook their heads. Flannel pj's caught on quickly. "Good God. Not that thing that's been on the news?"

"Yeah, *that* thing. There was a second attack at the first victim's house last night. I'm alerting the other victims. That's why I'm trying to find Sandy."

"Gee, we wish we could help you."

"How about a phone number for the former owner?"

"Hang on a sec." The man in the robe went to retrieve the number. Flannel pj's and I stood silently for a moment. "It wouldn't hurt to be vigilant yourselves," I said.

"Yeah, we will. Thanks."

"If anything happens, report it immediately to the police department and ask for Lieutenant Marcone. Here." I penned his name on the back of one of my cards. "Or you can call me." I handed him the card. "What's your name?"

"Barry. Barry Nelson. My roommate's name is Vince."

Vince reappeared and handed me the phone number of the previous owner.

"Thanks."

"Good luck. Hope you nail him."

My phone call to Sandy Devereaux's former landlord, Jeff Johnson, was also a dead end. Sandy had been his tenant, but he had no idea where she'd disappeared to. She had moved out the day after the rape. The experience had affected Johnson as well. He was unable to rent out the house again and within a month had put it on the market.

The only other lead I had from the police report was Sandy's occupation. There wasn't much to go on. The report listed simply, "beauty consultant."

I took a chance and dialed the Mary Kay cosmetic company. Wasn't the slightest bit surprised when the area manager had no information on Sandy Devereaux.

Finally I played my last card. I made a call to Joanne Friedman, a friend of mine who manages accounts for a national finance company. "Hey, Jo. I need to call in one of my chits."

"About time. What can I do for you?"

"Well, this one's for a good cause, a woman's safety. What can you find on Sandy Devereaux?"

"Can I put you on hold?"

"Sure." While I waited I pulled out the photo and looked again at the bull's-eyes etched into Sandy's chest. Meanwhile, the Muzak on the line piped out an innocuous version of "Mack the Knife." Ironic, but not at all funny.

Just as it was getting to me, Joanne popped back on the line. "Okay, are you there?"

"I'm here."

"Sandy Devereaux's last address is listed at one six two zero Arizona in University Heights."

"No new address after June of this year?"

"No," she said slowly. "In fact, she hasn't made any credit card purchases since June. As I look at this, yeah—she hasn't had *any* financial activity since June. That's really weird. It looks like Sandy Devereaux just disappeared."

I couldn't say I blamed her.

26

I had better luck with the next victim on my list.

Marisa Sanchez's fifteen minutes of fame had come and gone. The richly photogenic brutality that had catapulted her onto Halloween's eleven o'clock news had no doubt faded from the gnatlike memory of the television audience. The memory, like the scars, would live with Marisa the rest of her life.

Marisa's file was disturbing. The photograph of her face—savagely slashed, exposing the gums above her molars—was mounted behind the police report narrative. I found myself fingering gingerly through the file to avoid seeing the picture. As I dialed the phone number listed for Marisa on the cover of the report I secretly harbored a hope that she, like Sandy Devereaux, had started life over someplace else. My interviewing Marisa would force her to reexperience an ungodly event. I didn't want that job.

"Hello?"

Lucky me. A woman answered on the first ring.

"Marisa Sanchez?"

"Yes?"

There was long beat while I mustered the nerve to go on. "Hello, Marisa. My name is Elizabeth Chase. I'm working with the police department, investigating a crime you reported—"

She broke in on me. "Could you hang on a minute? One minute, please."

I heard a thump, an extended pause, and a click. Another pause, then Marisa came back on the line. "Sorry. I had to change phones. Please, go on."

"I need to meet with you as soon as possible. There's been an important development in your case. I could be there in ten minutes."

"No." The word shot out of her mouth. "Not yet. Could you wait a half hour, no, better make it forty-five minutes, to be on the safe side."

I looked at my watch. Forty-five minutes would put the little hand close to two. That would be cutting it pretty short if I was going to be ready to roll with Dietz and Billings on the three o'clock shift. "Is there any possible way we can talk sooner? I'm on a very tight schedule today."

"No, I'm sorry. I will explain this to you later. Please. Forty-five minutes. I will see you then."

She hung up before I could respond. What did she mean, "to be on the safe side"? Now I was curious. I figured if I had forty-five minutes to kill I might as well spend it outside Marisa's house, where I might get a clue as to what could be more important than urgent police business.

Even with the back-from-lunch traffic surge the drive took less than nine minutes. Kensington is just east of University Heights. There are no obvious geographical boundaries—no rivers, hills, or dales—that set Kensington apart from the rest of residential San Diego. The community is distinguished by quieter streets, larger houses, and lawns with better manicures. The Sanchezes occupied a beautiful adobe house on a street that wound through oak and acacia trees along the canyon rim. I parked halfway around a curve on the opposite side of the street, about a hundred yards from the house.

There was nothing much to see. Very little traffic passed this way. The street was quiet, save for the wind whipping through the branches overhead. The curtains of the Sanchez home were closed against the dark January day. I cracked my window. The draft that rushed into the car smelled like rain.

I studied the layout of the house. It occupied a beautifully landscaped lot. A deep front lawn lined with junipers buffered the front of the house from the street. Dense shrubbery provided privacy from the neighbors on the east and west sides of the property. I had to admit that it was a rather ideal place for a criminal to make a hit. Then again, a burglar or rapist trying to leave the scene would be conspicuous in a neighborhood like this. The canyon on the back side of the house, however, might provide a good escape route, particularly if the assailant were physically fit.

Again I reviewed Marisa's incident report, to see just how the crime went down. The rapist had used his established MO. Marisa had been asleep. He was on top of her before she even woke up. He held the knife to her throat and threatened to kill her if she made any noise. He pulled her gown up and raped her. It was during the act of intercourse that the rapist had slashed Marisa's face with the knife. She had called the police immediately following the crime, using her car phone. A search of the property revealed that all electricity and phone lines to the house had been severed.

I was twenty minutes into my reconnaissance when the front door of the Sanchez house opened. A man carrying an expensive briefcase and wearing a beautifully tailored raincoat walked out to the mailbox, opened it, and gathered several envelopes. He walked back into the house, and within a minute or two the garage door opened. A sleek silver-blue Mercedes rolled quietly out of the driveway as the garage door automatically closed. The car headed toward me along Canterbury. I slid down in my seat, keeping only my eyes above window level. As the car sped past I caught a glimpse of the driver, a dark-haired, brown-skinned man who stared grimly at the road ahead. I didn't think he saw me.

I wasn't patient enough to sit out the remaining fifteen minutes. I walked up the street and approached the front door. Large clay pots of lush ferns and purple orchids lined the entryway. I pushed the doorbell and put on my simpering smile. When I glanced up I was astonished to see that this time I was being monitored by a closed-circuit television. Before I could wave the door swung open.

"You are from the police department?"

Healing but cruelly evident, a purple-red gash bisected the left side of Marisa Sanchez's face from the top of her prominent cheekbone to the corner of her mouth. It was impossible not to notice, but I tried to keep the shock out of my eyes as I looked at her. "Working with the police, yes. Thanks for seeing me today." As I took in the damage on the left side of her face, it occurred to me that the rapist was probably right-handed. Gee, I thought, that eliminates a whopping ten percent of the population.

"My husband came home for lunch today. I had to wait for him to leave again for work." She escorted me across an entryway of hand-painted tile and into a spacious living room. "He does not approve of any police involvement. I'm afraid he does not trust the police in this city. He's very stubborn. He wants to handle this his own way." I wondered if her husband had installed the closed-circuit television security system after the rape.

Together on the carpet in front of the television a pair of twin girls—I would guess about age three—sat entranced by *Sesame Street*. Marisa clapped her hands for their attention. "Mommy has company. Upstairs with Rosa. Come on, let's go." She called out to Rosa, who appeared at the doorway and led the two upstairs.

I watched the girls run up the stairs and disappear into the second floor. "You have beautiful daughters."

"Thank you."

"Were they home when this terrible thing happened?"

Marisa cast her eyes to the floor. "Yes."

Had these precious girls, like the rest of television viewing San Diego, seen Marisa carted away on a stretcher in a blood-soaked nightgown Halloween night? I couldn't bear to ask.

Outside the plate-glass windows on the north side of the room a series of adobe arches framed a wide view of the canyon. I walked over to the windows and imagined how the view would appear at night, with the lights of Mission Valley sparkling below. It was a lovely home, insulated yet metropolitan.

Marisa saw me appreciating the view and stood with me in front of the glass. "We've been very fortunate. My husband owns a chain of restaurants in San Diego. Jalepeno's—perhaps you've eaten there?"

Jalepeno's Tex-Mex cuisine was fast, affordable, healthy, and delicious. The restaurants were clean and pleasant. I patronized them as often as time and opportunity allowed. "Are you kidding? I've *overeaten* there. The food is wonderful."

Marisa smiled on the good side of her mouth. "Thanks." She had swept up her thick dark hair into an elegant French roll and secured it with long black hairpins painted with gold. A few stray tendrils were escaping in a most bewitching way. Light from the window filled her eyes, which were large and expressive above her gorgeous cheekbones. With features this flawless and symmetrical, Marisa could easily get work in front of a camera. Could have.

She sighed. "So what is this 'important development' in my case?"

I met her eyes frankly. "He attacked one of the same houses again."

She crushed her eyelids shut. "*Dios mío.*"

"Marisa, perhaps you can take the girls and stay with relatives someplace until we apprehend this creep?"

She hadn't opened her eyes yet, but she shook her head. "No, no. He won't allow it."

"Your husband, you mean."

She opened her eyes. "Yes. He wants the rapist to come back so he can kill the bastard himself."

"Well, I don't blame him, but I don't think that's the safest plan. How do you feel about it?"

"Carlos has worked all his life for this." She indicated with a wave of her hand the house, the property, and the success they represented. "And what if the police don't catch this *pendejo*? Then what? I can't leave my husband, take his children away." She closed her eyes again. "I don't know." She placed her face in her hand, unconsciously covering the wound.

"I'm going to find this guy and make him pay for what he did to you." The words blurted out of me before I could think about what I was saying.

Marisa looked at me so gratefully I wanted to reach out and hug her. Instead, I opened my purse and pulled out a tape recorder. "Do you mind?"

She shook her head. "It was so awful. You can't even imagine."

She motioned me to the sofa. As we sat down I pushed the record button. I didn't pry, I didn't have to. Marisa Sanchez had mettle. I could hear it in her voice and in the straightforward way she offered up the whole ugly story.

"I'll tell you everything I know. I put the girls in bed at eight o'-clock, their usual bedtime. I took a bath and got into bed. I was reading for some time, then I became sleepy. I turned out the light and drifted off. It was maybe ten o'clock when I closed my eyes."

"Was your husband home?"

"No. He had business in Arizona. We're planning to open some restaurants there."

"So it was just you and the girls in the house?"

She nodded and closed her eyes tightly. "Then this horrible thing. I came out of my sleep with this knife at my neck and this monster on top of me. I was so frightened, I thought I would die. The girls, I could only think about my babies. I couldn't scream for fear they would come into the room. . . ."

Her voice caught, and she stopped to compose herself. I was grateful for the break. My own stomach had begun to churn. Discreetly, I took a deep breath. "Did he say anything to you?"

Marisa's eyes narrowed. "Yes, he told me if I made any noise he would kill me. He was a very heartless man. I have never seen such evil. He jerked my gown up—he was such a pig." The anger flashed in her eyes for a moment but quickly turned to pain and shame. "Then I made a terrible mistake. I could *not* endure it, do you understand?" She looked imploringly at me. "I was a fool, but I couldn't help myself. I spit on him!" She covered her face with her hands and began to cry.

"And that's when he slashed you?"

She nodded vigorously, crying louder now.

I hung my head. Such a nice planet I lived on.

Marisa wiped her tears and hissed bitterly. "At least he got off me then. He backed away as if I was suddenly too dirty for him."

I tried to picture it. "No, that's not why he backed away. It's not that you were dirty, not in the way you think. I'll bet he was just trying to keep your blood off his clothes."

I could see Marisa's tear-filled eyes considering that explanation. "Yes. That's probably exactly what that *pendejo* was trying to do."

A violent image of what I would like to do to Marisa's rapist flashed through my mind. It made spitting look like child's play. "You're not a fool, Marisa."

"I am. Again my hot temper gets me into trouble. Please don't tell anyone about the spitting, okay? Already my husband is ashamed of me. Oh, he doesn't say so, but I can sense his disgust. Things have changed between us. He's a very honorable man. He would never leave me. But he would be very angry if he knew what I had done. Promise me you will say nothing."

"I will say nothing to your husband, that I can promise."

"Another thing that I did not tell the police. I didn't remember until later, and then it seemed like such a small thing. I heard something in the bushes behind the house that night. It did cause me some concern, but I talked myself into believing that this was some Halloween pranksters."

"What did you hear?"

"Just . . . rustling. Too heavy to be an animal, but as I said, it was Halloween, I thought that maybe . . ." She let the sentence drift.

"But you didn't see anything? Before, during, or after your rape—can you remember any details at all about what this man looked like, smelled like, sounded like?"

She shook her head. "No. As I told the police, he was wearing a black mask and white rubber gloves. He was heavy and he was strong. And very evil."

Marisa's last word hung heavily in the silence that followed. I snapped off the tape recorder. "Marisa, I have a favor to ask. Not today, but at a time that's convenient for you, would you be willing to be hypnotized, to go back and see if you can recall any more evidence from the crime? It would be less traumatic—"

"No!" Her voice stopped me in midsentence. "I am a religious woman. I've been praying every day that God will remove that demon from my mind. Why would I allow you to let him back in? I'm sorry, I don't mean to raise my voice with you, but try to understand—"

I raised my hand to quiet her. "That's all right, really. You don't need to explain. I understand." I thought back to the horror that Thomasina Wilson had experienced during her hypnosis session. In a way I was relieved that Marisa had turned me down.

We went over the details of her nightmare one more time before she showed me to the door. She paused before pulling it open. "Thank you for letting me know what's been going on."

"You'll be extra careful, then?" The question sounded ridiculous under the circumstances, and I regretted it as soon as it left my lips. Marisa was already living in a state of justifiable paranoia.

"What else can I do?" She cracked open the door.

I took a deep breath and looked into her eyes. "You'll be in my prayers."

Her eyes moistened. "Thank you."

Walking back to my car I could not erase the image of Marisa's torn face from my mind. Could not stop thinking what a burden it would be to live with the constant visual reminder that a man's rage can be murderous.

27

"Thomasina Wilson checked out this morning."

Cell phone cradled on my ear, I had started to turn my ignition but stopped. This information gave me a scare. "Did she leave a forwarding address?"

"No ma'am."

"Surely you have information where to send her bill."

"I can't give that to you over the phone, ma'am." She had that *I'm hanging up now* tone of voice.

"Wait, listen. I'm a private in—" I didn't have time for this. I tried a different tack. "Is Dr. Goode in?"

"I don't see her on the floor."

"Could you page her? Please? It's important." Being a pest like this was one of the unfun aspects of my job. I waited several minutes before a familiar voice came on the line.

"Second Floor. Dr. Goode speaking."

"Dr. Goode, Elizabeth Chase, the detective working on Thomasina Wilson's case. It's imperative that I reach her."

"Relax. She knew you'd be looking for her. She'll be staying at her brother and sister-in-law's for the rest of the week. They left an address and phone number for me to give to you."

I breathed a sigh of relief as I took down the information. At least I wouldn't have to worry about Thomasina for a while.

Now my biggest problem was food. I'd heard McGowan complain loudly on several occasions that working patrol did not allow for regular, well-balanced meals. Hence the stereotypical doughnut-snarfing cop. All I'd had was a bagel six hours ago; a doughnut wasn't going to sustain me through an eight-hour shift. I pulled into a fast-food Mexican restaurant, ordered a chicken burrito and fish taco to go, and ate in the car on my way downtown. I checked in to the Sex Crimes department one minute before Dietz, Billings, and I were scheduled to roll. Problem was, they weren't around.

I explained my dilemma in animated tones to a weary-looking officer in the hallway. "Don't worry. They didn't leave without you. I just saw Billings around here somewhere. And Dietz is yacking with the department secretary over in Homicide. Come on. Follow me."

We walked a couple doors down, and sure enough there was Dietz, standing over the secretary's desk with a cup of coffee. If I were in an uncharitable mood I might say he was displaying himself. He did wear his uniform well. With his trim waist and bulging forearms, Dietz could be the police department poster boy. The cop who'd led me to him was a more normal human, with a bit of flesh bulging above his belt. He called across the room. "Your ride's here, Dietz."

Dietz looked over and gave me a wave. "Be with you in a minute."

As I waited I cased the department—the usual conglomeration of messy government-issue desks and mismatched furniture. My eye fell on a tiny crocheted sampler mounted near the cooler. I moved in a for a closer look. The precise blue-and-pink stitching spelled out the following motto:

WELCOME TO HOMICIDE
OUR DAY STARTS
WHEN YOUR DAYS END

I had to chuckle. It wouldn't make points with the community relations people, but gallows humor works magic for those who have to face tragedy day in and day out.

"You do think I'm funny, don't you?"

I turned to see Rick Billings smiling widely behind me. "Is that yours?" I pointed to the sampler.

His eyes twinkled. "Yeah. Some people have accused me of

turning this place into the San Diego Police Farce. I say that would be an improvement." His expression turned serious. "I just like to keep things light. The job's heavy enough. Guess you got a little taste of that last night."

"Yeah."

He motioned me toward the door. "Come on. While we're rounding up Dietz you can tell me how in the world you happened to find out about that break-in before we did."

The cavernous garage seemed even darker today. Somewhere a car door slammed, and the sound reverberated through the hollow expanse. I shimmied my shoulders in mock horror. "This place reminds me of an oversized dungeon." Dietz and Rick smiled but made no reply. We walked the rest of the way in silence, heading for a fleet of cruisers near the exit. Dietz approached an unmarked car and opened a rear door for me. When I was settled he slammed my door shut.

From the moment that door slammed and Dietz and Rick slid into the front seat I felt nervous. I sensed something, but I wasn't sure what. Was I picking up on an impending crisis? Several years ago I had refused to board a flight for a long-awaited vacation to Jamaica, *knowing* that the plane was destined for tragedy. *It's an end*, I kept hearing an inner voice say, *It's an end*. This was in my early twenties, before I'd fully laid claim to my gifts. For fear of being wrong, for fear of being ridiculed, for fear of inconveniencing others, I had kept my phobia to myself. There wasn't another flight scheduled for a day and a half, so I lost two full days of my vacation. The plane I'd refused to board went down just off the coast of Florida. Thirty-seven passengers lost their lives.

I tuned in now. Was the discomfort I felt as dire as all that? I didn't think so, but it was a hell of a gamble. I decided that if the feeling became too strong I would discuss it with them. If worse came to worst, I would ask to be let out of the car. They'd been trained to be heroes. I hadn't.

The officer manning the exit booth waved us through, and we pulled onto Broadway, then turned north toward the canyon area. Rick booted up the small computer mounted on the dash. He hung his arm over the back of the seat and turned to me. "Okay. We got three cops on this beat, so unless it's something hairy we'll let them handle the calls you'll see coming up on the screen here. We'll just be focusing on our investigation today."

Dietz pulled the two-way off the dash and touched base with the dispatcher. Rick turned around and looked at me again. "You hungry?"

I shook my head.

"Our shift runs three to midnight. Theoretically, we got an hour in there for dinner break. But don't count on it."

With that comment I felt a bit smug. It would take hours to digest the Mexican food I'd just eaten. "I can hang," I said.

The afternoon was cold and overcast, but the first thing Rick did was roll down his window. I made a grimace, which he caught in the extra-wide rearview mirror. "I always keep my window down. Like to keep my ear on the street," he explained. I pulled a pair of cashmere-lined leather gloves from my coat pocket and wriggled them on, then tried to wrap my coat more snugly without making a big production out of it.

"Gloves, in California?" Somehow Dietz had seen me slip them on.

"I just wear these to look cool." Only Dietz's eyes showed in the rearview, so I couldn't tell if he smiled or not. I tried to focus on the city but became more interested in the way the guys kept their attention outside, on the street. All business.

I wondered what further information there might be on last night's incident. "So Dietz, did Rick brief you on the rapist hitting the Hillcrest house again last night?"

"Yep."

"The department agrees, then, that it was the rapist?"

Rick nodded. "Oh, yeah. It's our guy all right."

"Did anything turn up with Richard Zimmer? The lock tampering at the scene sure points to someone with his kind of skills."

Again Rick nodded. "It sure does, doesn't it? As usual Zimmer's got a slick alibi, one nobody believed for a minute. After last night we put a full-time tail on him."

Our game plan was to canvass the Hillcrest neighborhood. Dietz parked in front of Cheryl's locked-up bungalow. We began by knocking on the door of the house whose backyard the intruder had escaped into last night. A man with a goatee answered the door. "Sorry," he said, "we weren't home. My wife and I just got back from the East Coast this morning. Guess it was a good time to be out of town."

After that we split into lopsided teams, Dietz taking the three blocks west of Cheryl's bungalow and Rick and I covering the three blocks east. Zimmer's white van had been seen parked in the neighborhood the day of Annie Drummond's rape. We were trying to find out if anyone had seen it—or anything else of interest—last night. The work quickly became a dreary routine of knocks with no answers or residents patiently listening, then shaking their heads and closing the door. As we walked Rick kept things lively with a stream of consistently poor jokes. "You won't take offense if I tell a psychic joke, will you?"

I stepped around a large crack in the sidewalk. "Heck no."

"Okay, why was the psychic late in making her prediction?"

"I don't know. Why?"

"She was delayed by unforeseen circumstances."

"That's awfully damn lame," I said.

"I know."

On the second block we hit such a long string of no-answers that I was beginning to feel people were shunning us like a pair of Jehovah's Witnesses. "Hey," Rick said as we started in on our third block, "why did the monkey fall out of the tree?"

"I don't know. Why?"

"Because he was *dead*."

I chuckled. Even lame jokes beat stony silence.

We hit pay dirt at the house on the end of the third street, right up against the canyon. "Yes, I did notice something unusual last night," said the gray-haired man who answered the door. "There was a strange car parked here that pulled away like a bat out of hell."

"What time was this, sir?" Rick asked.

"Well, the car was parked here around dinnertime. Red Toyota in front of the house here. Only reason I noticed it was because the numbers in the license plate spooked me. Six-six-six."

Rick took notes on his clipboard. "Do you remember the letters?"

"No, son."

"When did you see the car pull away?"

"Middle of the night. That's why I noticed it. We don't get much traffic on this street—it's a dead end. Sure don't get many cars leaving rubber on the street."

"Did you ever see the driver of this car, sir?"

"No, son, I'm afraid I didn't."

That was the only promising lead our work generated. We met back up with Dietz two hours later, when what little light had existed in the overcast afternoon had begun to fade to black. By that time my fingers and toes were so cold that I was beginning to lose touch with them. I was grateful to pile back into the car.

I let Rick fill Dietz in on what we'd turned up today. My headache was back, and my neck muscles were tighter than ever. I rested my head against the back of my seat and watched the 911 call data appear and disappear like ghosts across the computer terminal on the dash.

"So what now?" I asked.

"At this point we'll just be cruising, looking for anything suspicious. More like regular patrol," Dietz replied.

We spent the next four hours looping through the canyon neighborhoods and the business districts that surrounded them. As night came on a frightening state of mind descended on me. The horror of Marisa's torn face kept coming back to me. A delayed reaction to the stress of seeing her, I figured. I did a double take of a woman waiting to cross at a neon-lit intersection. I could have sworn it was Marisa. The woman saw me staring at her and glared back. Her face was unscarred. I quickly turned away.

My phobia intensified. Flashbacks of Marisa's nightmare superimposed themselves on my present reality. The radio static became the sound of the bushes rustling outside of Marisa's house. Distracted by my audial hallucination, I was only vaguely aware of the dispatcher calling for Dietz. I watched him take the call, but instead of seeing his hand wrapped around the radio mike I envisioned the rapist's hand wrapped around a knife. The case was getting to me.

I returned my focus to the street and managed to keep it there for some time. Finally the sheer duration of the patrol took the edge off my anxiety. Toward the end of the shift my attention to the street began to wane. My thoughts were beginning to wander when Dietz yanked the wheel so sharply that my shoulder banged against the car door. "Well I'll be damned," he said. "Look who we have here."

28

"Aw, come on now. I wasn't doing nothing against the law here."

Bobby Morgan, hands in pockets and shoulders slumping, was talking to Dietz but directing his comments at the sidewalk. Rick and I had rolled down our windows to hear the conversation.

"Get your hands out of your pockets and tell me what you're doing here," Dietz said coldly.

Under the streetlights Morgan had a yellowish cast to his skin, making him appear even more unhealthy than he had in the interview room two days ago. He held his hands out, palms up. "I was just going to go see the show here." We had pulled up near the corner of Fifth and Robinson, across the street from Hillcrest's old movie theater.

Dietz looked over and read the marquee. "So you were going to take in a screening of *Au Revoirs les Enfants*, huh?" He folded his big arms across his chest. "Sure you were, Morgan."

Bobby Morgan scratched a sideburn. "You don't got any right to be hassling me here." He sounded unsure.

"What were you doing last night?" Rick piped up from the front seat. "Just tell us that and we'll get out of your face."

"I was in the medical clinic," Morgan said. "I been under the weather lately."

Dietz sneered at him. "Shouldn't you be home in bed, then?"

"Which clinic?" Rick asked.

"Harbor View," said Morgan.

The men stood in a stalemate, Dietz glaring at Morgan and Morgan glaring at the sidewalk.

"Hey, Dietz, there's a call for you in here." Rick was full of it. There'd been no call for Dietz over the radio.

Dietz gave Morgan a hard stare. "Wait here."

When Dietz got into the car Rick said, "We can check out the medical clinic thing tomorrow. We're going into overtime here. Let's go home."

Dietz frowned. "I'm not so sure that's a good idea."

"What are we going to do, follow him around all night? Morgan's right about one thing. We *don't* have anything solid to be hassling him about. We'll have night shift patrol keep an eye on him. I gotta get some sleep. It's been a long night." I couldn't have agreed more.

"Okay," Dietz said, "but this could be a big mistake."

Rick rolled his eyes. "You're such a pessimist, Dietz. If you had the choice between two evils you're the kind of guy who'd take both."

By the time I drove from downtown San Diego back home to Escondido it was almost eleven. Whitman was waiting for me at the door, a concerned tone in his meow. Once he'd gotten a good ear scratching all was well. There were no messages on my machine, not even from McGowan. Then I remembered he'd said something about being unavailable for a couple of days. Still, it was unusual not to have even a call from him. Not the world's best timing, either. If ever I felt the need for companionship, tonight was the night.

I fell into bed but couldn't sleep. I counted sheep, I cleared chakras, I listened to a meditation tape—all to no avail. Scenes from the last three days appeared in my mind like a relentless slide show. Marisa's torn face. Bobby Morgan dispassionately describing his rape of a woman at knifepoint. The bloody bull's-eyes on Sandy Devereaux's chest. Cheryl Arendt's blacked-out house, the door secured shut from the outside. Richard Zimmer's disfigured hand and cold, disturbing glare. Dianna's mountain range of incident reports, describing nightmare upon nightmare upon holy living nightmare. The horror in Thomasina Wilson's eyes after reliving her rape under hypnosis. I tried sorting through what I'd seen to make sense of it all, find a pattern. There was too much to sort, and it was too late to think. I might be awake, but that didn't necessarily mean I was coherent.

I got out of bed and searched for something constructive to do with my insomnia, some nonintellectually challenging chore. Things were piling up on my desk. Pushing paper always had a way of making me tired.

I found a large envelope containing the contents of a task I'd put aside for just such a dull moment as this. Inside was a mailing list my mom and I had used to solicit contributions for the upcoming AIDS benefit. She'd pulled it from her resources file, a compilation of San Diego's "people to watch." Coveted names and addresses not found in public directories. Many of these folks were filthy rich, and the rest were up-and-comers, soon to be filthy rich. My task was to go down this list and compare the names against the pile of checks that had come in so we would know who and who not to hassle for prepledged contributions. Finally, I needed to fill out a deposit slip and get this money in the donation account.

There were about two hundred names. Nice eyelid wearying work. But my eyes popped wide open when I got to the N's. I rubbed them, just to be sure I wasn't seeing things. But there it was: Gary Warren Niebuhr, P.O. Box 1113, La Jolla CA 92037.

Could there be two Gary Warren Niebuhrs? A name like that? Impossible. This was a different address from the one I'd found for him on credit reports and agency listings. This was his *real* address, the one he used. True, it was only a post office box, but I had ways of getting around that.

Satisfied that the evening had been productive and I had earned enough peace of mind to deserve sleep, I returned to bed. I'd spent the week looking for criminals. A rapist. A thief. The search continued as I drifted into a nonsensical half dream. I saw the city of San Diego as a gigantic haystack, a psychedelic Monet miles and miles wide. I became lost in neon-lit straws, feeling the futility of searching for needles. Somewhere in the middle of it all I finally fell asleep.

29

I was still half asleep the next morning when an odd thing happened. Rummaging through my jewelry box for a pair of matching earrings, I pierced my finger on a long hatpin with an opalescent tip. I pulled it from the box and stared at it. It wasn't exactly a needle, and it certainly hadn't been found in a haystack, but given last night's dream vision, it seemed a good omen.

Bright and early I went across the street and rang Toby's doorbell, hoping to catch him before he left for school. His mom answered the door and after we exchanged pleasantries hollered down the hall for him.

"You still looking for work?" I asked when Toby's sleepy face came into view. Even in a rain-drenched January the kid had remnants of a tan.

He was pulling a baggy shirt over his head. "I gotta go to school right now." His head popped through, and his jaw-length sunbleached hair fell into place. He looked like he should be in one of those technicolor soda commercials with lots of sun and girls and manic sports action.

"I realize that, Tob. I'm talking about Saturday and Sunday, from seven to five."

"Seven to five! Those are slave-driving hours!"

When I told him how relatively simple the job was, and how much I (okay, my client) would be paying, he lunged at the opportunity. "Heck, yeah, I can do that."

I walked back across the street and puttered around the house waiting for Annie Drummond to arrive. I didn't expect her to be on time for our rescheduled ten o'clock session. While I hadn't bought into her father's uncharitable interpretation of her sleeping patterns, I did realize that Annie was suffering from sleep disorders and that she would probably be running late. So it wasn't exactly a shock when she hadn't arrived by quarter past. I whiled away some time leafing through the morning paper. Skimming the obituary page, my eyes paused at a picture of a young woman. Twenty-eight years old, a head full of curls, bright eyes. The text was longer than average, as it often is when family members have felt a death to be particularly tragic. The young woman had died of complications from Hodgkin's disease. As I moved on through the paper I realized that something in her face and hairstyle had reminded me of Sandy Devereaux, the missing victim. The whole thing left me with a funny feeling.

By ten thirty Annie still had not arrived. Maybe her father hadn't passed along my message about rescheduling our session. I dialed the number, hoping everything was all right.

"Hello." It was Roger Drummond's grim monotone.

"Mr. Drummond, Elizabeth Chase. I was calling to see if Annie might be on her way up here for our appointment this morning."

"Wouldn't hold my breath if I were you." Grimmer.

My heart thumped. "Why's that?"

He made a hissing noise. "I'll let her tell it." He put the phone down recklessly, so that it clattered in my ear. I waited a long, suspenseful minute before Annie came on the line.

"Hi, Elizabeth." Her voice was strained but apologetic.

"Is everything okay? You all right?"

"Sort of, I guess. Sorry I didn't call. I just got home a few minutes ago. My boyfriend and I went to Tijuana last night and my truck got stolen and it was this huge hassle. . . ." She ended the sentence with a loud, hopeless sigh.

I hoped she'd been able to keep up her insurance premiums. "Oh, no. That's the last thing you need," I said.

She didn't respond, but the despair I picked up through the phone line spoke loudly enough. "So is there no possibility for us to meet today?"

"Well, I don't have wheels. Dad's already told me there's no way I'm borrowing his car."

The eleven o'clock hour was approaching. I quickly weighed Annie's transportation alternatives, my own plans for the day, the logistics of it all. I had no desire to be a taxi service, but a hypnosis session in the Drummond igloo was out of the question. "All right," I said at last. "If I pick you up, can you get a ride home?"

Annie spent most of the ride up to Escondido slumped against the door staring vacantly at the road ahead.

"I met Kevin Knutsen at the bank this week," I said.

Her gloom lifted for a brief smile. "How is dear old Kevin?"

"I'm pretty sure he cares about you."

"I know. I didn't mean he was the rapist. Something about him just reminded me is all." She stared out the window for the next several minutes without speaking.

"So what happened last night?" I asked. *Come on, Annie, talk about it.*

She rubbed her forehead. "Syd—that's my boyfriend—wanted to party in Mexico. I didn't want to go, but he kept hassling me, so I gave in. We took my truck. He blames me for it getting stolen. Said I made a stupid choice in parking lots."

I got an energy read on Syd as Annie was talking. A toxic aura. "You don't need to be around negative people like him. Especially right now, when you're still healing."

"Healing. You crack me up. The rape happened last year. It's really not that big a deal."

"Who says that?" I asked. She reached for her cigarettes. "Sorry, Annie, not in my car."

She tossed the pack back into her purse. "*I* say it."

"Who else?"

She looked over at me, thinking. "Syd says that. He says I'm *making* it into a big deal."

Syd sounded a lot like her father, Roger. No wonder she felt a connection with him. Annie sat up as we pulled into my driveway. "What a cool old house!"

I had to agree. My house was built in 1888, back when Escondido was nothing more than a train station, a school, and a few vegetable farms. The structure has undergone minor revisions during restorations, but for the most part its original construction is intact. I finally gave in last year to community pressure to place the house on the Historical Society register. What this basically entails is opening the place to visitors once a year and promising not to put up a satellite dish.

Once through the door, Annie didn't hesitate to begin touring the house without me. As she headed down the hallway I called to her. "Hey, check this out." I walked over to a closet and opened the door. "Stick your head in here and take a look."

Annie walked over and peered into my closet, which was packed stem to stern with books, about equal parts hardcover and paperback. "Oh, my God! Are you a book collector or something?"

I laughed. "I think they collect *me*. I just wanted you to see how desperately I need that bookcase."

Her eyes circled the closet. "I hate to tell you this, but you're going to need more than one bookcase to hold all of these. Maybe I could build you some floor-to-ceiling shelving?"

I wondered what the Historical Society would say to that. "We'll see. Are you about ready for our session?"

"Yeah. I'm ready."

She settled comfortably into the recliner.

"Okay, Annie, take a deep breath. First, I want you to imagine yourself surrounded by a protective field of brilliant white light. Now, starting with your toes, feel a wave of relaxation moving through your feet, now up your ankles, your calves, over your knees. . . ."

As I finished Annie's body relaxation I thought about my approach. I was anything but confident about the reliability of memories recalled under hypnosis. Still, there wasn't much else to go on, and I continued to feel strongly that the key to this case rested with the victims. After my experience with Thomasina becoming retraumatized under hypnosis, I was concerned about what might come up for Annie. I had already decided to keep the questioning as far away from her physical torment and as focused on the rapist as possible.

"All right, Annie. We're going back to the day of your rape, earlier in the day. Did you go outside your house at all that day?"

"Yes."

"Tell me about that. Why did you go outside? What did you see?"

"It was a Saturday. I went out to mow the front lawn."

"Can you see yourself out on the lawn now?"

"Yes. The sun's out, but it's chilly. I'm hoping I'll warm up as I work. The motor on my lawn mower doesn't start right away."

"Look around the street, Annie. Do you see any cars parked in the neighborhood?"

"Yes. I see my neighbors' Honda Civic parked in front of my house, and their Jeep Cherokee behind that."

"How do you know they're your neighbors' cars?"

"I know it's the neighbors' Civic because it has a THINK PEACE bumper sticker. And the Cherokee has surfboard racks and a license plate that says BCHBUM2."

"Can you see any other vehicles?"

"There's a Ryder truck across the street where someone is moving out, and there's a white van."

A white van. Zimmer's van. Perhaps this part of Annie's memory, earlier in the day before the rape, would not be subject to the stress-related distortion my father had warned me about. "Let's look at the white van. Does it have lettering on the side?"

"Yes."

"Can you read what it says?"

In the pause that followed I was hoping Annie would magically come up with Zippy Lock & Safe.

"No," she said finally. "I can't make it out. It's parked too far away."

Rats. "Can you make out any other cars, maybe farther down or across the street?"

"Yes. There's a blue sedan of some kind . . . and at the end of the street there's a brand-new red Toyota Celica."

Another red Toyota. Interesting, I guess. Not that there weren't ten million red Toyotas in California. "Can you read the license plates on either of these cars?" It was a long shot, but I figured there was no harm trying.

"No."

Double rats.

"Okay, Annie. Good. Now, we're going to move forward to the time of your rape. You will just be looking. You won't be feeling anything. You will simply be viewing what happened. You are just going to help me look for physical evidence. Okay, what is the first thing you see when you look at your attacker?"

Annie took a deep breath, and her features stiffened. Her voice dropped, and she spoke in a slow monotone. All signs of numbness, which pleased me. "I see his mask. It's made out of black knit material, like the kind you wear when you go skiing. I can see the ridges in the knitting."

"That's good, Annie. What else can you see?"

"I can see his shirt. He's wearing a black turtleneck shirt, also knit, like cotton-polyester."

"Great. Now, look down at his body. He has to take his pants off, doesn't he?"

Annie nodded slowly, silently.

"Can you see what color his skin is? Can you see any body hair?"

Annie sat quietly.

"Breathe, Annie. I want to remind you that you are only looking, as if from a distance. You are not feeling anything. You will not feel painful physical sensations or painful emotions, either."

She shook her head. "I can't see his body because I'm not looking at it. I don't look down. I'm looking up at the ceiling. I see the ceiling for a long time. I forget to blink. My eyeballs start to ache because I haven't blinked."

Looking at Annie's rigid form it was too easy to imagine her stiffened body enduring the assault. I longed to get to the end of this. "Okay. Now, taking in all the knowledge that you have of this crime, is there anything you can see that might help me find out who this person is?"

"He's wearing rubber gloves. His hands feel cold and rubbery." Annie stopped speaking, but I sensed there was more she had to say. The red light on the tape recorder glowed steadily as the machine captured the silence. "Everything about him feels cold," she said suddenly. "He has a cold heart."

A cold heart. Certainly wasn't Kevin Knutsen. "Why does he remind you of Kevin Knutsen?"

She inhaled through her nostrils. "The way he smelled, I guess." She curled her lip in distaste.

"Like aftershave or cologne?"

"No. A bad smell."

Annie came out of her session without any frightening physical symptoms, but her mood was a lot quieter than when she'd arrived. A really zealous hypnotherapist will swear that the process always leaves the client feeling peaceful and calm. In most cases that's probably true. Some memories, though, just aren't that easily erased, even by white light and positive suggestions.

"How are you feeling?" I asked.

Annie sighed. "Right now? Not that great. I dread going home. My dad is really bent about my truck getting stolen. God, I hate my life."

The resignation in her voice concerned me. "Did you ever call that rape hot line number I gave you?"

She shook her head.

I couldn't rescue Annie, but Lord, how I wanted to.

I flashed on something I'd ordered from a catalog several weeks ago. At the time I wasn't sure why I'd bought it. Now I knew. "Hang right here, okay? I'm going to go upstairs for something. I'll be right down."

I dashed up the stairs and into my bedroom. In my dresser drawer I found the T-shirt, still wrapped in the clear plastic it had been shipped in. Painted in southwestern colors, the silk-screened shirt depicted a coyote howling against a backdrop of mesa cliffs. The lettering beneath the art read, "You Are Not Alone." If you looked closely you could see other coyotes howling on other distant cliffs.

When I reached the bottom of the stairs I saw that Annie had gotten up from the recliner and was staring glumly out the living room window. I called across the room to her. "Hey, catch."

She caught the shirt just before it hit the carpet. She held it up and stared at it for a long time without speaking. Finally she shook her head. "That's one of the things people kept asking me after the rape: 'Why were you alone?' "

I sighed. I'd meant to cheer her up, not trigger more painful memories. "I know. As if being alone is a sin. But I'm not surprised people asked you that. It's one of the four most common questions rape victims get asked. Want to know the other three? This is based on a recent survey. Ready?"

"Sure. What are they?"

"Number one: 'What were you wearing?' Number two: 'What were you doing there?' Number three: 'Why were you alone?' " Do any of these sound familiar?"

She stared at me solemnly. "All of them do. But I mean, they're reasonable questions, aren't they?"

"Reasonable? Hardly. They deflect the shame of the crime onto the victim. Reason would tell you it's the rapist, not the victim, who should be scrutinized. Like, what was *he* wearing? What was *he* doing there? See what I mean?"

"Yeah, I guess I do. Why don't people ask those things?"

"I think because those are the harder questions. If people can believe that a woman has been victimized because of her own mistakes it gives them a sense of security—however false—that if they just don't make those same mistakes, then they'll be safe from this hideous crime."

Annie frowned. "You said there were four questions. What's number four?"

" 'Are you kidding?' "

Annie looked puzzled. "No, I'm not kidding. I want to know. Tell me."

I shook my head. "No, Annie, that's *it*. That's the fourth most common question people ask when they hear about a rape: 'Are you kidding?' "

She screwed up her face. "Like a woman would kid about something like that."

"No kidding."

30

Annie carefully folded her new T-shirt and put it into her knapsack. "Guess I should call a cab."

I'd been pondering a hunch and formulating a plan as I watched her. "No, don't bother. I have an errand I need to run in San Diego anyway."

An errand. Yeah, right. As if a trip to the coroner was on a par with picking up dry cleaning and returning videos.

"You sure?"

"Positive."

Annie sat up a little straighter on our way back down to Clairemont but sank into a brooding silence as we neared her parents' house. I had to admit I was relieved to drop her off. Her depression was getting to me.

As luck would have it the San Diego medical examiner's office was conveniently located not more than a mile from the Drummonds' house. I drove up Overland Avenue looking for the California State and American flags that marked the functional county building. I had a feeling I was getting warmer as I pulled into the parking lot, but this was one hunch I hoped would be wrong.

Death certificates are public records, but if I found what I had a feeling I might find I'd want to see the autopsy report too. Getting your hands on one of those can be tricky. I showed the clerk my license and gave him a brief summation of the serial rape case and my involvement with it. Dropped Lieutenant Marcone's name. The clerk came out from behind the counter and walked me over to a computer terminal, where I began my search.

I typed the subject's name, watched it glowing on the monitor. Waited a beat before clicking the Search box, just enough time to send up a futile prayer. Within seconds the computer found a match and brought my dark hunch to light:

Name: Devereaux, Sandy
DOB: 11-30-68
DOD: 07-15-93
Cause: Suicide

I stared at the screen in a daze for several moments. Then took slow steps back to the counter, where my earlier politicking paid off. The clerk retrieved the autopsy file and investigation report with no further questions.

The report was relatively brief, five pages. Sandy Devereaux had died of multiple lacerations, primarily to her inner wrists. Evidence supported the medical examiner's conclusion of suicide: Wounding to the right wrist was less severe, consistent with a right-handed person's suicide. Fingerprint and blood splatter evidence also pointed to suicide. The investigation and police reports, too, supported the medical examiner's cause of death. A note had been found by the body ("Just tired of the pain. That's all."). The police report cited a statement taken from Tina Robbins, Sandy's last roommate, who confirmed that Sandy had made vague references to taking her own life in the last few weeks prior to her death. The autopsy report had noted the bull's-eye scarring on Sandy's chest, describing it as "old scar tissue." It surprised me that this hadn't been looked into more closely. Maybe the doctor presumed the bull's-eyes were kinky body markings, much like the tattoos on Sandy's left ankle and right buttock. What's a little old bull's-eye scar on a woman's chest? The physicians at the medical examiner's office have seen it all.

I went over the file one more time before handing it back in. It was reasonable to believe that Sandy had taken her own life and that her death was not the direct work of the rapist. The emotional pain that led her to make that decision, however, was at least in part his doing.

I called Lieutenant Marcone from the public phone in the lobby to let him know where and how I'd found one of the case victims. His brief response, "Christ," was not an expression he used frequently.

I exited the medical examiner's office and squinted against the light. For the first time in days the sun had broken through. I welcomed the sun but not its blinding reflection off the wet pavement. The glare gave me a headache on the drive home. That, and the thoughts spinning in my head. Information overload. As soon as I walked through my door I sat down and pulled an old trick that often goes a long way toward calming the control freak in me: I made a list. Pulling together information from my tapes and notes, I sifted that which was substantial from that which was mere slippery terror and lined it up like this:

Notes on Thomasina's hypnosis

During rape, Thomasina sees/feels:
 —rubber gloves
 —knife on neck (blade fat on top)
 —sand under her thighs
 —rapist's bulky neck, crazy eyes

Notes on Annie's hypnosis

Mowing lawn, Annie sees the following vehicles:
 —Honda Civic (neighbor's): THINK PEACE bumper
  sticker
 —Jeep Cherokee (neighbor's): BCHBUM2 plate
 —Blue sedan
 —New red Toyota Celica
 —Ryder truck
 —White van

During rape, Annie sees/feels/smells:
 —rubber gloves
 —black knit ski mask
 —black turtleneck (knit) shirt
 —coldness
 —bad smell

Notes on interview with Marisa

—white rubber gloves
—knife on neck
—black mask
—electricity cut

Notes on this week's incident at Hillcrest bungalow

—electricity cut
—shattered stemware
—doors locked from outside
—neighbor sees red Toyota tear away three blocks from
   scene: 666 on plate

Not many tangible clues to pursue. The only solid evidence I could follow up on at this point were the vehicles. I put in a call to Sex Crimes at the SDPD. Dianna was off again today, but Dietz answered his extension on the first ring. "Dietz here."

"Elizabeth here. How goes it?"

"Fine. How're you doing?"

"I'm fine, but I've got some sad news on our case. One of the victims committed suicide."

"Yeah. Marcone phoned me after you called."

He didn't ask for further details, so I didn't offer. I got the feeling I was interrupting something more important. "You busy?"

"Yeah, pretty much. I've been double-checking Morgan's medical clinic story."

"And?"

"I don't know. It's kind of screwy. He was at the clinic Tuesday night but not during the hours the Hillcrest place was broken into. I gotta make a few more calls."

"I won't keep you. I was just following up on some leads and wondered if you might run a few plates for me."

"Sure. Happy to help out. Whatcha got?"

"Vanity plate, BCHBUM2."

He repeated it back to me. "Anything else?"

"I'm not sure. Is there a way you can search for a vehicle with a partial plate number? Rick and I ran across a guy who'd seen a red Toyota tearing away Tuesday night three blocks from the Hillcrest place. One of the victims remembers seeing a red Toyota the day of her rape. It's a sketchy connection but it may be worth a try."

"How many numbers have you got?"

"Just three, but they're unusual. Six-six-six."

There was a long pause. I wondered if Dietz was writing this down. I was just about to speak when he said, "Yeah, okay. Could be scattershot, but I'll search that for you."

"Thanks. Wish there was more physical evidence to go on."

He laughed. "Frustrating, isn't it? There is some stuff, just not much that's useful. We got sheets, bedclothes, carpet fiber, rape kits from every scene. Got a whole little section reserved for this case in the evidence room."

My inner ears pricked up. "Is that like the sanctum sanctorum, off-limits to mere private investigators like me?"

"Usually. But for you we can make an exception. Come by tomorrow and Dianna and I will take you down there."

Things were looking up. If I could hold a gift-wrapped box in my hands and see the present inside, maybe by holding physical evidence from the scenes I could *see* who was committing these awful crimes. It was certainly worth a try.

31

I was awakened by the rocking, rolling sensation of being at sea. I heard the sound of water slapping and sloshing against the side of my craft. I opened my eyes, it was just dawn. I recognized a gray morning in the middle of an endless, colorless ocean. The horizon was socked in by a heavy cloud layer. The sky was light, but it was not bright. This was not the peaceful beginning of a new day. Already the water was turgid and churning, restless and menacing.

I looked down to see myself, to view my feet or hands, to ground myself in this tenuous state. I could not see my body. Instead I began to float up, up, up, above the boat. I looked down and saw busy gray waters, tiny frustrated caps on innumerable wavelets. Nothing but ocean, as far as the eye could see. From above, the undulating body of water appeared as a restless grid in motion, a liquid kaleidoscope. Staring down, I felt hypnotized. I looked for my boat, but it was gone. Higher and higher I floated, several hundred feet above the water.

Suddenly, as if some universal power had called out an unspoken command, the choppy waves dissolved, and the sea became as smooth and immobile as glass. The water laid flat, preternaturally still. A terrifying silence filled the air. From far above I looked into the perfect reflection of the dead-still sea. In the mirrorlike surface of the water a face appeared. It was a face I recognized immediately.

The waters began to stir again, and I started falling into the sea.

On my way down I wondered if it would hurt when I hit the surface or if I would feel anything at all.

I woke groggily, the dream replaced by a general feeling of insecurity. I remembered coming home early that evening. Still no call from McGowan. It was two days now that I hadn't heard from him. The silence was starting to eat at me. I would be glad when we reconnected.

What had I just been dreaming? It seemed important to remember. I lay patiently—eyes closed, not moving—in hopes that the dream would come back to me. An image of the sea flitted through my mind, and bit by bit I began to piece it back together: the restless ocean, the moment of calm, the glassy surface. I remembered that I'd seen a face, the face of someone I'd seen before. In my dream I had known who it was. *Who?* Fully awake now, I shut my eyes, chasing the memory. Faster and faster I ran to catch the face in the dream. I was losing ground.

I could not remember who it was. I could not see the face.

32

I sat at my kitchen table Friday morning racking my brains to bring back the face in the dream. The elusiveness of the image frustrated me no end. Finally I consoled myself with the thought that even if it were the rapist, even if I *had* seen his face, that wouldn't necessarily solve the case. I needed physical evidence. In a world that physicists are rapidly discovering to be more ephemeral than solid, hard physical evidence still rules in the criminal justice system. Suspect identifications are a crap shoot. Victims' memories can lie. Physical evidence does not lie. Reality is anchored in stuff.

The phone rang. I welcomed a distraction and jumped up to answer it.

"Hello, Elizabeth." It was Thomasina's voice, clear and strong. Not McGowan's, I realized with a pang of disappointment. "You know that hypnosis we did?" she asked.

"Yeah."

"I've been seeing things, remembering things, since you put me under the other day."

"What kinds of things?"

"I know this sounds crazy, but I keep seeing myself looking right at his face. No mask. But when I try to identify who it is, I can't."

This sounded very much like a certain dream I'd had recently.

Thomasina sounded excited. I didn't want her to get her hopes too high. "It turns out that memories from traumatic events aren't always that reliable." My tone was cautious. "So we're sort of stumbling around in the dark here. I'm interested in your impressions, but I just want you to know that they might be more symbolic than literal."

"This wasn't any symbolic thing. I saw the guy. It was real." Her no-bull tone made a believer out of me. "I want you to do it to me again, take me under again."

Another hypnosis session? Some serious doubts slowed my response time. "Why?"

"I swear I think I'll be able to make the ID. I really do."

"You don't have to go through that again, Thomasina."

"You gotta understand one thing about me. I'm a fighter, not a quitter. I am not giving up on this. I'll tell you one thing: That man seriously, seriously underestimated me."

Something in the tone of her voice inspired me. "Okay. If you're really up to it, let's do another session. When?"

"How 'bout we do it after my karate class tomorrow? Better yet, come along to class with me. I want you to meet my teacher. I have a feeling the two of you will hit it off."

"Karate class? You were just released from the hospital two days ago!"

She laughed. "I told you, girl, use it or lose it!"

The invitation intrigued me. "Okay. Where should we meet?"

"Why don't you come by here first, meet my family?"

"I'd love to."

She gave me directions and then fashion advice. "For class tomorrow? Wear loose-fitting clothes."

33

"Hey, Elizabeth. You know what Dietz's idea of law and order is?"

We were standing near the north wall of the Sex Crimes department, waiting for Lieutenant Marcone and Dianna to arrive for our Friday morning meeting. "Oh, no," moaned Dietz. "It's too early for us to pretend you're funny, Billings."

He hung a thumb toward Dietz. "Rounding up a few suspects? No way. His idea of law and order is rounding up a few *beers* at the corner bar."

I chuckled. Rick smiled at me appreciatively and turned to Dietz. "*She* thinks I'm funny."

Dietz was clearing an odd assortment of SDPD T-shirts, paperwork, and abandoned snack wrappers off a table near the window. "She's either polite or gullible, one of the two." He gave me a just-kidding smile. "You've been on this case all week, psychic detective. How long does it usually take for you to tune in to the solution?"

"Some cases go unsolved for me, just like they do for you."

"Hmph." Dietz was being polite, but I could bet what he was thinking: *Oh, sure. That's an easy out.*

"But in fact a revelation came in this morning that puts me on the verge of unraveling this sucker." This was a huge, overinflated bluff, stated in total jest. I liked the sound of it though.

Dietz gave me a dubious smile. "Oh, *real*-ly. What've you got?"

"I've got a victim who is close to identifying the face."

Dietz looked puzzled. "That's impossible. He was masked."

"That's what all of the victims have reported. But one of the victims I put under hypnosis swears she could make out a face."

"I don't get how that's possible," Dietz repeated.

"I have two theories. One is, she saw the face during the rape but blocked the memory when she was reporting the crime to the officer on the scene—trauma amnesia. Another possibility is that sometimes in hypnotic states people can tap in to psychic abilities they don't have during normal states of consciousness. It could be that Thomasina is 'seeing' under hypnosis the way I can sometimes see."

"Thomasina Wilson, this is?" Dietz may have been skeptical, but at least he was paying attention. Still I hadn't convinced him. "Come on, Chase. You gotta admit those are pretty far-out theories—trauma amnesia or a psychic vision. Isn't it enough to have a psychic investigator on this case? Now we gotta have psychic victims, too?"

"I'll be the first to admit that I'm reaching. There are other possible explanations. A conservative interpretation of Thomasina's seeing the face would be that she's attempting to regain control over what was an utterly powerless event in her life."

Dietz nodded, apparently liking that theory.

"Hey," Rick said. "Do you know why hypnotists go out of business so often?"

I had a feeling what was coming. I turned and looked into his face. Total deadpan. "Can't say that I do."

"No one really knows for sure. They just tend to go under."

I started to chuckle, but Dietz shot me a look. "You're not actually going to laugh at that, are you?"

"Looks like you people are ready to go." Lieutenant Marcone was striding toward us, back straight and head high, looking very much like the military man he undoubtedly once was. Dianna, looking relaxed after a couple days off, followed behind, carrying a cup of coffee. She took a seat at the table next to Dietz, and Rick and I sat next to the window. The lieutenant sat at the head of the table and pulled out a notepad. "I've got to be in another meeting in fifteen minutes, so let's move quickly. Updates, everybody. We'll start with you, Elizabeth."

I sat down and reached into my briefcase. "Okay, you guys know that physical evidence is where it's at, so these are my notes from the case, itemizing tangible clues." I placed the list I'd drawn up onto the table.

"No . . . *insights?*" Marcone asked.

"Some, but not enough to go on yet. As I said before, the intuitive stuff comes when it comes. I can't force it. I'll let you know when I get something substantial. Speaking of which," I turned to Dianna. "Did I tell you that under hypnosis Annie Drummond confirmed that she saw a white van in the neighborhood the day of her rape? She wasn't able to make out the writing on the van so I can't be sure it was Zimmer, but she did see lettering there."

Dianna took a swallow of her coffee. "I've been working on Zimmer. He's up to his old tricks. Our tail tracked him to a meeting with a known player in the kiddie porn business. We're in the process of setting up a buy from this guy. If we can arrange to catch Zimmer in the sting, we'll have probable cause to search his place. Maybe turn up some latex gloves or a ski mask or something."

Lieutenant Marcone made a note on his pad. "Good, Dianna. Dietz, how about you?"

"I've been following up on our boy Bobby Morgan. He's got that rape record—"

"Aggravated assault," I corrected.

"Yeah, but that was a technicality. It was sex-related. Anyway, Wednesday night was the second time he's turned up in a crime scene area. I spent time yesterday checking out his story about being at the medical clinic the night the Hillcrest place was hit again. It's half-baked. Morgan was seen at the clinic that day, but they didn't keep him overnight."

There was silence around the table for a moment. I thought about the Hillcrest incident. "Anything turn up when you ran those license numbers, Dietz?"

"Yeah, just a sec." He went to his desk across the room. While he was gone I posed a question to the others. "Did the fingerprint lab ever turn up anything from the Hillcrest break-in?"

"Nope," said Dianna. "Not that we were expecting any."

"Well, at least that tells you it's probably our guy. The typical bumbling residential burglar usually leaves a few prints, right?"

Lieutenant Marcone nodded. "Unless they're professionals, yes they do. And a professional probably wouldn't waste time on a little place like that."

Dietz returned and handed me a list. "No red Toyota with three consecutive sixes, but plenty with combinations of three sixes. Here." He handed me a list five pages long.

"Oh, my."

"Well, we knew it was a long shot, right?"

Marcone was writing on his pad. He looked up when he was done. "Billings?"

"I eliminated that whole stack of new suspects you gave me this week, Lieutenant." The jokester had disappeared. The man who spoke was all business, respectful of his superior's time. "I'm keeping my eye on the target areas and doing what I can to turn up prospects. So far nothing substantial." He looked at his watch. "I'm taking the swing shift again tonight. Friday night, maybe I'll get lucky."

34

All physical evidence from the scenes of San Diego's crimes—the bullets and blood and fibers and flotsam and jetsam—eventually end up in an enormous storage room on the underground parking level of the SDPD. I was standing with Dietz and Dianna on the threshold of all that evidence.

Just inside the door a crew-cut officer sat reading a magazine behind a counter. He looked up and smiled. "Greetings, aliens."

Dianna gave the Vulcan salute. "What's happening, Scully?"

"Oh, lots, lots. The grass is growing unusually fast today." He looked at me and smiled.

I smiled back. I liked a guy who could make the best out of a boring job.

The towering walls behind Scully were lined with row upon row of shelving, each brimming with sealed packages. Hundreds of bundles filled with valuable evidence. I suddenly saw Scully as an armed shepherd watching over a tempting flock. Off to my side I noticed what looked like a mail drop. Just above the drop a printed sign read:

DID YOU SEAL IT FIRST?

Someone had scrawled a *T* so that it read:

DID YOU STEAL IT FIRST?

"What's that?" I asked.

"After-hours drug drop. You know, where you dump the contraband after one of those traffic stops at three in the morning that turns into a drug bust."

Scully ran the palm of his hand across his buzz cut. Must have had it done recently. "So what are you three after?"

Dietz jerked his head toward me. "This lady wants to see the goods from the White Fingers case."

The White Fingers case. First time I'd heard it.

Scully unlatched the little gate that led behind the counter. "Over this way."

We walked down several aisles of wrapped-up goodies. In a caged area I saw an arsenal of guns, presumably confiscated from bad guys.

"Here we go." Scully motioned to a corner of shelving filled solid with sealed plastic bags of varying sizes. "This whole section is the evidence from your case."

I walked over for a closer look. "Have you got an inventory of what's here?"

"Now you ask me. The inventory list is back at my desk."

While Scully went back for the list I examined the evidence from the rape case. There were bundles and bundles of bedsheets. The sheets were bulky and took up a lot of space. On a top shelf were several tiny vials. I turned to Dietz. "What are these?"

"Fibers from the scenes. They're for the lab. The clothes are here." He handed me some larger packages. Marisa's blood-soaked nightgown. Annie's T-shirt and undies. The tape the rapist had used to seal Sandy Devereaux's mouth. As I held each item, the horror of the victims came back to me—along with the sadness, the utter sadness. But no insight as to the rapist himself.

Scully returned with the evidence list. I looked it over, sensing a cold trail. "What I want—"

"Huh?"

"I'm just thinking out loud here. These are the victims' things. What I really want is something that belonged to the *rapist*, something that came specifically from him. Thomasina Wilson told me that she felt sand under her thighs. That most likely came from him." I turned to Scully. "You got any sand from the Wilson case?"

Scully took the evidence list from my hands and pored over it.

Twice. Finally he shook his head. "Nope. No sand here."

"It might have been in the sheets. Would it still be wrapped up in the sheets?"

"No. Fibers and dirt particles—that would include sand—are removed and logged separately. If there'd been sand in those sheets we'd have a vial for it and see it listed here." He held up his paperwork.

No sand. Odd.

35

Just like that, he was dead.

That I read about it in the morning newspaper made the shock all the more severe. But there it was. Not just in black and white, either. *The San Diego Union* had blazoned a full-color photograph above the story. Yellow crime scene tape in the foreground, a crowd of officials hovering over the body on the stretcher. The copy beneath it read:

MASSIVE HUNT STARTS FOR COP KILLER

The killing of a police officer who was found fatally wounded in his patrol car triggered a massive manhunt Friday night by 80 San Diego County law enforcement officers.

Officers in police cruisers staffed roadblocks and observation points in a two-square-mile cordon around the residential area where Officer Richard Billings, 31, was shot and killed about 1:30 A.M.

Billings, who had been with the San Diego Police Department for three years, was the 28th officer shot to death in the line of duty in the city's 105-year history, an official said.

"We are deeply saddened by this event. Richard Billings was an outstanding police officer, well liked by both his colleagues and the community," said San Diego police Lt. Douglas Marcone.

Police on foot were aided by search dogs, and a helicopter circled the rugged, bushy hills adjacent to Mountain View Drive, the street on the canyon rim where the killing occurred.

Investigators say a "distant witness" may have seen an assailant fleeing on foot, said Officer John Weston, a spokesperson for the San Diego Police Department.

Police moved on the assumption that the killer may have fled on foot into the canyon that borders the residential area.

I put the paper down and remembered his face, his voice.

Why did the monkey fall out of the tree? Because he was dead.

After a solid hour of dialing and leaving messages, I finally got a call back from Dianna. "Sorry I haven't been in touch," she said. "All hell has broken loose around here."

"I know only what I saw in the paper. Can you tell me what's really going on?"

She sighed. "I don't know." Her voice was gravelly, as if she'd been up all night. "They're talking now about this maybe being a drive-by. He took a shotgun blast through his open window."

I always keep my window down. Like to keep my ear on the street.

"I'm sorry, Elizabeth, but right now this takes priority over our case. We'll get back to you when things settle down."

I sat staring at the telephone long after we'd hung up, unable to get the image of Billings's grinning face out of my mind.

Why was the psychic late in making her prediction? She was delayed by unforeseen circumstances.

36

Dianna had said that the investigation of Rick Billings's homicide took precedence over the rape investigation. After I hung up the phone I realized I'd been too stunned to ask if she thought the two might be related. Clearly it was possible. Rick had been killed in the target area, a part of town not known for drive-by shootings. Before the rapes began it had been a fairly decent place to live.

I felt shaken and in need of support. I knew a call to McGowan would be futile, but I dialed anyway. No answer. Sometimes being psychic is a real drag. I didn't leave a message. Instead I allowed myself to indulge in a half minute of self-pity that he'd disappeared when I needed him most. Then another half minute of anger—the guy'd better remember we had brunch plans tomorrow. After that I turned my thoughts to making myself useful. My plans for the day included taking in a karate class with Thomasina and doing another hypnosis. Maybe she would remember the face of her attacker today. Maybe it all tied in to Rick's death.

I was scheduled to pick her up at one o'clock. I drove right by Robert and Robin Wilson's house the first time. I probably would have driven past it again had I not seen Robert Wilson walking down the driveway to fetch his paper. I hadn't been expecting a house this size, an enormous two-story affair, six bedrooms at least, with a three-car garage. That Thomasina had been forced to move from her own home was regrettable, but from the outside this appeared to be a pretty decent crash pad.

The inside was another story.

A big guy with a pleasant face answered the door. His strong, square features were set off nicely by tasteful eyeglasses with fashionably small lenses. "Can I help you?"

"Hi. I'm here to see Thomasina."

"Hi. I'm Clay." He hollered upstairs to his sister and motioned for me to come in and sit. A television tuned to the Discovery channel blared from the corner of the room. The camera was sweeping through grasslands, focusing on a lion stalking prey. The eyes behind Clay's small lenses became riveted to the screen. "Watch this. He's about to go for the kill. Can you believe something that weighs over three hundred pounds can move forty miles an hour? Here he goes. Watch."

I watched for a few minutes. And a few more. I began to feel antsy. "Are you sure she heard you?"

"I don't know," he mused. "Maybe not."

Some children were arguing in the kitchen, and their voices now climbed into the obnoxious zone. "Keep it down in there!" Clay frowned toward the offending racket, then upped the volume of the television. The narrator boomed facts about the lions of the Kalahari into our ears. The kids raised their voices to compensate for the roaring television. I felt as if my head might explode.

"Mind if I mosey on upstairs to find her?" I asked.

Clay nodded absently, his eyes still glued to the tube. I wandered back to the front hall and had just placed my hand on the railing when a small tempest of young ones blew past me and up the stairs, their feet pounding the steps like a runaway herd of animals. A woman's voice rose above the thunder. "No running in the house!" Thomasina appeared at the top of the stairs, hands on hips, glowering. The crutch was gone, and her limp was hardly noticeable. She spotted me and managed a sheepish smile. "Welcome to Bedlam."

I could only marvel at her. Her eyes were bright, her dark skin radiated health. "God, you look great. How're you doing?"

"Pretty good, considering I'm recovering in a zoo. How long have you been here?"

I glanced at my watch. "A few."

"You'd think my damn fool brother would tell me, now, wouldn't you?"

"He hollered, but . . ."

She moved quickly down the stairs. "Can't hear a thing in this house. We'd better hussle, girl. You still up for this?"

I nodded enthusiastically. "My body has the kind of tension that only exercise can cure."

We were running late so I pushed against the upper edge of the speed limit on our way to the karate class. "Let me know if my driving gets to you," I said.

"Who me? You kidding? Lead Foot is one of my nicknames."

I maneuvered into a hole in the fast lane and relaxed into cruising mode. I felt so comfortable being with this woman. I longed to confide in her my feelings about Rick's murder, Sandy's suicide, Marisa's torment, McGowan's disappearing act. I had to remind myself that I was here for *her*. "Thomasina, that's such a pretty name. How'd you happen to come by it?"

"My dad had his mind made up he was gonna have four boys. Had all our names picked out for us before we were even born. Robert, Brett, Clay, and Thomas."

"So you're Thomas, huh?"

"That's me. The youngest, best, and brightest." She laughed at herself.

"So what do you do for a living, if I may ask?"

"I'm a horn blower, can't you tell?" I glanced at her face. Her white smile brightened an otherwise cold, gray day.

"Public relations?"

"More or less. Community relations director for a housing project in South Central. You want to hear something ironic?"

"Sure. I love irony."

"Over the last year I have tried every trick in the book to try to get coverage for some of the newsworthy things our organization's been doing—making mortgages available to low-income families, creative fund-raisers for day care centers, you name it. I can't tell you how many of my letters and phone calls to newspapers and radio and television stations went unanswered. Then this rape happens and damn if I don't hear from every single one of these people."

"I hate hearing stories like this."

"I just shake my head. What a world."

"So. How are you getting along living with Robert and Robin in Bedlam, as you call it?"

Thomasina groaned. "I'm not getting along. I'm moving."

"Moving! When?"

"Tomorrow. In fact, I hate to do this to you, but I really have to reschedule that hypnosis thing we'd planned for this afternoon. Brett's gotta go to work and I agreed to baby-sit. Since he's gonna help me move I figure I'd better be nice to him."

"Brett, your other brother. Those were his kids?"

"Yeah. Clay's watching them while I get to class here."

"So where are you moving?"

"Redding Street. A little closer to State University."

Zimmer's neighborhood. I didn't mention it. Thomasina didn't even know who Zimmer was. It was a long story. I didn't think she needed to hear it.

"But you're still healing. Do you think this might be, I don't know, a little premature?"

"I love my family, but not enough to live with them. Moving's gonna speed my healing process. Trust me, girl. Besides, my brothers are going to do all the hard work. I'm just supervising."

"You want some company tomorrow, some moral support?"

"On a Sunday? You don't have anything better to do?"

I'd *thought* I was going to be having brunch up the coast with McGowan. Heck with it. I wasn't going to put my life on hold for a date that was looking more and more dubious. Right now Thomasina was my best bet for cracking the case. "I'm due to practice some good deeds," I said. "Besides, once you're settled in maybe we can take some time and do the hypnosis session. If you're still up to it."

Thomasina smiled bravely. "Yeah, that'd be great." But I could sense that she felt anything but great about it.

We pulled into the parking lot of the Mira Mesa campus two minutes past the hour. Thomasina led the way. "You sure all this physical activity is a good idea when your wounds are still healing?"

"I'm here today as much for my *mind* as anything else. You'll see when you meet Master Janice."

"Master Janice?"

"Yeah. Janice Somera-Reinhardt. She's been training in martial arts for more than thirty years. Seventh-degree black belt. She's even been given a white satin belt, the only woman in the country to have been honored that highly."

I'd never heard of a white satin belt, but it sounded impressive. I followed Thomasina into the auditorium. "I take it that's a hard-earned credential."

"That's for sure. She earned some of her credentials on the street. A six-foot-six, two-hundred-fifty-pound guy tried to rape her. He ended up in the hospital with a broken nose and permanently damaged testicles. But her real power isn't in the belts and diplomas, or even the fact that she put that guy in the hospital. Her authority's a lot deeper than all that. You'll see when you meet her. We don't call her Master for nothing."

Around the auditorium about two dozen women stood in small groups, talking and laughing. A few were doing stretches on the floor. Several rubber mats were lined up along the wall. Thomasina and I sat on one.

The room became silent, and I turned to see a woman scarcely more than five feet tall walk through the doorway. Her skin was dark, her features an amalgam of Chinese, Filipino, and Hawaiian. Her large smoky eyes turned up at the corners like a cat's. Blessed with a delicate nose and full lips, Master Janice was a beauty. Yet there was intensity behind her catlike eyes. Power in her walk. She put her hands together and bowed slightly to the gathering. "Good afternoon." Her voice was gentle and at the same time commanding.

"Good afternoon," came the chorus from the assembled women.

Master Janice turned and smiled at Thomasina. Tremendous compassion filled her eyes. "It is good you could come."

Thomasina simply nodded.

"Who is your friend?"

"This is Elizabeth."

Again Master Janice placed her hands together and bowed, this time toward me.

"Thank you for allowing me to sit in," I said.

The cat eyes sparkled. "It is no coincidence that you are here."

Ah, now here was a woman who spoke my language. "I don't believe in coincidences."

Master Janice responded to my comment with a wink. She clapped her hands, and five men dressed in loose white pants and tunics came forward. "We will practice the moves we worked on last week. Vickie, would you like to demonstrate?"

A pretty redhead and one of the men stepped forward. "All right," Master Janice went on, "this move is for freeing yourself if you are attacked from behind. We call it 'Down and Out.'" She gave two short claps, and the man rushed at Vickie from the rear, grabbing her around the chest and pinning her arms to her sides. The impact was intense—he lifted her entirely off the ground. Master Janice raised her voice above the scuffle. "Now, at some point he must put you down, so plant your feet firmly."

With that, Vickie spread her legs and stomped her soles on the carpet.

"Your attacker will be expecting you to push against his arms, outward. You do the unexpected by clasping your hands together and thrusting your arms *forward*, then down."

In a flash the slender woman had slipped from her assailant's grasp. My eye caught her fist slamming into the inside of his thigh. It seemed to have a very real impact on him.

"Very good." Master Janice turned to me, as if reading the question in my mind. "Yes, he did feel it. As you can see my assistants wear no padding or protective gear like in other self-defense classes. All these men hold advanced belts in my martial arts school. They have been conditioned to handle the tough physical strikes I encourage my students to deliver. This is essential to my teaching of rape prevention, since actual body contact is much more realistic than hitting heavily padded opponents." She let out a chuckle. "My targets here are not so easy to hit. Come, you're next."

"*Me?*" I wasn't sure I was ready for this.

She placed a reassuring hand on my shoulder. "It's all right, woman. Again, plant your feet firmly, thrust forward." She demonstrated in slow motion. "Now strike down with the fist, like so. The surprise and impact should cause him to release you. That's why we call this move the Down and Out. Ready? Walk."

I stepped across the matting, trying to remember everything I'd just seen. I did my utmost to prepare for the attack, but when the moment arrived my assailant's crushing arms knocked the breath out of me. For a second I was stunned, completely helpless. Then I fought like hell.

Uselessly.

I squiggled and squirmed, but the arms that gripped me might have been made of cement. My own arms burned, and I broke out in a sweat. I became dizzy, and the room began to spin.

Master Janice appeared in my vision. Responding to the slightest raising of her finger, my assailant let me go.

Her eyes locked onto mine and stopped the frantic busyness in my mind. I could feel hot tears standing in the corners of my eyes.

"You're struggling." Shrugging and shimmying her shoulders, Master Janice imitated me with movements that looked as inept as I had felt. Then she stopped and stood silently, the compassion returning to her eyes. "Do you know why you struggle?"

I shook my head.

"Conditioning. As women, from the time we are little, we struggle. We struggle to be accepted. We struggle to be respected. We are not treated with the same privilege that the men of this world enjoy. We struggle to attain that privilege. We struggle and we struggle. Is this not so?"

The truth of her words rang through my mind, harmonizing with years and years of memories. I could not speak but answered her with my eyes.

"Elizabeth, you are *powerful*. You do not need to struggle, woman. Move from here." She pounded her lower abdomen with a fist, her eyes blazing. "Here is where your power lies. Here—and within."

She clapped her hands, and my assailant resumed a striking position behind me. I started to walk. This time when the impact came I stayed in my body, concentrating on the power spot in my lower abdomen. When I thrust my arms forward I moved from *that* place and was amazed to find myself slipping right out from under the cement arms. Of course I forgot to thrust down with my fist and ended up in another crushing stronghold, but that I had escaped at all thrilled me no end.

"You did well." Thomasina was smiling at me like I was the five-year-old daughter who'd just passed the school play audition.

"Thanks. That was a little frightening. Frankly, I'd rather just rely on my gun."

"Can't always count on your gun." She got a bitter, faraway look in her eye. "Then again, can't always count on your karate training."

37

The phone was ringing when I got home. I ran to catch it. Whitman leaped out of my way as my feet pounded the floorboards. "Hello?"

"Hi, Elizabeth. It's Toby."

Again, disappointment. Where the hell was McGowan?

"Hey, Toby. You're supposed to be keeping your eye on that post office box."

"Chill out, man. I did. That's what I'm calling about. Somebody did come and pick up mail from that box."

"Are you sure it was the right box, number one one one three?"

"Positive."

Some people were charmed. I'll bet I could have staked out that post office for three weeks without any action. "Do you have a description of this person? Did you see the license number on the car he was driving? Were you able to follow him and get the address he went to?"

"Slow down, man, jeez. Yes and yes to the first two questions. But it was a *woman*, red hair, in her twenties or thirties I guess, driving a red Miata with license number three ESG four five six. I don't have an address, though—"

Oh, well, I thought. He was just a sixteen-year-old kid, after all, not a trained tail.

"—because I followed her to the marina. I do have the number on the pier where her boat is docked."

Hot damn. "Toby, you just earned yourself a big tip."

He laughed happily. "All *right*. And I only worked half a day. Yah-hoo!"

"Okay, bud. I'll give you the money tomorrow. Don't spend it all in one place. See you then."

The phone was almost back in its cradle when I heard Toby's tinny little voice calling out, "Wait!"

I put the receiver back to my ear. "Yeah?"

"Um, I thought I had something else to tell you, um. . . . Crap, now I forgot."

I sympathized. That happened to me often. "Something about the woman? The boat? The marina?" I ventured.

"No, no . . . not that. Oh, well. Guess it wasn't that important. I'll call ya if I think of it."

"Okay. Thanks, Tob."

I spotted the red Miata in the parking lot as I pulled into the Oceanside Harbor marina. The thick gray cloud cover had made for a gloomy drive over to the coast. It was nearly sunset now, dusk would come quickly. I pulled my coat from the backseat and put it on as I hurried to the dock.

Damn it. The gate to the boat area was locked. I was standing there composing a plausible story that might get me in somehow when a couple approached, keys jangling. "Hi," they said.

"Oh, great!" I said, genuinely thrilled to see them.

"Forgot your key?"

I rolled my eyes as if I were the silliest thing on the planet and nodded. The guy held the door for me and the woman smiled. "I just hate it when I do that," she said.

"Yeah, me too." Not exactly airtight security at this place, I thought. I took off down the pier and tried to look like I knew where I was going. I noticed that the slip numbers were going in the wrong direction but didn't turn around until my Good Samaritans were out of sight. After one more try I found the slip I was looking for. With a boat in it. So far my luck was holding.

It was an average boat with an average name. *Sea Witch*. A redheaded woman in a navy and white warm-up suit was standing topside adjusting the ropes. She looked down onto the dock and saw me but continued working as if she were accustomed to spectators. "Excuse me," I called. "Have you got a minute?"

She gave the rope a few hard tugs. "Sure. What can I do for you?"

"I'm wondering if you've seen Gary anywhere."

"Gary?" She looked puzzled.

"Yeah, Gary Niebuhr." I watched her eyes. Totally blank.

"Don't know a Gary Niebuhr," she said. I believed her.

"Shoot," I said. *Now what?* "Maybe I got the wrong forwarding address."

Something clicked in her mind. "Are you an investigator?"

To lie or not to lie? That was the question. I pondered it a second too long. "You are, aren't you?"

"What if I am?"

"I've got something for you. Just a minute." She disappeared belowdecks. When she came back up she was carrying a small white envelope. "He didn't say what his name was, but the guy who rented this slip before me left this and asked me to give it to the investigator who would come looking for him."

"Didn't you think that was a little strange? I mean, did you think to call the police?"

"The police? Why? He said the investigator was a friend who might come looking for him here." She began to see her mistake and frowned. "I didn't know. I figured if he was making the effort to leave a letter for this person it probably *was* a friend."

"That's okay. What did he look like?"

"Hmm. Let's see. Receding hairline, glasses, funky sideburns."

It was Niebuhr, all right.

She handed me the envelope. "Here."

I opened it and read:

Dear Friend:
Well, well. You *are* smarter than the average bear. But not smart enough. Not nearly, chump.

Yours,
Gary Warren Niebuhr

"What's it say?" she asked.

"It says I'm a chump."

The woman laughed and returned to her ropes.

I clutched Niebuhr's note in my hand and walked back up the pier. At the horizon's edge the heavy cloud cover gave way to a strip of clear winter sky. The sun dropped into the opening, and the marina was suddenly bathed in brilliant orange light. I stood against a piling to watch the sun's rapid descent into the sea, hoping to catch a glimpse of the famous green flash. I'd seen the elusive phenomenon only once in my life.

As I stared at the horizon I saw a phenomenon, but it wasn't the green flash. Instead, 22X22 popped across my field of vision.

I knew the sequence had significance. Reading numbers was one of my strongest gifts. I reached into my purse for a pen and jotted the sequence onto the back of Niebuhr's note. Perhaps it was a partial license plate number that would provide a clue to the rape case—or to Billings's death.

I thought about Rick Billings on my drive back to Escondido. Wondered what kind of person could brutally kill a sweetie like Rick. Wondered how the homicide investigation was going. By the time I got home it was past six o'clock, but I took a chance that Dianna might still be around the department and placed a call. She was there.

"No, nothing new, not really," she said to my question. "I talked to the 'distant witness' who reportedly saw someone running into the canyon after the shooting. She was two hundred yards away, couldn't even venture a guess as to what sex this person might have been, so that's nothing. The dispatcher noticed pretty quickly that Billings wasn't responding, so we were able to cover the area almost right after it happened. People gave plenty of descriptions of the search dogs and helicopters and cop cars that descended on the area after the crime. Nothing before, though."

"You think Billings's murder is related to the rape case?"

"Definite possibility. The tail lost Zimmer the day before Billings was killed. I guess Zimmer got on a plane and our investigator wasn't authorized to follow. Budget decision."

"Where was the plane headed?"

"Vegas."

"So theoretically it's possible Zimmer could have lost the tail and come back in time to kill Billings."

"Possibly. But as of this morning his van was still in long-term parking at the airport."

I heard another phone ringing somewhere near Dianna. "Before you go, I wondered if you could run a partial license number for me."

"Sure."

"It's two two X two two."

"Sounds like a customized plate. Where'd this come from?"

"Don't laugh. It popped into my head."

"Hey, I'm not laughing."

"So when's Rick's memorial service?" I asked.

"His wife was saying maybe Thursday. A lot of family to round up in the Midwest."

"Are they going to have a stand-up comedian for any of it?"

She laughed softly. "Doubt it. But he would have liked that, wouldn't he?"

"Yep." There was a moment of silence while we remembered. "If he were here you know what I'd say to him?"

"What?"

"I'd say, 'Hey, Billings, that small medium is not the only guy at large.'"

Dianna laughed, but her heart wasn't in it. "You're not any funnier than he was, you know that?"

38

Before leaving for Thomasina's Sunday morning I called the Escondido Police Department, just in case, and discovered what I already knew: McGowan was marked off the schedule until Monday. A call to his pager had yielded no response. I didn't know whether to be worried or angry, so I tried to deliver my message to his machine in an impartial voice: "I thought we were having brunch today. I can't seem to reach you, so I'm going out."

Once in Thomasina's neighborhood I cruised up Redding Street and zeroed right in on her new house. Didn't even consult the curb-side street numbers. Hardly surprising. I shared an uncanny connection with this woman, after all. Of course it didn't hurt that a Ryder moving truck was double-parked in front of the place. I got out of my car and said hello to Thomasina's brothers, who were hoisting a sleeper sofa out of the back of the truck and up the front steps.

"Hey, Clay. And you must be Brett. Is Thomasina here?"

Both men nodded. "Yeah, she's inside," Clay said. "Follow us."

I trailed behind the sofa and into a house already filling with boxes and furniture that didn't quite know its place yet. Brett, as tall as his brother and a good thirty pounds heavier, bellowed over his shoulder as he set the sofa down. "Tommie! You've got company!"

Thomasina appeared in the doorway, put together even on moving day. Wrapped around her head was a fabric swath in vivid browns, purples, oranges, and greens. She wore a matching purple

T-shirt and a stylish pair of jeans. She took in my own casual—some might call it ratty—attire. I was wearing a paint-splattered extra-large T-shirt and roomy sweats. "You came prepared to work, I see."

In fact I had. Any excuse to dress down.

"Was Brett decent enough to introduce himself? Brett, this is Elizabeth Chase, the investigator I was telling you about."

Brett and I exchanged formal hellos. Then he turned to Thomasina. "We've got a couple more chairs and a dresser and we should be outta here, sis." With that the brothers went off to retrieve more furniture.

Thomasina surveyed the littered rooms with a defeated expression. She looked over at me and rolled her eyes. "Oh, man, I hate moving."

"That's why I'm here. Let's start with the kitchen. As long as you have a bed made, a few dishes and a towel or two unpacked, you can survive the chaos. Where are your dishes?"

Thomasina hunted up a box with FRAGILE scrawled along the side. "This looks promising," she said, pushing the box my way. When she leaned over I could see the wide white chest bandage beneath her T-shirt.

"How much are you supposed to do, physically, given your injuries?"

"The doctor says no lifting or reaching over my head for a few more days. But I'm fine, really. The pain lets me know when enough's enough." She busied herself opening another box. "Oh, good. Pots and pans. These go in the bottom cabinet. These I can handle." She began taking pots out and tossing them carelessly into the cabinet, where they banged to a landing. "So how's the investigation going? Are you getting any warmer?"

"I don't know. Sometimes I think so. Then again . . ."

I didn't finish the sentence about sometimes feeling utterly clueless. But Thomasina read it in my face. She turned to me and stood, frying pan in hand, unflappable. Fixed me with her intense, wide-eyed stare. "Don't give up, Elizabeth. Don't you *ever* give up."

"If I were giving up, I wouldn't be here." I unwrapped a few more dishes in silence. Toward the bottom of my box I found a flat parcel wrapped in newspaper. I removed the paper to uncover a framed picture of a beautiful child whose wide eyes shone with precocious wisdom. Her hair was braided up and adorned with white ribbons, matching an exquisite little dress with a full skirt of white tulle. A paragraph was mounted under the photograph:

I solemnly promise that, to the best of my ability, I will help this child to grow up with love for the right and the courage to do the right; with the ideals of integrity and large-mindedness; with love for others of whatever race, nation, or creed; and with faith that the power within her is stronger than any power without her.

"With faith that the power within her is stronger than any power without her," I read aloud. "That's wonderful. Wonderful! I'd love to have a copy of this."

"That can be arranged."

"I take it from the gleam in the eyes that the little girl is you?"

Thomasina grinned. "Yeah. My parents had that made. The words were from my christening ceremony. Hard to believe I was ever such a bitty little thing, isn't it?"

I looked at the photo of Thomasina as a little bitty thing. The toddler, like her grown-up counterpart, was solid and strong. "I'm sure you were a handful, even then." When I looked up Thomasina was staring at me. In that moment I knew for a certainty that the fiery soul behind her eyes was no recent acquaintance.

She didn't look away but instead intensified her gaze. "I never forget a face. So I know we didn't meet before this week. But I could swear I *know* you. You just feel so damn familiar."

I looked at my old friend. "You spoke my own mind."

She squinted dubiously. "Past life?"

I began stacking unwrapped dinner plates into the cabinet above the sink. "Who knows, Thomasina. Who really knows? All I know is we've got our hands full with this life, eh?"

She sighed heavily. "That's for damn sure. So what have you found out? Anything? You know I have this feeling I can remember his face, even though it doesn't make sense. I mean, I know he was wearing a mask, but—"

"I told you. Even if you could identify him perfectly, that wouldn't necessarily be enough to nail him in court. What I'm looking for is solid, physical evidence that can link this sicko to your rape, Annie's rape, Marisa's rape, Sandy's rape."

Thomasina froze. I looked over and saw the whites of her large eyes. "How many women has he attacked?" She spoke softly.

"We don't even know." The horror of that gaped between us like some immeasurable, dark dimension. But I wanted to stay on track. "Back to this physical evidence thing. For example, one victim remembered seeing a—" I caught myself here. Wouldn't want to sway her with the power of suggestion.

"A what?" She put the last of her pans into the cabinet and shut the door.

"A specific vehicle in the neighborhood that day, which matched the description of the vehicle driven by one of our primary suspects. Do you happen to recall what cars were parked on your street that day?"

"I have no idea."

"I didn't think so. These aren't things we generally pay attention to."

But I could tell from her faraway expression that Thomasina was scanning her memory. "Actually, I do remember thinking that Robert had come over, because I thought I saw his Toyota parked across the street that afternoon. But it turned out not to be his car."

Toyota. That rang a bell. "How do you know it wasn't Robert's car?"

"Oh, when I really looked at it, it was newer than his."

"What kind of Toyota? What color?"

"Oh, that snazzy model. I forget the name. Red."

I felt my pulse quicken. "You wouldn't happen to have seen the license plate?"

"No."

As I emptied the last few dishes from my box I reminded myself that there were literally millions of red Toyotas on the road. "Are you sure you're up for this hypnosis today? I know it was hard last time."

"It's harder to live with knowing that guy's wandering around out there. Let's do it now. I know I can see that face."

We sat on the sofa surrounded by boxes in Thomasina's new living room. I said a silent prayer before putting her under.

Thomasina's eyelids fluttered, then relaxed. "Remember now, you are perfectly safe. You are seeing this like a movie, and you will feel no emotional or physical pain as you review this event. Now let's begin with the afternoon before the rape. What do you see yourself doing?"

"I spent the afternoon going over funding applications for the housing project I was working on."

"Can you see yourself doing this? Where are you sitting?"

"I'm sitting at my dining room table in my old house on Montezuma."

"Do you have any sense that anything is unusual on this particular afternoon?"

"No."

"Tell me about the cars you see on the street that day. Do you see any cars?"

"I look out the window and think I see Robert's car across the street, but then I look carefully and see that it's newer than his car."

"Robert's red Toyota is an older model?"

"Yes."

"Can you see the license number on the Toyota?"

"No."

"Do you notice any other cars?"

"Yes. There's a Volkswagen bug and a Volvo."

"Have you ever seen these cars before?"

"Yes. They're my neighbors' cars."

Neighbors' cars. This line of questioning seemed futile. "Is there anything else unusual about that particular afternoon that you remember?"

"No, not really."

"All right. Let's go forward to the point where you're getting ready for bed. Do you notice anything unusual then?"

She didn't answer for some time, and I thought she might have drifted into a sleep state. Just as I was about to prompt her she said, "I'm double-checking that my doors are locked. I don't usually do this. For some reason I'm very insecure. I'm double-checking all the windows and doors."

I remembered that Thomasina's sliding glass door had been lifted right out of its tracks. "Did you see or hear anything that might have made you insecure?"

"No, it's just a feeling."

"All right. Let's go to the next important incident."

"I hear a loud noise. Wakes me right out of my sleep."

"What noise?"

"Like something heavy falling on the floor. Something breaking. My heart starts pounding."

Another new detail. Every time I had Thomasina review the rape it seemed she came up with different versions of the event. "Okay, Thomasina, take a deep breath and remember that you are just watching this like a movie. You are perfectly safe. After hearing the noise, then what happens?"

"I roll off the bed. I'm trying to hide behind the other side of the bed. I'm very frightened. The room is light, there's a lot of moonlight coming through the window. I'm hiding, but I'm afraid he'll see me."

This wasn't just a new detail. This was an entirely new story. I felt hopeless and a little disgusted. Dad was right, these trauma victim memories were about as reliable as the weather forecast. I was tempted to bring her out of the trance but figured I might as well let her play it out. If nothing else, perhaps it was good therapy. Maybe she was going to rewrite history for herself and come out the victor. More power to her. Whatever gets you through the night.

"Okay. So you're hiding behind the bed now?"

She nodded her head in tight little jerks. Her breathing had become shallow and fast.

"Take another deep breath, Thomasina. That's good. Now, what happens next?"

"I see him coming through the doorway. He sees me. He's coming around the bed, his eyes are bulging in his face. I try to kick him, but he's too fast. He jumps back and kicks me. Now he's got his hands around my neck. . . ."

Again, labored breathing. "Take a deep breath again, Thomasina. That's good. Just breathe now for a while. You said you saw his face. What does it look like?"

"He's got those crazy hollow eyes, and a hawklike nose, and a mean, tight mouth, thin little lips."

"Any facial hair?"

"No, he's clean shaven."

"What color is his hair?"

"I don't know. He's wearing a hat."

"Is there anything else to distinguish him?"

Thomasina paused. "There's something strange about his eyes. He's got evil eyes."

"You can see all this, even though he's wearing a mask?"

"He's not wearing any mask."

What? "No mask? What about the gloves?"

"Oh, he's wearing the white rubber gloves."

"Can you see his left hand?" Thinking about Zimmer now.

"It's wrapped around my neck. He's got a knife in his right hand. I can't breathe, I . . ." There was a long silence.

"What happens next, Thomasina?"

Once again her eyelids fluttered. Her face began to tighten, but she didn't speak. I waited for her to answer in her own time. After several seconds, a pair of large teardrops rolled down her face.

Maybe it was time to wrap this up. "Thomasina," I said gently, "can you tell me anything else about what happened?"

"I lose!" she cried. "I lose!"

I decided then and there to nix hypnosis from my investigative bag of tricks.

After the hypnosis session Thomasina was very quiet. She hunted up two cups and made us some herbal tea. I stayed on until her bed was made, her kitchen was navigable, and her bathroom was stocked with towels. We weaved through the boxes and scattered furniture in the living room and stood near the front door. She looked discouraged. "What a mess."

"Just needs some civilizing touches." I lifted a lush philodendron in a colorful ceramic planter onto a tall plaster pedestal in the center of the front hall. The leaves tumbled artfully down the column. "There. Warms the room right up, don't you think?"

"Yeah, it sure does." She smiled halfheartedly.

I hated to leave her here. She caught my feeling. "It'll be all right once I get settled. These transitions are always a pain."

"You sure?" I still felt reluctant to leave.

"Haven't you got your own work to do?"

I laughed. "Now that you mention it, my cat needs to be fed. And I suppose my yard could use some attention."

"Well then go, girl." This time her smile was warm and wide. I was sure that smile had won her many friends and influenced a lot of people. My name could be added to that list. Her smile was the last thing I saw as she waved me out her door that afternoon.

39

Thirteen inches of rain had fallen during the last half of December and the first half of January. In a normal year this would be more than San Diego's total annual rainfall. A couple of kids had nearly drowned playing on their boogy boards in the city viaduct system. Several California cowboys had stranded their four-wheel drives trying to cross washed-out roadways that in any other year would have been a piece of cake. The downpour had wreaked havoc with my backyard. Dammed like a reservoir against the side of the house, the water had drowned my African daisies and was now threatening to ruin the siding. As I pulled into the driveway I resolved to spend the remainder of the afternoon digging a trench to drain the flooding into the gutter along the street.

That's what I was doing when Zimmer came to call.

I was shoveling liquid earth, work that made a loud, sucking sound. I had just been pondering how the rainy weather might be affecting the fresh crop of newly deads who had insisted on burial instead of cremation when I felt eyes on my back. I shoveled on without turning around, trying to guess who it might be. A little game us psychics like to play: Name That Presence. I knew it was someone familiar—not a family member, not a friend, but not a stranger, either. "I give up," I said out loud. "Who are you?" I spun around and looked into a pair of hinky black eyes.

"Bet you've got a pretty nice place here when the sun's out." Richard Zimmer stood smiling at me, his arms folded across his densely muscled chest, legs spread slightly.

Instantly I felt on guard.

"You're a hard woman to find, you know that?"

Apparently not hard enough. "Oh, really? You been looking for me long?"

"All my life, baby. All my life." His top lip curled back to reveal a dazzling white smile.

I was grateful to be holding a metal shovel in my hands.

When I didn't reply, the smile left his face. "I got a bone to pick with you, lady."

"Is that right?"

"Yeah, that's right. I'm getting damn sick of being followed everywhere by that fucking unmarked cop car."

I slid my eyes up and down the street. "I don't see any car."

Zimmer stepped forward—a little too far forward—and smiled again. "I lost her."

I moved sideways and held the shovel between us. "Congratulations. Then you can go now." Something about him looked different.

"I don't think so. You see, I really don't appreciate being followed by a bunch of fucking idiots."

I put my shovel back into the earth and resumed digging. "That's too bad. I feel for ya. I don't like idiots following *me*, either."

"I'm going to ignore that insult." He looked down his nose at me as he said it. That's when I noticed it. No mustache now.

"It's not like I invited you over for tea, Mr. Zimmer." I slopped a shovelful of mud precariously close to his shoes.

"No, you didn't. But I'd make better company than those pigs at the police department. Why a woman like you is hanging with those morons—"

"I'm helping them apprehend scumbags and slimeballs," I interrupted. "Just so that you know."

"Well, while you're at it, get those scumbags off my back."

"Now why would I want to do that?"

"Because they're violating my privacy."

Violating his privacy. From a guy who'd made a career out of violating the property and person of others, a whine about his loss of privacy. I stopped shoveling and looked him in the eye. "You forget I've seen your record. My heart's not exactly bleeding for you, bro."

"Doesn't it bother you that the cops are wasting time trying to nail the wrong guy? They should be looking for the real rapist, don't you think?"

I took a hard look at Zimmer. More than anything he appeared to be working hard—too hard—at appearing innocent.

"Look," he went on. "They hauled me in for questioning after that house in Hillcrest was broken into again, okay? I was in Las Vegas the night that happened, visiting my mother. You can even ask her."

I'm not necessarily touched by mothers' testimony. Mothers will lie through their teeth if they think it will do their kids any good. "Oh, I see. So your very own mother can vouch for your whereabouts that night? Not exactly an impartial witness, Mr. Zimmer."

"My mother wasn't the only one who saw me in Vegas. Other people saw me there, too. The police could check them out if they wanted to. But they don't. They seem to have a vested interest in getting me behind bars."

It sounded weak. I thought back to the doctor's description of what Zimmer had done to his girlfriend, Belinda. *The elbow and shoulder were ripped apart like a chicken wing.* Thought back to her frightened voice on the phone. "Gosh," I said, "that's such an awful shame. Who'd want a nice guy like you behind bars?"

He narrowed his eyes. His face began to redden, and for a minute I was afraid he would lunge at me. "I offered to give them blood, semen, whatever they wanted to put this thing to rest. The cops aren't interested. Don't you find that a little strange?"

The media, and therefore the public, didn't know that there was virtually no DNA evidence to go on in this case. I didn't mention it to Zimmer, either.

"What's preposterous is the thought of me chasing down women. Like I'm that desperate. I can get it anytime I want it."

It.

My shovel dove deep into the wet earth and hit a rock with a resounding clank. A big rock. I pried the large stone loose and hurled it into my backyard reservoir, where its heft landed with a satisfying splash. "Rape is not about sex," I said. "It's about power and control."

"Okay, like I'm that desperate for power and control. I mean, driving all over the city for it? Too much trouble. Let the babes come to me." He pointed to his chest with his three-fingered hand and chuckled. Again he was trying to be funny. Enduring Zimmer's humor was like being strapped to a chair, having your eyelids pried open, and being forced to watch the rankest stand-up comic in the history of the world. On acid.

"Sorry you can't stay. Let me walk you to your car." I walked briskly toward the driveway to let him know I meant business. Zimmer's white van was parked out front. It disturbed me that I hadn't heard him drive up. Could he have cut the engine and rolled into the driveway? Once again I eyed the sloppy lettering on the side of his van. "So tell me what happened to Zippy Lock & Safe."

His weird eyes studied mine. "They took my locksmithing license when the robbery verdict went down. Fucking pissed me off. I didn't steal a damn thing from that bitch."

When he called the woman he'd battered a bitch, my blood began to simmer. "Save your breath. I don't have time for liars."

With that he *did* lunge at me. I was ready for him and spun around, shovel out. He jumped back with amazing speed and avoided the impact. The commotion triggered a ferocious barking in the van. I looked up to see Zimmer's pit bull hurling his snout over and over against the window. The glass became wet with saliva. I could hear the clicking of the dog's fangs on the glass.

Zimmer was watching me now, his white smile gleaming, delighted by the fear in my face. He rounded the van to the driver's side. "You call off your dogs, I'll call off mine."

40

I hurried back into the house and watched through the kitchen window as the white van backed out of my driveway and disappeared down Juniper Street. After my encounter with Zimmer and his dog I felt dirty all over.

I looked down and saw that I *was* dirty all over. Mud had already begun crusting the edges of my pants legs, and I'd managed to work the kind of grit under my fingernails that only a hot bath will soak out. My filthiness was more than skin deep. Zimmer had a tainted aura, a sleazy vibration that hung in the mind the way a foul odor hangs in the air. Charles Schulz, the cartoonist of *Peanuts* comic strip fame, created a character named Pigpen who walks around in a cloud of dirt. Some people walk around in energy fields like that. Richard Zimmer was one of them.

I put a call in to Dianna's voice mail. "Zimmer's back in town. He came by the house and threatened me that I'd better *call off my dog.* I'm quoting him, Dianna, so don't take that personally." I hung up the phone and ran a bath.

The bath helped my body feel cleaner but didn't dispel my icky mood. I put on some flannel pj's and went to the living room to light three white candles for meditation. On ambitious days I meditate sitting in the lotus position. Today was a lying-on-my-back day. My lower spine was already starting to complain about the morning's hard labor. Much is made of the ascetic posture, but to tell you the truth I get just as much benefit meditating flat on my back. The important part is quieting the thoughts. Getting past the daily mental newsreels. Getting to the quiet, getting to the light. Always, the light.

But I couldn't get to the quiet today, let alone the light. I closed my eyes, committed myself to centering, and breathed consciously, just the way my yoga teacher had instructed me over the years. No matter what I tried I could not find peace.

This meant something, of course. It was simply a matter of tuning in to what I was repressing and inviting the feeling to come bubbling to the surface. Usually that feeling was sadness or anger. Today it was fear. It started as an icy wave, paralyzing my face first and then moving down through my body, chilling my arms and legs until they were numb. Every inch of me froze except for my heart. It was pounding stronger and faster, keeping step with my rising panic. Somehow I remembered to breathe.

Something terrible was going to happen. I knew it.

My rational mind quickly tried to dismiss that knowing. Maybe this was just backlogged anxiety from the horrors I'd been exposed to this week, my rational mind said. Sure, my brain rationalized, just a little unprocessed dread. It was only logical to feel this kind of phobia given the uncertainties about this case.

Something terrible was going to happen and I knew it.

I got up and fixed myself some chamomile tea. Wanted to be in touch with the police but knew Dianna wasn't available. It was Sunday and after five, but I thought that perhaps with Billings's death Dietz might be keeping long hours. I called his number at the SDPD. No luck. Lieutenant Marcone, however, was still in the building, and the desk sergeant was kind enough to page him for me.

"Thought that might be my daughter," he said after we'd exchanged hellos.

"Daughter, huh? How many kids you got, Lieutenant?"

"Just one I think," he laughed warmly. "If you can call a twenty-five-year-old living at home a kid."

"Sure you can. They're always your kids."

"That they are." He paused. "It's been a hellish couple of days around here."

"I have a feeling it's going to get worse."

"Hard to imagine that. Not to tempt fate." He sounded battered, defeated, in need of rest. "I shouldn't be so pessimistic. We have had a positive development that could relate to the case you're working on. Dietz has been keeping a pretty tight rein on Bobby Morgan. Last night it paid off. Just after dark Dietz caught him breaking and entering into a ground-floor apartment near Fifty-second and El Cajon."

"The rapist doesn't hit apartments. And he prefers the wee hours."

"True."

"Were the doors secured from the outside? Was the electricity cut?"

"No."

"Hmm. That's not the rapist's part of town, either. Did Dietz have enough charges to hold Morgan?"

"Yes. Caught him trying to escape through a busted window carrying a VCR and camcorder."

"It's not exactly a carbon copy crime, either."

"True. We're in the process of getting a warrant to search Morgan's place. We'll be keeping an eye out for evidence to link him to the rapes. You never know."

"True. You never know."

I heard a muffled yawn on the lieutenant's end. "Have you turned up anything since we talked last?"

"A couple of things. First, I'm working on some promising plate numbers."

"Uh-huh." Marcone didn't sound too excited about that.

"Then I hypnotized Thomasina Wilson again. The three-gabled house, remember? This time she thought she saw the rapist's face. Practically a full ID—'crazy hollow eyes, thin lips, hawk nose, clean shaven.' "

"But her rapist was masked."

"I know."

"Doesn't make sense, then."

"I know."

Whitman jumped onto the table and knocked some papers over the edge. The noise startled me. I shooed him down. "I guess I'm frightened, Lieutenant. Zimmer came by my house this afternoon, angry about the police tail."

"I'm sure that didn't help your serenity any. By the way, Zimmer has facial hair."

"Not anymore. The mustache was gone when he came by here today. Ever since I've had this terrible feeling. Like something bad is going to happen."

"Something bad has already happened. We lost an officer this week."

"I know. Something else, I mean."

There was a pause on Marcone's end. I could picture him. He'd be sitting straight in his chair, no matter how many hours he'd worked. "Can you tell me where this bad thing is going to happen?" he asked.

"No."

"Can you tell me who it's going to happen to?"

"No."

"Can you tell me when it's going to happen?"

"Soon. How's that for being a big help?" I felt a little foolish.

"Don't be hard on yourself. You're not the only one who's been flying blind lately. We don't have a single decent lead in Billings's homicide."

"So, Lieutenant, are you thinking Billings's death is related?"

He sighed. "We just don't have enough information to know that. Why, do you think it is?"

The feeling had been with me from the moment I'd read the news of Billings's death. "If I had to guess, I'd say yes."

41

The shrill scream of my cordless telephone had an ominous ring to it. My eyes popped right open. The digits glowing by the bedside said three-thirty. I felt a fluttering in my rib cage, like some panicky bird wanting out. I reluctantly picked up the phone.

"Elizabeth. It's Dianna. There's been another attack. You'd better come down. We're at one oh oh three Redding Street."

The address didn't register. I wouldn't let it. It was too terribly familiar. I refused to connect it with anyone I knew. I was sitting up now. "Okay. I'm on my way." I hung up before Dianna could tell me anything else. I didn't want to know the rest. I desperately wanted *not* to know.

My movements were rigid and mechanical. I pulled on a shirt and a pair of jeans. Scooped my car keys off the dresser. Bravely marched to my car. I drove down to San Diego silently observing the sparse early morning traffic. By the time I left the off-ramp near the university I had admitted to myself that I was on my way to Thomasina's new house. By then the feeling had started to leave my body. I felt the numbness in my fingers first, then observed, with considerable detachment and curiosity, as the feeling left my toes and feet. Then my limbs, then the very core of me. I wondered just what, exactly, kept me sitting upright in my seat, working the turn signal, steering the car onto the freeway off-ramp. I made a left turn, then a right. For a moment I completely lost my bearings. South seemed north, east seemed west, as if someone had spun the city around like a vinyl record. I slowed and saw a pair of police cruisers. I pulled up to the curb.

Déjà vu.

I floated up the walk, unable to feel my feet. Dianna appeared at the door looking haggard. Her blond hair needed washing. "Glad you could make it," she said. When I looked into her face she averted her eyes and shook her head.

"How long ago did this happen?" I marveled that I had somehow spoken. I didn't feel connected to my vocal cords at all.

"About an hour and a half. She was able to dial nine one one but couldn't speak. It took patrol a while to get here." She put a hand on my arm. "Where's your jacket? You're freezing. It's cold out there." I glanced down at myself. Until now I hadn't noticed I'd forgotten my coat. Dianna stepped sideways to let me into Thomasina's house.

The plaster pedestal had been knocked over onto the tile entryway, and the ceramic planter I'd put there yesterday had shattered. Brightly painted shards littered the tiles. Dianna sighed, then began, "We think he knocked this over on the way in. The lock on the front door was dismantled. This attack was a little different—"

I interrupted her. "I know. She tried to hide behind the bed, tried to fight him off. But he was too fast for her, too strong. He didn't even rape her. He just choked her." My voice sounded so far away. A most annoying sensation, like I had water in my ears. "And he stabbed her. Repeatedly." I delivered it all in a dull monotone.

Dianna's mouth hung open. "How do you *see* all that?"

I stood dumbly. I was listening to an internal rushing sound, as if someone had boxed me in the ears.

"I'm amazed you can see that."

"I didn't see it," I answered. "*She* did." And then the tragedy of it hit me right between the eyes. "I didn't see it." My faraway voice was a distraught whisper. "*I* didn't see it. She laid it all out for me and *I didn't see it!*" Cold was traveling down my spine. Fear stomped down on me, crushed me like a heavy boot. "Is she dead?" A small whisper.

Dianna bit her lips together and squeezed her eyes shut. When she opened them she said, "Her condition is listed as extremely critical." I now noticed the small crowd in Thomasina's house. Cops. Police photographer. Crime scene techs.

"I want to see the bedroom." Some new voice now was taking control of me. This voice was strong and sure of herself. I was relieved to have her on board.

Dianna followed along behind me. "Careful not to disturb anything."

"Of course. Believe me, I care as much about the purity of this evidence as you do."

The bed I had so neatly made for Thomasina yesterday afternoon was disheveled. The top sheet was stretched diagonally across the mattress, as if Thomasina had pulled it with her on her way over the side of the bed. The floor behind the bed was a riot of bloodstains. Had I not been so thoroughly detached from my feelings, I knew this sight would have been impossible to bear. As it was I viewed the tableau from a safe distance, an observer watching the surgery from high above the operating table.

A technician was already busy with the scene. I called to him. "Excuse me. Do me a favor?" He looked up, the overhead light shining in the small round lenses of his glasses. "Be extra meticulous with this case?" He nodded and returned to his task.

42

I was sitting on a padded bench in the pastel-painted corridor outside of the recovery room. Thomasina's life hung in the balance. She had survived the seven hours of surgery that were required to repair twenty-one stab wounds. Some time ago an exhausted resident surgeon had informed me that her condition was still extremely critical. He said it brusquely with a shake of the head, a gesture that had me leaping to the conclusion that he didn't expect her to live. I wondered vaguely how long I'd been in this spot. Time was distorted to me, as if I'd been dropped here out of eternity and had arrived at this hour—two o'clock on Monday afternoon—completely by chance.

I didn't even see Lieutenant Marcone until he was nearly on top of me. He took a seat beside me on the bench. When I looked over, his eyes were filled with sorrow.

"I saw this coming," he said. "Damn it."

"You weren't the only one."

"Dianna told me how you saw everything there, at the crime scene."

I shook my head. "No. I didn't see. It was Thomasina. *She* saw it. She saw the whole thing under hypnosis. I didn't recognize it at the time. I thought she was distorting her memories of the first rape. Posttrauma hallucinations, whatever. God." I buried my head in my hands and left it there even after I felt Marcone's hand on my back.

"The scene was the same as always. No prints, no hair, nothing left behind. Except . . ." He gave my back a little squeeze and I heard a tiny note of hope in his voice. I looked up. "This time he left a bite mark on the victim's back."

A bite mark. I remembered the red patch that had appeared on my right shoulder the night McGowan had come home out of the rain, the night I'd done surveillance on Zimmer's house. "Was the bite mark on her upper right shoulder, by any chance?"

Marcone nodded, curiosity lighting his gaze. "The victim saw that, too?"

"No, I did. Sort of."

"That's amazing."

I hissed in disgust. "Too little, and way too late."

"You're being awfully hard on yourself." An orderly wheeled a cart past us, empty plates clattering on the metal shelving. Marcone watched the cart disappear down the hallway. "I understand the victim moved into that house just yesterday."

Shut up with this victim shit! I wanted to scream. "Her name is Thomasina."

"Sorry."

"I helped her unpack boxes yesterday."

"So he followed her. From a police perspective that's good news. A stalker is a lot easier to track than a random rapist. Any pattern helps."

I knew I should think about who might know where Thomasina had moved to, who might have the motive to attack her again. In time I would. Right now, though, every fiber of my being and every ounce of my will were organized around a single desire: Please, please let Thomasina live.

Marcone was talking again. I hadn't been listening. ". . . gathering up what we could find that might be related. Which reminds me." He took something out of his inside jacket pocket. "We found this on the vic—Thomasina's—dresser, thought you might like to have it." He placed an envelope in my hands and looked as if he suddenly had someplace important to go. As he got up to leave he patted my back. "Keep your chin up." With that he disappeared down the hospital corridor.

Square and bright white, the envelope was addressed simply, "Elizabeth Chase," as if Thomasina had intended to give it to me personally rather than mail it. I pulled out and unfolded a piece of paper and read again the words from her christening ceremony:

> . . . *with love for the right and the courage to do the right . . . with faith that the power within her is stronger than any power without her.*

I leaned back against the wall, too drained and devastated to cry. From the end of the corridor, Dr. Goode approached the bench. Her eyes were compassionate behind the large frames of her glasses. "For you," she said, "a special exception to the no-visitors rule. Would you like to see her?"

I nodded.

"Two minutes tops. In and out, okay?"

Again I nodded.

I walked through the door. Thomasina was lying in a tangle of IV lines, oxygen tubes, and bandages. I felt her presence in the room, though not entirely in her body. Clutching the envelope, I stood behind the IV pole. "I'm so sorry—" Here my voice caught, cracked, failed me entirely. It seemed important to finish saying it out loud, so I pushed myself. "I'm so sorry I let you down."

Thomasina's closed eyelids looked just as they had during our hypnosis sessions. They filled me with an aching tenderness. I moved closer to the bed, leaned over, and put my mouth next to her ear. "I don't know about you," I said softly, "but I'm not giving up. I'm not *ever* giving up."

43

Never underestimate the value of a good night's sleep.

Depression and exhaustion had begun to eat away at my can-do attitude as I drove home from the hospital. By the time I went to bed Monday night I was feeling utterly hopeless. It's truly amazing what a little rest can do. I woke up Tuesday morning as angry as I was determined. The powerful mood was a welcome surprise, like finding a big check in the mail.

I called the hospital first thing. There had been no change in Thomasina's condition during the night. I pressed Dr. Goode for a prognosis, and all she would say was "guarded." But by God Thomasina was hanging in there.

Clearly the attack had not been a random act. Statistically it might be possible for lightning to strike the same place, but the same victim in two different places—? No way. Who had known that Thomasina had moved? Who had access to her new address? Was this attack malicious terrorization, or was there a motive behind the attempt on her life? And if there was a motive, was she safe in the hospital? I called the PD to make certain they were thinking along the same lines. None of my people was in, but I got some assurances from the desk sergeant and was told somebody would call me back soon.

I was sitting at the kitchen table taking notes and trying to make logical connections when the phone rang. I assumed it was Dietz or Dianna.

"Are you all ready for your big performance tonight?"

It was my mother. Shit! I'd completely forgotten about the AIDS benefit. "Oh, God. I mean . . . Hi, Mom. Whew. What a week. How are you?"

"I'm fine, but you don't sound so good. What's going on, dear?"

"Critical things with this case that I don't want to go into right now."

There was a worried pause. "You're not going to cancel on us, are you?"

I thought about it for a moment. For me, a commitment's a commitment unless it's life or death. True, this was life or death. Then again there were several experienced investigators working this case. It wasn't all up to me. I had other responsibilities too. I took a deep breath. "Of course not. I'll see you tonight."

"Before you go, what are you planning on wearing tonight?"

I grinned. "Oh, you know, the usual. Long flowing robe, turban, crystals hanging around my neck."

"You're kidding."

"Yes, Mom, I'm kidding."

The Ninth Annual San Diego AIDS Benefit was being held at the new Hyatt in the Golden Triangle, so named for the lucrative quality of this particular hunk of real estate. Central to everything, the area is marked by the much-criticized new Mormon Church. The gothic monolith rises like some surreal anachronism along the freeway, its gleaming alabaster spires as ostentatious as they are spooky.

My dance card for the night was full—sixteen clients between eight and midnight. While I would be reading charts the charity guests would be dancing in the hotel ballroom. After the predictably lousy banquet meal (chicken en croûte, what else?) I went to set up my laptop in one of the adjacent conference rooms. On the wall above the table a discreet sign read, ASTROLOGICAL READINGS. My first client was already waiting for me when I walked in.

She wore a dress of peach silk and matching pumps. Light bounced off several diamonds on her ears, neck, and fingers. That was the only light bouncing off her, though. She gave me a tight smile. "Hello. I'm Myra Roberts."

"Hi, Myra." I entered the birth data she gave me into my computer, and her chart came up on my screen. Instantly I saw the problem. Not only was the sun in Capricorn right now, but six other planets—Moon, Mercury, Venus, Mars, Uranus, and Neptune—were as well. All of these transiting planets were crowded at the bottom of Myra's chart, squaring a group of natal planets she had in Cancer. "You must feel like Job about now, Myra. A lot of endings. Too many endings all at once. A man, a woman who was very close to you, a work situation—at least one of these endings was rudely abrupt. Ouch."

Her eyes got teary. "Is it ever going to end?"

I consulted my ephemeris. "You ought to be feeling some relief by the end of next month. But you're going through a somewhat prolonged phase of reevaluating your priorities. That will be going on for another two years. Keep breathing. Try to get through this period one day at a time, and remember it will definitely pass."

My next client, Mrs. Richard King, was perhaps ten years older and wearing proportionately larger diamonds. She offered to double her donation if I would compare her chart with her beloved Richard's. "Sure, happy to oblige." I brought up her chart first, printed it out, then pulled up her husband's chart and superimposed his planets onto her wheel. I found myself staring at an unmitigated astrological disaster. "Hmm, interesting," I began.

She bared her teeth in a big fake smile. "He *is* an interesting man. We have such a unique marriage."

Well, that was one way to put it. From the looks of it they probably came close to murdering each other every few months. "Do you find that there's a little tension around money issues?" I ventured.

"You see that in there?" Teeth still bared in a smile, she looked like a mannequin.

I nodded.

"We don't really have any problems that way," she lied.

Ah, one of *those* clients. "What are you hoping to gain from this reading, Mrs. King? Is there some question you have, any particular problem you'd like me to address?"

"No. I just thought this might be fun is all." Still smiling.

A thousand bucks for a little fun. Hmph. I looked at what the gang of planets in Capricorn was doing to this couple. Yikes. Trouble ahead. Perhaps the universe had assigned me the job of warning her. "Your marriage is going through some challenges right now," I said. The word *challenge* is New Age–speak for *painful as hell*. "There may be a major transition in the marriage over the next two years." Read: *Prepare to meet your lawyer*.

She was still baring those teeth as she walked away from the table, as if I'd given her the greatest news in the world.

I became completely absorbed in the readings and the hours passed quickly. Again and again as I read the charts I saw the effects of the extraordinary stellar line-up in Capricorn. For some people it was energizing, for others rough, all depending on where they fell on the wheel. Cosmic roulette. The readings energized and inspired me. They reminded me that there was order in the universe, when everything else this week had appeared so cruelly random.

I was packing up my computer when McGowan stepped up to the table. "Surprise."

It was the first time I'd ever seen him dressed in a tux. The effect on me was predictable. In that moment all anger and doubt were poised to disappear. My heart became a wheel, ready to roll in whatever direction he cared to spin it. Disgusting.

I did my best to mask this as I continued my packing. "Whatever you have to say, it better be good."

His wide goofy smile dissolved as my mood registered in his brain. Then something clicked, I saw it in his eyes. "Toby didn't tell you, did he?"

"Toby didn't tell me wha—" I flashed back to the kid's memory lapse. "No, he forgot."

"Oh, jeez. I'm sorry." His enormous brown eyes had never looked more sincere.

I wasn't melting just yet. "I do have a phone machine, you know."

"Couldn't use phone lines. That's why I left the message with Toby."

"The message."

"Yes. The one that said I had to go out of town through Monday but would see you at the AIDS benefit. With bells on."

I could swear the eyelashes fringing those huge brown irises had grown since the last time I'd seen him. "So where are your bells?"

"Show you later. Hey, can I have a reading?"

"Readings are over for the night. Besides, you know I can't read for people close to me. I'm too invested to be objective."

He took a seat. "Nice necklace, by the way."

I was wearing the tanzanite he'd given me. "Thank you. In more ways than one." I was beginning to get acclimated to the dizzying effect of his evening attire. "Where in the galaxy have you been, Tom?"

He smiled apologetically. "Can't tell. Not yet." Then he winked. "Maybe you can look at my chart and tell me."

Worth a try. I pulled up his chart, not that I hadn't memorized his planets by heart. Still, the wheel itself was a centering tool for the intuitive part of the reading. The Capricorn stellium was transiting his eighth house. The insight came to me in a sudden flash: *Career, government, secret.* I looked him straight in the eye. "You're not working for the feds now, are you?"

He reddened. I'd gotten my answer.

"So how is this going to affect us? Does this mean you're moving to Washington or Quantico or something?"

He stood up and took my hand. "This is not the time and place to talk about it. But I promise we will talk. Soon. Right now let's just get over to the ballroom. If we hurry we might catch the last dance."

44

There was a pattern here, a definite pattern.

I was poring over the astrological charts of the rape victims, charts showing what was going on astrologically at the times of their assaults. In each chart I kept seeing the same things that had popped out at me from McGowan's chart last night. An association between the rapes and *government, secret, career*. I wasn't sure what to make of it. That these serial rapes were part of some larger conspiracy? Come on, Chase. Get real. The phone rang, interrupting my thoughts.

It was Dianna. "Have I got news for you."

"Don't tell me. You matched that partial plate number I gave you to America's most wanted criminal, who just happens to be our rapist."

"No, I didn't turn up a thing on your number. But we are making progress elsewhere. The sting operation we've been setting up for Zimmer is almost ready to go down. It's even worse than we thought."

"In what way?"

"It's not just child pornography. Zimmer's trafficking snuff films, too."

"Snuff? As in murder on camera?"

"As in rape and murder on camera. They're foreign made, Philippines, from the looks of it. But Zimmer's the distributor. Anyway, something is expected to break loose today. If we nab him

I want you to be available to, you know, vibe out his house before the evidence guys tear it down."

"Sure. Why don't I just drive down and hang out at the department? I wanted to check the new report on Thomasina's last attack anyway."

"She's hanging in there, by the way."

"I know. I've been staying in close touch with her doctor. Anything new on Rick Billings's case?"

"Dead ends, mostly." Rick would have appreciated the pun. "Very demoralizing around here. Everybody's wearing sad faces and black tape across their badges. It's the second shooting like this we've had in the last three years. Makes the paychecks look too small, you know?"

"I'll bet. You going to be in your office when I get there?"

"Should be."

During the drive downtown I thought about last night with McGowan. He'd seemed warm, loving, and genuinely glad to see me. Still he wouldn't talk about where he'd been or why he couldn't come home with me. All he would say was that he'd be able to tell me more at the end of the week. I drove myself nearly crazy thinking up possible explanations. By the time I pulled into a metered space across from the SDPD, I was feeling grateful to have work to keep my mind occupied.

The place was beginning to feel like home. The officer at the front desk recognized me and waved me through. I rode the elevator up to the third floor. When I got to the Sex Crimes department Dianna was busy making phone calls. Her desk was piled higher than I'd ever seen it before. "Too much going on," she explained. "All happening in triplicate. Thomasina's new report is over on Billings's old desk."

I walked over to Rick's desk. Almost immediately I sensed his essence. Made me smile—he'd been a good guy. I sat down in his old chair and shuffled through the papers. The report of the recent attack on Thomasina was right on top. Underneath that was the file on the second break-in at the Hillcrest house, the attack McGowan and I had averted. True to form, I began snooping inside Billings's desk.

Most of his personal items had been cleared out. A few pens and pencils rolled around in the top drawer. The second drawer was empty save for a smattering of paper clips. As I pushed it shut I heard the crumpling noise of paper stuck along the runner. I reached in and pulled out the culprit. It was one of the pages from the listing of red Toyotas I'd had Dietz run for me. Hmm, Rick must have had my same thought and done the same homework. My eyes skimmed the page and stopped short about halfway down. There it was, plain as day: 3XEA666.

Okay, what did this mean? Could Dietz and I have missed it? I pulled my copy, the one Dietz had given me, out of my briefcase. A slightly different type style. With 3XEA666 missing. My mind was slow getting it, but already goose bumps were rising along my thighs.

Government, secret, career.

Cold, conscious, calculating.

Rick must have found the real list, the one that hadn't been tampered with. Before I went leaping to conclusions I thought I'd better get some substantial evidence, goose bumps or no goose bumps. I called across the room. "Dianna, can you get the registered owner on another plate number for me?"

"Sure. What've you got?"

"Three XEA six six six."

"Just a minute."

While I waited I looked into the report on Thomasina's last attack. It was tough reading. Midway through the file was a list of every item that had gone to the evidence room. Something popped out at me from that list, too: sand.

The realization struck me with such force that I had to catch my breath. Thomasina had felt sand beneath her thighs in our hypnosis sessions. I now understood that she'd been seeing visions of her future, not her past. On my trip to the evidence room I'd looked for sand from the scene of her first rape. Of course it hadn't been there. The sand she had felt under hypnosis was from the scene of this most recent attack, at the house she had just moved into on Redding Street. In a brand-new house, where would sand have come from? Her brothers could have tracked it with them as they moved furniture, but I didn't think so. That sand came from the rapist. I knew it, with the intuitive certainty that circumvents logic. An analysis of that sand might even help convict him. Sherlock Holmes had amazed Dr. Watson by identifying what section of London a man lived in on the basis of the mud the man wore on his heel. In San Diego there was a lot more sand than mud. Most of it comes from the beach communities.

In my dream I had seen a face appearing against the backdrop of the ocean. A face I knew. "I like to spend time with the ocean," he'd said.

He'd blanched when I'd told him that under hypnosis Thomasina thought she might be able to see the rapist's face. That was when he knew she was getting close, way too close. He'd intended to kill her.

And if Rick had identified the red Toyota parked near the scene as his, he had motive to kill him, too.

"Robert Caffey."

It was Dianna, calling from across the room. "What?" I called back.

"Robert Caffey. That plate is registered to Robert Caffey of Oceanside."

Robert Caffey? Big letdown. I shook my head. Was I losing it?

"Why, whatcha got?" Dianna asked.

I shook my head in confusion. "Nothing, I guess."

I closed my eyes and pinched the bridge of my nose. Tried to rub away the tension between my eyes. On my inner movie screen I saw Rick standing by his patrol car, waving me forward. As if to say, Come on, keep going. Don't stop now. Then the vision faded. "Come back," I said under my breath. "I need to ask you some things."

Dianna walked over, stretching her arms. "Been sitting in that chair since six this morning, putting this thing together. I'm getting desk butt." She grabbed a hunk of flesh on her rear thigh and frowned. "Need to get some exercise. I'm psyched about getting Zimmer, though. I admit it, I'm psyched."

My mind was elsewhere. "Hey, where is the car that Rick was shot in?"

She pulled her eyebrows together. "Down in the evidence area of the garage. Over by the chain-link fencing. You don't want to see that, do you? It was pretty messy."

"No, I just want to stand near the car and see if I can get in touch with what happened to Rick. I know it sounds weird, but I think he's trying to reach me. Will you walk me down there?"

She stared at me for a moment before answering. "Sure." In that one hushed word I could tell how deeply Rick's death had affected Dianna. "I was just saying I needed exercise, wasn't I?"

On the way down I went over it again in my mind. Damn! I'd been so sure whose name was going to show up on that registration. It would have been a shock, but it also would have made a horrible kind of sense. The elevator doors dinged open, and Dianna and I stepped out into the black expanse. Dianna's chatter sounded strange here, too, upbeat for the surroundings. She was still talking about the sting operation for Zimmer. "I'm going to go as the girlfriend of the guy who's making the videotape buy. Sometimes it's fun to play these roles."

"Are you nervous?"

"Sort of. Even though I'll be wearing a wig and staying in the car, I'm a little worried that Zimmer might recognize me from the interview. I just don't want that jerk to slip away. Okay, here's Billings's car."

It was a standard cruiser. The windows were rolled up. I tried not to look at the bloodstained upholstery inside. Dianna checked the number on the vehicle. "Yeah, this was his car." We stood quietly for a moment. She watched my face. "So?"

Just then her beeper went off. "Oh, shit, that's the call. I know that's the call." She pushed a button on the pager and glanced at the readout. "This is it. I gotta go. Sorry."

"That's okay. I'll find my way up. I just need a minute here."

I watched Dianna walk toward the elevator until she was out of sight. Then I stood very still, inviting information from the subtler realms. Almost as soon as I leaned against the car, images began to come. Rick sitting inside, watching the Hillcrest neighborhood. Turning and seeing his killer's face through the open window. I saw it now, too. The face I'd seen in the dream.

I heard the grinding of a motor coming around the corner. Its mechanical rhythm was amplified in the large, empty space. When the car came into view I saw the face again.

Dietz glared at me from the driver's side of the cruiser. He was propping his Sig against his thigh, pointing it through the open passenger window at me. He'd fitted the gun with a silencer. "Get in the car," he said.

45

I know the kind of damage a nine-millimeter does at point-blank range. After all, I own one. To my profound dismay my Glock was upstairs in my purse, on Rick Billings's old desk. I looked into Dietz's eyes, sickened by the coldness in his vacant stare. "You'd be a fool to shoot me right here in the police compound."

Dietz shrugged. "Not really. It's not as risky as you think. This is a damn good silencer." He turned the barrel slightly so that I could appreciate the apparatus. "No one ever drives by this corner of the garage. My trunk is empty. I'd just stuff your body in there and drive out. The guard at the exit booth knows me. He'll wave me through."

I was searching my peripheral vision for a way to duck, roll, escape.

"Get in the car. Now." He punctuated the last word with the end of his gun.

I got in but all the while was formulating a plan. The roar of Dietz's engine in the underground tunnel drowned out the slamming of my car door. We drove past the chain-link evidence area and circled upward.

Dietz sat back almost casually. "You made it easy for me today, Doctor. I thought I was going to have to nab you in broad daylight."

"You've been following me, then."

"Yep."

We made another loop, passing below street level where the officers parked their cars. One more loop up and we'd be nearing the exit. I knew there would be no time to hesitate. As soon as the guard came into view I would have to make my escape fast. If I was shot, there would be a witness. It was my only chance.

The exit booth came into view. My heart was pounding, and I willed the muscles in my limbs to appear relaxed so that Dietz wouldn't anticipate my next move. Twenty feet away now. My heart pounded faster and louder. Then skipped a beat.

The exit booth was empty.

Dietz saw my horror and laughed low and mean. He looked straight at me with soulless eyes. "Guess my guard buddy had to go take a piss." More laughter.

The cold fear set in again. My limbs became numb. I had a strange, floating sensation, as if I were already dead. My heart rallied against the numbness, beating wildly. I focused on that beat, the sound of life, drew strength from its rhythm. I tried not to look at the end of the barrel still pointing directly at my chest. We were heading west across town on Broadway. I had no idea where he was taking me.

Dietz pulled to a stop as a yellow light turned red. He was talking now. "Yeah, you were starting to make a believer out of me." He laughed. "You and your black girlfriend. If she'd died I would have had no problem. Well, less of a problem. She's the only one who saw my face. Pulled my damn mask off." He turned to look at me. "That girl should have died." He shook his head, genuinely puzzled. "She *really* should have died." My head jerked back against the seat as Dietz accelerated into the intersection. I hadn't seen the light change. I wasn't paying attention.

Dietz continued to talk. "Even if she did die, you'd heard her description of me. You were catching on. I did my best to cover my tracks with the damn car. Billings caught on to that one. I sold it pronto. But it was only a matter of time till the car thing would come back to haunt me, I knew that."

I wondered why he hadn't just killed me in the garage. Taking me away like this was risky. With a sinking heart I realized that he meant to rape me first. I forced myself to breathe, to keep him talking. "Covering your tracks included getting rid of Billings?"

"What else could I do? I could see he didn't buy my story about a mistake in the sale date on the registration. He was going to take it to Marcone that next morning."

We turned up Ash Street. Must be headed for the freeway. I was eyeing the control panel, wondering if I could possibly trip the emergency transmitter that was standard equipment in these cars. The one that said to the dispatcher, *Don't believe what you hear on the two-way—I'm in trouble.* Dietz saw me staring at the switch. "Don't even think about radioing for help. I've cut the wiring. This is my custom cruiser." From the corner of my eye I saw his hawk-like nose bobbing up and down, his mean thin lips curled in laughter.

"So you began to believe in me, huh?" I tried to keep the fear out of my voice. Tough to do.

"Yeah, about the time you pulled the name of that battered woman out of thin air, just by looking at the husband's photo. Gave me the creeps. Couldn't figure out why you didn't see it was me, plain as the nose on your face."

Appeal to his humanity. Yes, that's what I'd do. "Maybe I didn't want to believe it was you, Dietz. Maybe I thought you were a better person than that."

He laughed.

What humanity?

He repositioned his gun, adjusted his wrist. "Now you're sounding like all those ministers who tried to save my soul back in church school." In one lightning-swift motion he grabbed my jacket and pulled me toward him. I felt the gun jutting into my chest. "Fuckin' teachers pissed me off. Don't *you* piss me off." His breath was foul. Annie Drummond had said her rapist, like the bank employee Kevin Knutsen, had a "bad smell." Too late I made the connection.

I felt my arms and legs begin to tremble. "Okay, I won't piss you off."

"Good." He let me go, keeping the gun trained directly at my heart.

I shrank back against the passenger-side door. Dietz was way, way over the edge. I wondered how long he'd been that way. What had started it. "Why?" I heard myself whisper.

He looked at me coldly. Pointed to my shaking hands. "That's why. You should see the fear in your face. It's beautiful. I get off on it, always have. That's one of the best things about being a cop. People fear you."

I tried to fathom his psychosis. Couldn't. My head was pounding now with as much intensity as my heart. It occurred to me how many headaches I'd had this week, all in Dietz's presence. My body had been trying to talk to me—I just hadn't been listening.

I flashed back to our patrol ride, when I'd imagined the rapist's hand holding the knife instead of Dietz's hand holding the radio mike. I hadn't been hallucinating, I'd been *seeing*.

We were heading past Beech Street and on toward the entrance to Highway 5. It was dawning on me that this might be the end of my life. No gun, no karate training to save me. Then I heard a voice in my head. Maybe it was Thomasina, maybe it was Master Janice, maybe it was a guardian spirit. Maybe it was just me. Didn't really matter. The message was more important than the messenger. It said, *The power within you is stronger than any power without you.*

I looked over at Dietz. "Did you have a grandmother you were pretty close to? She died several years ago?"

He narrowed his eyes, keeping them on the road. We were just about to the freeway. "What if I did?"

"I can *see* her. She's talking to me. She loves you, Dietz. She's saying you don't have to do this."

Dietz pulled the wheel with his left hand and accelerated into the curve of the on-ramp. "You see my grandmother?" His voice was higher, surprised. For a moment the tough guy let down his guard and little Jeffrey Dietz came through. That was the moment I pulled the door handle and bailed out of the car.

46

Ice plant: a soft, spongy succulent consisting mostly of water. It's a common Southern California ground cover and grows thickly alongside many of San Diego's freeways. Unfortunately I missed the ice plant by about a yard and connected with the pavement at thirty miles per hour. A concerned citizen saw me roll from the cruiser and pulled over. He must have assumed I was a criminal attempting to escape custody. That's the only thing that could explain why he pinned my already bruised shoulders to the ground and yelled at the lookie-loos to call the police. I screamed with pain and turned my pounding head toward the freeway. The last thing I saw before passing out were all those cars politely pulling aside to make way for Dietz's police car speeding northbound.

I came to as I was being loaded into the ambulance. It had started to pour again—the rain on my face was probably what brought me around. "Call Lieutenant Marcone at the San Diego Police Department. Emergency development on the rape case." My voice was slurred. I hoped the medics wouldn't take me for a drunk. Someone was doing something incredibly painful to my right shoulder. "Hey, that hurts," I snapped.

The medic gave me a pitiful smile. "That's not me making it hurt, honey. That's a broken shoulder."

Lieutenant Marcone stood beside my hospital bed, arms folded across his chest. I was doing my best to swim up through the Demerol. I knew the situation was critical, but the drug wasn't allowing me to express that urgency. "Dietz killed Billings, he tried to kill Thomasina, he was going to kill me. Put a silencer on his Sig. Made me get in his cruiser. He was getting on Five north when I jumped out of the car."

"How did you manage to get out of the car without getting killed?"

"I dunno." At that moment it felt like I might die yet. "Um," I tried to remember and started to drift. Talking through the drug was a major chore. "Oh, yeah. I told him his dead grandmother was speaking to me, telling him things. It gave him just enough pause for me to get out."

"His dead grandmother was speaking to you?"

I waved my good arm. "No, no, no. That was total bullshit. I was just trying to get away."

Marcone smiled, then became serious again. "We'll get an APB out on Dietz's cruiser right away. You'd better rest."

The next time I came to it was Dianna sitting beside the bed. When she saw my eyes open she took my hand in hers. "Hey, partner. You took quite a tumble, didn't you?"

"Guess so." My voice box sounded like it needed new batteries. "Did they tell you what the damage was?"

She arched her brows. "Broken right shoulder, two broken ribs, punctured lung, bruised kidney, and a few other tender vittles. Plus the usual scrapes and scratches." She smiled and squeezed my hand. "Playground stuff."

I blinked slowly. "Beats a bullet in the chest."

"They found Dietz's cruiser in a commuter parking lot in Mission Bay. No leads yet what vehicle he might be driving now. Got fifty states looking for him, though. Marcone put a team on all the leads you gave him. The Toyota *was* registered to Dietz before the current owner. Dietz's work schedule is tracking with the rapes exactly."

"I gave him leads?" I didn't remember.

"Yeah, you did. And we've got a forensic dentist working to find a match between Dietz's dental records and that bite mark on Thomasina Wilson."

Something worrisome in that name. "Thomasina?"

Dianna gave my hand another squeeze. "She regained consciousness this afternoon."

I let my head fall back on the pillow. "Oh, good."

"She was even able to make a photo ID of Dietz."

"That's great." My eyelids were feeling heavy. "Hey. What happened with Zimmer?"

Dianna flashed a big smile. "We bagged him but good. It went down perfectly. Caught him red-handed and cleaned house with a fresh warrant. It was sweet."

I nodded. "That's good. That's really good. I'm just going to close my eyes, okay? I'm still listening."

I felt Dianna give my hand a little pat. "Now if we could just bag Dietz. I can't believe . . ."

Her voice faded on me. Behind my closed eyelids I was seeing the ocean. Endless ocean, a soothing visual. I had a vague impression of the Oceanside Harbor marina nearby. But mostly I saw just ocean. Undulating, hypnotic water. In time something white appeared in the upper right corner of this liquid inner movie screen. A boat. I moved closer, as if I were flying some extraordinary machine that was navigated by my curiosity alone. I saw a figure on the boat. A man. Curiosity pulled me even closer. Close enough to see his face.

My eyes popped open. "I found him."

". . . to get the—huh?"

I'd interrupted Dianna in midsentence. "I found Dietz. I mean I just got an image of him taking off on a boat from the Oceanside Harbor marina."

She gave my hand another squeeze and stood to go. "Worth a try," she said on her way out.

I had no idea how much time had passed when I heard his familiar voice. "You sleeping?"

"Mmm."

"You gonna wake up?"

"Only if you promise to tell me what the hell's been going on with you this past week."

"Okay, I'll tell."

I opened my eyes. It was hard to see him behind all the flowers. Carnations, chrysanthemums, zinnias, heather, baby's breath, cosmos. An armful of colorful winter blossoms nestled between lush sprigs of evergreen. "They're beautiful, Tom."

He put the arrangement on the broad windowsill and sat in the chair beside the bed. "To sum it up in a nutshell: I've been double deputized."

"What does that mean?"

"That means I was on a special assignment that I really couldn't—can't—talk about. Not even with you. That's just part of the life."

"The life?"

"I've been cross-sworn as a federal agent."

"Federal agent, as in FBI?"

McGowan nodded.

"I was right, then. Thought so."

He smiled. "I know. Pretty tough to get anything past you."

It dawned on me how godawful I must look. I tried not to think about it. "So how does this affect your life?"

He rested his hand on my leg. "My life? Or our life?"

"Okay, our life."

He ran his fingers along the blanket as if suddenly fascinated by the woolly fabric. "Not drastically in the near future. Cross-sworn means I'm staying on with the Escondido Police Department."

"When might the not-so-near future begin?"

His chin came up. "I don't know yet. But as soon as I do, you'll be the first person I tell. Okay?"

"Okay."

His hand moved to my face. He stroked my cheek. "Gave me a royal scare when they told me you were thrown from a car."

"I wasn't thrown. I jumped."

"Okay, whatever. Scared the bejeezus out of me."

"Welcome to having a lover in law enforcement."

He ran his fingers along the blanket again. Chuckling now. "Fair enough."

I reached across the bed with my good arm and caught his hand. Tried to look him in his big brown eyes but they were still studying the blanket. "This fed stuff. This is something you really want?"

He looked up and nodded. "I do."

It wasn't the kind of "I do" most women wanted to hear. But I really love a man who knows what he wants. I smiled. "Cool, then. Congratulations."

EPILOGUE

The sun, I noticed with pleasure, was almost hot. It poured out of a brilliant blue sky through the windshield of my car. The rays bounced off my wrists and hands, revealing just how pale my skin had become during an overlong California winter. Another week and spring would arrive officially.

It had been two months since the Coast Guard had cut Dietz's Mexican cruise short with a capture and arrest at sea. As rumor had it, the captain of the SDPD had stripped Dietz's badge, spit on it, and ground it under the heel of his shoe. Dietz had been charged with thirteen counts of aggravated rape, two counts of attempted murder, one count of first-degree murder, and enough additional charges to make his defense attorney, Joe VanDerhoff, work hard for his money. During the last several weeks VanDerhoff had filed the usual motions—mental incompetence, illegal search and seizure, and a few truly creative legal shenanigans—all in an effort to delay the inevitable. The inevitable had finally arrived, however, and Dietz was having his day in court. *Days*, to be precise. The trial had already spilled over into a second week. I sat in the parking lot of San Diego Superior Court, waiting for the prosecution's star witness.

I'd returned to work two weeks ago, albeit with a stiff shoulder that had me feeling about twice my age. Fortunately I'd managed to close the Gary Warren Niebuhr case without even leaving my desk. At some point it had dawned on me that the number I'd seen as I'd clutched Niebuhr's note and stared out to sea might have something to do with the clever little dweeb's whereabouts. I asked my client, Mark Clemmens, if 22X22 had any meaning to him. It turned out to be the secret password to a program in Niebuhr's old computer at MicroLight. When the screens opened up they revealed enough information to track Niebuhr down in Austria. So far nearly half of the missing sixteen million had turned up in Switzerland. MicroLight had rewarded me handsomely. Best of all, Niebuhr had been wrong about me being a chump.

A musical, five-note tapping on the passenger-side window interrupted these happy thoughts. I buzzed down the glass. "You're early," I said.

She smiled through the window. "You are, too."

"Come on. Let's go be early together." I locked up the car and we headed toward the courthouse. She walked with an even stride, head held high on her elegant neck. Again I marveled at her. "Can you possibly feel as good as you look?"

"No! It's all a front, believe me. I'm a frightful sight under my clothes. And my lung's still damaged. Won't be running any marathons this year."

I'd gotten rid of my sling only last week. I put my good arm around her waist as we walked up the cement sidewalk. She returned the gesture. Arm in arm, we neared the building.

She sucked air through her teeth. "I'm nervous."

I sighed. "I would give anything to be able to be in there with you when you testify." I also would be testifying in Dietz's trial as a witness for the prosecution. Because of that I was barred from hearing anyone else's testimony.

"I wish I knew what was going on in there. I mean, I know the case is strong, but I can't help but worry. What if he gets off on some technicality? What if—"

I held up my hand. "Stop. Don't even think about that. Besides, it's going great. I have my spy in the courtroom."

"Oh, yeah?"

"Yeah. My boyfriend, McGowan. He sat in for me a couple of days last week. Insisted he was attending the trial for reasons of his own. I didn't really believe that, of course. Anyway, he wouldn't discuss particulars about the testimony—he's very straitlaced about stuff like that. But he was able to, shall we say, convey the flavor of the trial to me."

My companion was all ears. "Tell me."

"Okay. Remember that blond woman in her twenties I was telling you about? Annie Drummond? McGowan said she was amazing. If she was intimidated at all she didn't show it. Looked right into the eyes of the audience, he said. An audience that included that blaming, shaming, idiotic father of hers."

"What about the Hispanic woman, Sanchez?"

"Marisa Sanchez. Outstanding. She came to court with a lot of female relatives, I guess. No husband. McGowan said she handled some really tough cross-examination. He was sure that the content of her testimony didn't even matter. That scar running down her face spoke more powerfully than any words."

At the mention of scars Thomasina fell silent. I wanted to pull my foot out of my mouth and kick myself with it. A moment later, she gave me a huge grin. "Think I should do some striptease for the jury? Show 'em my slice-'n'-dice chest? Will that work?" It was the old gallows humor again. She was milking it for all the comfort it could give.

I shook my head. "You amaze me, Thomasina Wilson. And, no, I think the prosecution's photos will be adequate." We stopped behind a small crowd waiting to enter the building. "You're so strong."

"I told you, honey. That man seriously, seriously underestimated me." She looked over. "Underestimated you, too."

"I can't wait to take the witness stand and watch his face when he realizes that." I smiled at the thought.

We sat on a bench outside Courtroom 126. We amused ourselves by people-watching, a pastime for which there is no better location than a public courthouse. Humanity runs the gamut there. Your average shopping mall can't begin to compare. In time a deputy leaned his head out of the courtroom door. "Ms. Wilson? They're ready for you now."

The muscles in Thomasina's face froze, and a lump pumped up and down her throat. She exhaled loudly. Then she was up off the bench.

Just as she reached the door I called out to her. "Hey."

She turned back.

I gave her a thumbs-up. "Go, girl."

The last thing I saw before Thomasina Wilson disappeared into the courtroom was the bright white flash of her winning smile.

When Sergeant Tom McGowan of the Escondido Police Department needs help in exploring the not-so-accidental death of an old friend, he turns to parapsychologist P.I. Elizabeth Chase.

Instantly, Elizabeth is absorbed by the case, and searches the stars and her sensitive psyche for answers. Janice Freeman, the dead woman, had a lot of friends, but as Elizabeth meets the people she knew, she begins to pick up a few unpleasant auras that have the unmistakable color of evil. Trying to pin down Janice's last fateful day of life, Elizabeth charts her final moves—and follows the celestial signs to cold-blooded murder.

MURDER IN SCORPIO

MARTHA C. LAWRENCE